The name of the vi

The name brought a who[...] flitting forward. But Nolar[...] that now. Now he needed to focus on learning everything he could about the criminal who'd attacked her.

He could hear another NYPD officer talking to the victim just around the corner. He couldn't see her face. "Detective Clayman will speak with you now. Tell him everything you already told me, then he'll see you home."

"Thank you," she said.

The timbre of the woman's voice shook him, making the memories he tried to forget burn bright.

No. It can't be the same woman—the same family.

Nolan stepped forward. His heart dropped to the floor.

Sitting in front of him was the brown-haired beauty who'd haunted him for years.

Her wide blue eyes lifted to meet his. The wariness and fear were swiftly replaced with anger. "You!"

She shot to her feet and the soft lines of her face morphed into hard, jagged angles. "No way in hell I'm talking to you."

Dear Reader,

I may be a small-town girl from Ohio, but I've always loved the hustle and bustle of the city. I love to spend time getting lost in the shuffle and discovering new places. I love the sounds that come together to create a soundtrack for the lives people live in these fabulous places.

I was lucky enough to be exposed to New York City when I was in college. When writing *Driven to Kill*, I knew I wanted to make a soundtrack for New York as well, and what better way than by writing a heroine who uses her love of the city as inspiration for her music?

I'm not a musician and never will be, but I understand what it's like to have a passion that drives you. A passion that is as much a part of your life as breathing. I hope I was able to convey that when giving Lauren her passion for music and piano. I hope when you dive into these pages, you can get lost in this world with all its amazing sounds. And I hope you all always tend to the passions in your lives.

With much love,

Danielle M. Haas

DRIVEN TO KILL

———

Danielle M. Haas

HARLEQUIN®

ROMANTIC SUSPENSE™

Recycling programs
for this product may
not exist in your area.

ISBN-13: 978-1-335-73845-5

Driven to Kill

For questions and comments about the quality of this book, please contact us at CustomerService@Harlequin.com.

Harlequin Enterprises ULC
22 Adelaide St. West, 41st Floor
Toronto, Ontario M5H 4E3, Canada
www.Harlequin.com

Printed in U.S.A.

Danielle M. Haas resides in Ohio with her husband and two children. She earned a BA in political science many moons ago from Bowling Green State University but thought staying home with her two children and writing romance novels would be more fun than pursuing a career in politics. She spends her days chasing her kids around, loving up her dog and trying to find a spare minute to write about her favorite thing: love.

Books by Danielle M. Haas

Harlequin Romantic Suspense

Matched with Murder
Booked to Kill
Driven to Kill

Visit the Author Profile page at Harlequin.com.

To my father, Michael Pennington, and his lovely wife, Christal. Thank you for always being proud of me and cheering me on. I hope you both always hear the music of life and continue dancing through the years with as much joy and kindness and love as you have today. You both are truly one of the biggest blessings in my life. Love you both forever.

Chapter 1

Frustration had Lauren Mueller tightening her arms around the mess of sheet music she hugged close to her chest. She'd give her right leg to go home and collapse in a warm bed, but that wasn't an option. Not tonight when another gig waited for her across town from the upscale lounge she played four times a week.

The blast of horns and drunken yells of New Yorkers and tourists rang into a Friday evening, mingling to create the soundtrack of Manhattan. A song that it had sung to her since before she could remember. A song that lived inside her, inspiring her to choose her own melody—and musical path—that she could pound out on the ivory keys of a piano.

But tonight, the cacophony of the city she loved so much didn't inspire her. Instead, it weighed down her already exhausted body. Her day had been long, first eight hours on her feet selling high-end jewelry, followed by a two-hour set playing piano for a crowd that hadn't even noticed she was there.

The door to the bar swung open and an onslaught of music and a group of giggling thirtysomethings poured onto the sidewalk.

A long-legged blonde with a face as smooth as stone stopped in front of Lauren and stared wide-eyed then wagged a finger in her direction. "You! You're the woman who played the piano in there. You were amazing." The light drawl on her words told Lauren this group of women were far away from home.

Pride straightened her spine. Okay, so maybe not everyone inside had ignored her. "Thanks. I'm glad you enjoyed the music."

"Enjoyed it?" A striking brunette, whose hair was a touch darker than Lauren's mousy-brown locks, cut in with a laugh. "We sang along to every song." She pressed a hand to her black sequined top, awe clear in her green eyes. "Will you play here again tomorrow? We only have one more night in the city. We'd love to watch you play again."

Her heart swelled. This was why she'd devoted so many of her twenty-nine years to her music. For moments like these, when strangers approached her with praise. Okay, maybe not the whole reason. She didn't have the ability to articulate the desperate need in her soul to sit on a hard bench and let her fingers fly over the keys. It was simply a part of her.

But having her talent recognized definitely didn't hurt. She flashed a bright smile as she struggled to keep her overstuffed tote bag high on her shoulder and the sheets of music in her arms from billowing away on the warm summer breeze. "Not tomorrow. I'm so sorry. But enjoy your time in the city."

As she watched the group laugh and waltz down the busy sidewalk, she snagged her phone from her pocket. She'd had the forethought to order a car on the At Your Service app before loading her arms down with all her crap. The picture of the driver and information about his car were front and center.

Standing on the edge of the sidewalk, she stood on the toes of her ballet flats. But she was too short to see over the Friday-night crowd, no matter how high she went on her tiptoes. She struggled to catch a glimpse at her watch, then blew out a long breath, the wisp of air pushing her layered bangs out of her sight line.

She'd nabbed a coveted late spot at a bar in the Meat-packing District. A trendy place that could put her in front of people with the means to change the trajectory of her career. But if she didn't make it there on time, it wouldn't matter who showed up to watch her play. She tapped her finger against the back of her music as irritation zipped through her body.

A silver sedan cut a path through traffic and glided to a stop in front of her. The small neon sign in the windshield broadcasted the name of the ride-sharing service she used. *Finally.* If they didn't get caught at too many red lights, she should make it to the bar in time. Before stepping off the sidewalk, she glanced at the license plate and confirmed she had the right car then struggled to reach the handle. Sheets of music spilled from her arms, and she bent to pick them up before they blew away.

A car door closed. Jean-clad legs and name-brand sneakers caught her attention. A man with a Yankees baseball cap crouched beside her and plucked pieces of paper from the sidewalk, gathering them in his arms before handing them over. "Here ya go, miss. Sorry. I should have opened the door for you so you didn't drop your things."

Securing her music, she stood and offered the driver a smile. The bill of the hat hid the top of his face in shadows, but the light skin and blond scruff on his chin matched the photo on her app. "Thank you so much. I would have been in a whole world of trouble if I'd lost that."

The driver dipped his chin then opened the back passenger door wide. "Not a problem. Go ahead and hop in."

She slid onto the cloth seat and rested her head on the seat back. Time wasn't on her side, but she'd take the precious minutes she had to relax.

The driver jumped back in the car and drove into the bustling traffic.

Although grateful for his assistance, she stayed quiet, taking in the colorful lights outside her window. Small talk wasn't something she enjoyed on a good day. On a day like today, filled with annoyed customers and rude patrons, the idea of making chitchat with a stranger made her teeth hurt.

A few minutes passed, and the lights became less pronounced. The amount of foot traffic decreased. She sat taller, paying attention to each turn. She might not be super familiar with the area where they headed, but she'd grown up in the city and had a general idea of the direction they should be going, so the scenery around them made less and less sense as they continued.

"Excuse me? Sir? Are you sure you have the right address?" She didn't want to be a rude backseat driver, but she couldn't sit back and let him take her to the wrong destination. No GPS blurted out directions. Maybe he was confused about where to go.

"Sure do. Just trying to get you there a little quicker."

She stayed on the edge of her seat. Uncertainty bounced her foot up and down on the carpeted floor that rumbled over uneven concrete. She moistened her suddenly dry lips and tightened her hold on the sheet music pressed to her chest.

"Almost there. The place is around the block. I'm just driving in from behind. The front entrance is always crowded—so many bars and restaurants popping up in this area now. Let me park on the side street. I can get closer that way."

Anxiety bubbled in the pit of her stomach. Something wasn't right, but she didn't know what. She just needed him to park so she could get out of the car and put the whole weird vibe she was getting behind her.

The driver turned into a dark alley, parking the car against the curb. "Here we are."

"Thanks. I'll leave a tip on the app." With her arms loaded down, she struggled to reach the handle.

"Oh, I'm not worried about that," he said. "But let me help you out."

Before she could protest, he climbed out and ran to her side of the car.

Her heart pounded and instinct had her inching her fingers toward her purse.

The door swung open, and the driver launched himself into the car. His hands circled her neck, and the weight of his body pressed her against the seat.

Her arms flung wide, dropping her belongings to clutch at the hands on her neck. The light inside the car didn't flicker on—something that hadn't registered before—and long shadows were cast over the man forcing her down.

"Help!" she croaked, the word barely squeezing through her constricted throat. Air leaked from her burning lungs. She thrashed, clawing at the tough skin over his knuckles. She tried to connect her knee to his soft middle pinning her to the seat, but she didn't have enough range of motion. Couldn't move her legs beneath his bulky frame.

Not enough oxygen was making it to her brain, making the world around her spin. No. She couldn't die. Not like this. Trapped under a strange man in a dark alley, with no one around to hear her cries. "Stop. Please." The words caught on a silent sob.

His face was close to hers. His warm breath on her cheeks turned her stomach. "I'll teach you a lesson," he said through clenched teeth. Anger radiated from his every pore.

Blackness edged her vision and pain pounded against her skull. His hands squeezed impossibly tighter. She sputtered and gasped, trying to block out what felt like razor blades scarping against her throat. She focused on her fingers as they moved through her purse still hung on her shoulder until she found the cylinder-shaped spray attached to her keys. Using all her strength, she yanked it out of the bag, aimed the can at his face and pushed down on the little plastic trigger. Holding her breath, she closed her eyes, turning her head to escape as much of the blast of fiery spray as she could.

Pepper spray pelted his skin, and he rose up, creating space between their bodies, and wiped frantically at his eyes.

She kept the can trained on his face as she struggled out from underneath his body. The pungent spray hung heavy in the car, burning her eyes and making her nose run.

"Sonofabitch!" he cried, leaning away from the onslaught of potent chemicals.

With her legs free, she brought her knees to her chest, pressing them outward in unison, screaming with the effort and pain as her first fresh breath broke through her bruised throat. The soles of her shoes connected with his torso and propelled him farther back with a thud and a grunt. He stumbled against the broken sidewalk, choking against the blast of chemicals she'd delivered.

She scrambled for her bag, opened the opposite door and flew onto the road. "Help!" she called again as she fumbled for the phone in her purse.

She rounded a corner, desperate to find anyone on the eerily quiet street.

A low growl sounded behind her. She glanced over her shoulder and panic tightened every muscle in her body. The man was after her. She'd knocked the hat off his head. His eyes were red and hatred twisted in the lines on his face. She fought for focus as she sprinted down the sidewalk. Searching for anyone to help her. Tears fell from her burning eyes, mingling with the warm night air. But she couldn't fall apart. Not when her life was on the line.

She sprinted forward. A convenience store sat on the corner of wherever the hell he had taken her. Her ballet flats pounded on the uneven sidewalk, each footfall vibrating her shaking legs. She didn't chance another look behind her, but heavy breathing and curses reached her ears, confirming the man was still after her.

Adrenaline zipped through her veins and pushed her harder, faster, until she reached the store. She yanked open the door and practically fell across the threshold. "Please. Someone help. Call the police. I was just attacked." Each word scraped against her raw throat, but she spit them out. Desperately seeking someone to aid her.

A man with a wrinkled brow and kind eyes behind the counter ran to her side, a phone in his hand. "Are you all right?"

She drew in a shaky breath then winced as the air sliced through her esophagus. "I am now," she said, bending at the waist as she struggled to keep her composure.

"I'm calling the police. Everything's going to be okay."

The summer heat hadn't gone away when the sun went down. And for reasons unknown, when the heat simmered in the concrete jungle of Manhattan, the predators came out in droves. Detective Nolan Clayman was on the hunt for one of those predators, a killer who'd stolen a young woman's life and discarded her in an alley like she was nothing more than the trash he'd left her in.

Two days had gone by, and Nolan was no closer to finding the bastard now than he was when he'd stood over the poor woman's body and promised to get her justice.

But all that changed the second he received the phone call that tore him from a quiet night at home, poring over notes. The red and blue lights of the squad car parked in front of the convenience store in the Lower East Side urged him forward.

Creating his own parking spot next to the cruiser, he jumped out of his SUV and approached the officer who stood guard by the door. A few pedestrians strolled by, curiosity slowing their pace, and Nolan scowled and waited for them to pass before addressing the young woman in uniform.

"Evening, Officer…" He let his words hang, fishing for the woman's last name.

"Jeffery. Evening, sir. Victim's inside with Officer Stanley." She kept her stance wide, her hands clasped behind her back.

He glanced over the woman's head and spied Officer Stanley standing in front of someone seated in a folding chair. Only her slim calves and black shoes were visible from this angle. "Any sighting of the suspect?" He'd ask more questions once inside but might as well get what information he could now.

"No sightings that lead anywhere," she said. "A teenage couple witnessed the man running after the victim before she reached the store. Couldn't provide a good description of him or the vehicle he left in. But the victim got a visual, as well as the information on the car service app she used to identify both."

Nolan took a step back and studied the tops of the

buildings. "We'll need access to the security footage. Let's see if we can uncover which way he went." If the driver brought his target to the Lower East Side, he had a reason. And that reason might be more than just the maze of quiet alleyways and nooks he could use to get his hands dirty.

Officer Jeffery nodded. "I'll put in the request right away. A few officers are going door-to-door, searching for more witnesses. But gaining permission for the security feed would be a better use of time."

"Agreed. I'll want all the information and data sent my way. But first, I want to speak with the victim. Grab her statement so she can head home. I'll touch base with you when I'm done." He entered the store and made a beeline for Officer Stanley.

The older man turned and took a few steps away from the victim as he approached, the movement allowing Nolan a better glimpse of the woman seated in front of him. Officer Stanley offered a stiff smile. "Clayman," he said, in greeting.

"Evening. I got the rundown from your partner out there." He nodded toward the doorway where Officer Jeffery took up her post again, the stiff set of her shoulders oozing authority.

"I'd like to talk to the victim." He kept his voice low, not wanting the woman sitting a few feet away to overhear them discussing her and what she'd just endured.

"Ms. Mueller," Officer Stanley supplied. He'd angled his body toward Nolan and spoke low. "She's pretty shaken but has kept herself together. She'll need a ride home once you're finished speaking to her."

Mueller. The name brought a whole host of bad memories flitting forward. But he couldn't dwell on that now. Now he needed to focus on learning everything he could about the criminal who was out there, searching for his next victim.

"Can do. I'll take it from here."

Officer Stanley turned back toward the woman. "Detective Clayman will speak with you now. Tell him everything you already told me, then he'll see you home. I'm sorry this happened, but you can rest easy knowing we won't stop until we find this guy."

"Thank you."

The timbre of the woman's voice shook him, making the memories he tried to forget burn bright.

No. It can't be the same woman—the same family.

Officer Stanley clapped a hand on his shoulder then skirted around him to the exit, and Nolan's heart dropped to the floor.

Sitting in front of him was the brown-haired beauty who'd haunted him for years. Her wide blue eyes lifted to meet his. The wariness and fear were swiftly replaced with anger. "You!" She shot to her feet and the soft lines of her face morphed into hard, jagged angles. "No way in hell I'm talking to you."

Chapter 2

Not much had changed in the four years since Nolan first laid eyes on Lauren Mueller. Her straight brown hair was a little longer, but not even the sickly purplish ring around her neck could diminish the fire in her light blue eyes. And it looked like she still hated him.

But that didn't matter. Nolan had a job to do. And dammit, he was hell-bent on doing it. He couldn't allow himself to get caught up in the past. He was a different person—a different officer—now.

Ignoring her clenched jaw and tight fists balled at her sides, he approached her with as much profession-alism as he could muster. "Ms. Mueller. I hate meeting you again this way. Did you have someone take a look at your neck?"

She folded her arms over her chest. "I'm fine. And I already told you, I'm not talking to you."

He struggled not to squirm under her hard stare. He'd faced down some of the toughest criminals in the city, but something about this spitfire of a woman made him feel he was the piece of scum who needed locking up in a cage. Dealing with her disdain had nearly destroyed him once. He couldn't make the same mistakes again. "Unfortunately, you don't have a choice. I'm sorry this happened to you, and I'm even sorrier you don't trust me because of what happened in the past. But I'm pretty sure you aren't the only woman this man has hurt and I'm the best chance we've got of finding him before he hurts someone else."

She cut her gaze to the ground and the tears that shimmered over her dark lashes punched him in the gut. He wanted to offer her comfort but knew it wouldn't be well received. Not from him.

A quick glance behind the counter a few feet to his right showed him a stool. "Give me a second," he said, then approached the older gentleman who stood behind the clear partition, manning the register. "Sir, can I take this seat for a few minutes?"

"Take anything you need," the man said. "Poor lady. Came running in here like a bat out of hell. Glad she got away. I'll help any way I can. Just ask."

"Appreciate it." Nolan grabbed the circular top of the black seat and dragged it over to the folding chair Lauren had leaped out of at the sight of him. He sat then dipped his chin toward the vacant chair.

She watched him, her body practically vibrating with mistrust and anger.

"Please. Take a second. Sit. Forget you know me. Forget we've ever met. And tell me what happened so

I can help you." He spoke soft and slow as if he were speaking to a scared animal.

Working her jaw back and forth, she lifted the tips of her long, slender fingers to touch the nasty bruises along her collarbone. Slowly, she lowered herself to the chair, her gaze fixed ahead. "I ordered a car from At Your Service when I left a gig in Midtown."

Keeping his feet flat on the floor, he leaned forward and rested his forearms on his thighs. He didn't want to invade her personal space, but she spoke so quietly he had to make sure he didn't miss a single word. "Have you used this service before?"

She nodded. "Many times."

"What about this driver? Use him before?"

She shook her head, then winced—from the memory, the pain, or both, he wasn't exactly sure. "No. But the app provides a photo of the driver and information about the car. The license plate checked out, and the guy matched the photo."

"Did anything strike you as odd? Off in any way?" he asked, needing a full picture of what transpired before the shit hit the fan.

Her mouth swished to the side as if she were biting the inside of her cheek. "We didn't seem to be going in the right direction. I asked if he knew the way, and he said yes. But it was too quiet, too deserted on the sidewalks. I got nervous. He stopped in an alley, claiming to want to avoid the crowd, then came around to open my door."

He furrowed his brow. He'd taken countless taxis and driven in cars from ride-sharing services, and no one had ever opened a door for him. "Did that surprise you?"

"I guess," she said with a shrug. "But I was carrying a lot. Had actually dropped my music when he picked me up, and he hurried out of the car to help." Her face fell into a grimace. "Crap. My music is in the car. And I'm a no-show at my job."

He made a mental note that she had left some things of importance in the car but prompted her for more. Time was ticking, and he needed to move quickly. "What happened next? After he parked then opened your door."

Her hands dropped from her neck down to her lap. She drew in a shuddering breath, finally meeting his gaze. "He lunged at me. His body on mine, pinning me to the seat. Then he choked me."

He steeled himself from reacting to the pain in her eyes, the quiver in her voice. But damn, it was much harder than it should have been. "How did you get away?"

"Pepper spray. I don't know how he could even see to drive away. I unloaded most of the can while in that car."

That explained the redness flaring in her face. "Did he say anything?"

Tears fell down her cheeks, but she kept her hands folded on her lap. "That he wanted to teach me a lesson. His voice was hard, like he had an edge to his words. No pronounced accent, but if I had to guess, I'd say he was from Brooklyn."

"Can I see the information on your phone?"

A slight hesitation tensed her hand before she fetched her phone from the bag and turned the screen toward him.

"Do you mind?" He extended his hand toward the phone.

She handed it over, careful not to touch him.

The information from the app knotted his stomach. He gave back the device and ran a palm over his face. "We ran the app before and saw his picture. You're very lucky you got away. This isn't the first time this guy has attacked a woman he'd given a ride to, and the last woman didn't escape."

Ms. Mueller crossed one arm over her chest and propped her chin on her free fist, biting her thumbnail. "I can't believe this happened. How could such a trusted service let a man like this slip through the cracks?"

"That's a good question, and one I plan to answer."

A derisive snort puffed from her mouth and spiked his blood pressure, but he wouldn't take the bait. She had reasons to be cautious with him, but there was no need to rehash the past. "I have all I need from you right now. Would you like me to take you home?"

She sandwiched her plump bottom lip between her teeth, not answering him.

"I can call someone, if you'd like. A friend? Family?"

Her eyes narrowed and her body went rigid. "Family? Who in my family would you like to call? My father, who had a heart attack from all the unnecessary stress heaped on his shoulders over the last four years? Or my mom, who worries so much she barely leaves her house? Wait," she said, holding up a palm. "Let me guess. You'd like to call my baby brother to come get me. But you can't because you arrested him when he didn't do a damn thing wrong and then he died in a stupid jail cell fight before his name was cleared."

The high pitch of her voice rang in his ears and pricked at his conscience. He couldn't look at her, couldn't argue his side of the story, because she was right…he had been the one who'd sent her brother to jail. And nothing would bring back the life of an innocent man he had a hand in ruining.

"All I can say is I'm sorry about all the pain I've caused you. But now, in this moment, I just want to make sure you get home safely. Will you let me do that?"

She rose, her chin tilted in the air, and grabbed her bag off the grubby tile floor. "Fine. Take me home. Then I never want to speak to you again."

Rising to his feet, he nodded and led the way to the SUV waiting outside. He handed a business card to Officer Jeffery, who still stood outside the store, promising to be in touch soon, then opened the passenger door for Ms. Mueller. She passed by him, and a hint of sweat and lingering pepper spray wafted up his nose, setting his nerves on edge.

He hoped she didn't live too far away because he had no doubt this would be the worst ride of his life.

Thirty tense and uncomfortable minutes later, relief loosened Lauren's shoulders at the sight of her building. What were the odds she'd experience two car rides from hell in the same night? One from a man who'd tried to kill her. One from a man whose actions had resulted in her brother being killed.

The heat of his gaze singed the back of her neck until she escaped inside with a nod goodbye, putting much-needed distance between them. She'd never dreamed she'd see the handsome officer again. The fact that he was the one she must trust to find the man who'd attacked her sat like boiling oil in her gut.

She couldn't think of that now. Not when she felt as if she'd just swallowed glass, the skin around her neck still tender to the touch. Exhaustion weighed down each step she took as she made her way through the lobby and down the hall to her first-floor apartment. She hadn't let the officer accompany her inside, but she suspected he was watching and waiting.

"You're finally home! I've been scared to death." Rebecca, her roommate and best friend, launched herself across the living room and into Lauren's arms. She hugged her tight. "I wish you would have let me take a taxi to come and get you. Sitting here waiting drove me crazy."

Lauren melted against her friend, adrenaline finally fleeing from her system. The reality of what she'd just survived crashed against her like a wave on a rocky cliff and a sob caught in her raw throat. "What was I going to do? Ask you to take a car to come get me after what had happened?"

Rebecca rubbed a palm between her shoulder blades. "Good point. Let's take a seat." She led her to the charcoal-colored love seat pressed against the wall in the square room. "Can I get you anything?"

"A sedative?" she asked, only half joking. She sat and waited for her friend to take the spot beside her before resting her head on Rebecca's shoulder. She stared straight ahead at the white curtains they'd attached to the walls surrounding what should have been a breakfast nook. Her bed was nestled inside, with just enough space to squeeze in a narrow nightstand and dresser. All she wanted was to climb into her bed and pull the covers over her head. Forget this entire night had ever happened.

She was usually stronger than this, more capable of keeping her emotions in check, but tonight had rocked her to the core—in more ways than one. "This guy killed someone, Rebecca."

Rebecca's arm hooked around her shoulders, and she squeezed her tight. "Thank God it wasn't you."

Sissy, Lauren's fluffy Himalayan cat, meowed and jumped into her lap, patting her way in a circle before settling into a giant fur ball. A dull purr vibrated her body.

Lauren smoothed her fingers through the silky gray and tan strands, letting the motion calm her nerves in a way nothing else could.

After a few minutes of silence she said, "Officer Nolan Clayman is the man in charge of the case. Sorry, he's a detective now." The thought of him obtaining a promotion after what he'd done to her family made her bristle.

"Who?"

She pinched the bridge of her nose, trying her hardest to keep the flood of emotions from breaking free. "The officer who arrested Charlie."

Her brother's name came out on a sob, and just like that, the dam burst. Tears fell down her face, making the strands of hair stick to her cheeks.

Sissy jumped to her feet and butted her nose against Lauren's hand.

"Oh, honey," Rebecca said. "I'm so sorry. Coming face-to-face with him after all this time is the last thing you needed to deal with tonight."

She sniffed back her tears. The worst was behind her. She needed to get a grip and a little perspective so she could just go to sleep. "I never wanted to see Nolan Clayman again. Not after everything that happened. And the thing that upset me the most was the way my stomach dipped at the sight of him. Not in a 'I'm so upset that I want to throw up' way. But in a 'riding in a roller coaster, my stomach is flipping' way. What the hell is wrong with me?"

"I'm sure that was just shock from seeing him and all the adrenaline in your system. Don't be too hard on yourself."

"Maybe," she said, not believing it. The flutter in her gut had more to do with the way Detective Clayman's once buzzed hair had grown out a bit, making the sandy-blond locks long enough for her to grab a handful of if she'd wanted. His brown eyes had looked at her with kindness and regret, a lethal combination she couldn't forget.

But she had to. Finding a man attractive wasn't a sin. Hell, she couldn't control her physical reaction to someone's looks. That didn't mean she should waste any of her time keeping the image of his handsome face in her mind. Feeling anything other than contempt for Detective Clayman was a betrayal of her brother, even if he was the one charged with finding the man who attacked her.

Scooping Sissy into her arms, she rose to her feet and aimed a small smile down at her friend. "I just need to go to bed. All this crap will be waiting for me in the morning."

She left Rebecca's worried hazel eyes behind her and unhooked the curtains, letting them fall and provide her the little privacy she had in their one-bedroom apartment. She placed her cat on the deep navy throw at the end of her bed. "Go ahead and lay down."

Her body was zapped of energy, but she used what little she had left to slip out of the simple black dress and yanked on a pair of shorts and a sleeping tank. The thick straps brushed against her neck, and she winced. Her brain spun as she thought of all the terrible ways this night could have ended.

Ways her life could have ended.

Peeling back the covers, she slid under the cool sheet and Sissy curled into her usual spot at her side. She concentrated on the sounds of the cars honking outside and Sissy's purr so close to her ear. She closed her eyes, willing sleep to come and bring this horrible day to a close.

An image of Detective Clayman with his long, lean legs and chiseled jaw crashed against the backs of her eyelids. Sucking the air from her lungs. She wanted to make it disappear, to pull forth a different memory to fall asleep to, but he refused to leave. Refused to let her rest in any kind of peace.

But that wasn't different from most nights since Charlie died. Detective Clayman had robbed her of any peace she'd ever have. And nothing he'd do would ever change that.

Chapter 3

The midmorning sun beat down on Nolan, causing beads of sweat to gather at the back of his neck. He'd kill to rip off his dress shirt—even if it was rolled up to his elbows—and throw on something a little more comfortable and a lot cooler. A dream that wouldn't be achieved until the day was over. For now, he stepped into the long shadows of the alley and shoved his sunglasses high on his head.

A tall man with a full head of thick black hair climbed out of the back of the abandoned car, rubber gloves covering his hands.

Grinning, Nolan shook his head then slapped his buddy's back. "You sonofabitch. What are you doing here?"

His friend, and former roommate, Detective Jack

Stone was a homicide detective. Not someone who was called out to investigate a car that was ditched in an alley in the Lower East Side. Not that Nolan wouldn't accept any help he could get. Jack was one hell of a cop, and ever since Nolan's partner retired last month, he'd been hitting the streets solo.

"I was in the area when this was found. I knew you were the one heading up the case, so figured I'd lend a hand. Didn't want anything to contaminate what's inside." Jack sealed an evidence bag. "I sent the officer who found the car out to get whatever video footage they can of the area. Told them I'd see to this."

"Appreciate it," he said, rounding the front of the car. The vehicle matched the description of the one used in the attack against Lauren, as well as the car driven by the man who killed Ashley Banford—a driver who he'd confirmed had been behind the wheel when Ashley was murdered but hadn't been seen since. A man named Malcom Carson. An employee of At Your Service with no prior arrests and a clean record. "Officers searched this area last night. Malcom must have come back. Left the vehicle and split."

"How far are we from where the last attack was committed?" Jack tossed him the bag, which was filled with sheet music.

"Not far. A couple blocks." He peered inside the bag. "This is Lauren Mueller's. She mentioned leaving it behind. Was pretty upset about it. I'll dust for prints then see about getting it back to her."

Jack arched one dark brow. "This is the sister from the Charlie Mueller case, right?"

Nolan nodded and wiped the moisture from the back

of his neck with his free hand. Jack knew all about what had happened with Charlie Mueller. How he'd been caught driving the getaway car for his friends who'd robbed a liquor store. Nolan had arrested Charlie, not knowing the boy'd had no clue what his friends had been up to. He was an innocent guy caught up with the wrong crowd.

His family had been adamant the police clear his name. Figure out exactly what had happened. Lauren had been the most vocal of them all, going as far as blasting his name and reputation all across town. He'd listened, nearly killing himself to find the truth of what'd gone down, but it had been too late.

"Yep. She wasn't happy to see me, not that I blame her." He lifted the bag and stared at the cluster of musical notes, wishing he could hear her play. Wishing she didn't ooze hatred at the sight of him.

"You have to stop beating yourself up over what happened," Jack said. "You did the same thing any officer would have done. Anyone driving that getaway car would have declared their innocence. Hell, I've caught a man with a bloody knife still in his hands who claimed he didn't stab the dead woman at his feet. You did the job, then you worked like a man possessed every single day until you uncovered the truth."

He'd heard it all before, but the words did nothing to untangle the knots in his stomach. Now wasn't the time to rehash an old case anyway. It was time to focus on a new one. "All the good it did. I couldn't stop Charlie from dying, but I can stop the man who attacked his sister. I owe him that much."

Jack slammed the back passenger-side door closed.

"Finding the car is one hell of a start in finding the driver. Can't pick up any more unsuspecting women if he doesn't have a vehicle."

His friend was right, but something didn't sit well with him. Malcom didn't have any other vehicles registered in his name, which meant he had no way to make a living. "Maybe Malcom was spooked. Had to know the victim gave us his information. Even if it was dark and she was scared, she still got a look at him. So even if we weren't sure he was the one who murdered Ashley, there'd be no doubt he'd attempted to kill Lauren. We have his face. His car. Hell, I got his damn address from At Your Service—not like it helped. No one home when I showed up."

"He can only hide for so long. We both know that. And I can lend a hand on this, if you want. Unless Max and I catch a big case, I've got a little extra time."

Jack had been one of the city's best cyber crimes detectives. Nolan would be a fool not to accept his help. "I'd appreciate it, man. I'm up to my eyeballs in paperwork and follow-up calls. Not to mention the new security footage we pulled in."

"Anything you need, let me know," Jack said, pulling off his gloves and shoving them into the pockets of his jeans. He nodded toward a duffel bag by his feet. "I bagged some other evidence and stuffed it in there. Receipts, an old burger wrapper, stuff I found crammed in the glove box. Feel free to go over the inside yourself, but I took out anything that could be useful."

He trusted Jack's judgment and didn't want to waste time on something that had already been done.

"Thanks, man. I'll take everything back into the station for processing."

A large van with the NYPD logo stretched across the sides turned into the alley and parked.

"Crime scene unit's here to finish," Jack said. "I'm taking off. Call when you have details on what you need me to handle."

Nolan stood on the sidewalk and watched his friend leave as two CSI members walked toward him. He stared back into the evidence bag still in his hands, and his subconscious nagged him. His suspect might not have a vehicle any longer, but that didn't mean he wasn't still a threat. Especially to the woman who'd gotten away.

A scribbled note attached to the sheet music caught his attention. Securing his hand inside a glove, he snatched out the paper and read the neat writing.

Dovetail Lounge. August 6th and 7th. 10:00 p.m. BIG BREAK!

He considered the message. Lauren had been on her way to a gig the previous night, and from the looks of things, she was scheduled to play at the same place tonight. She said she never wanted to speak to him again but returning her things may start a bridge to building some trust. Okay, so it'd be one of those dilapidated old wooden bridges, but it was better than nothing.

Besides, if he saw this note, Malcom might have read it as well. Nolan promised to keep Lauren safe. He'd start tonight, whether she liked it or not.

A different kind of nerves jumbled up Lauren's insides. Not the usual kind she experienced before stepping onto a stage. No, this was the kind that made the hairs on her arms stand at attention. As if someone was watching her.

Of course, she was being ridiculous. She *wanted* people to watch her while she pounded out a melody on the keys. She must have residual fear from what happened the night before, which was understandable. She just had to make sure she didn't let this new kind of terror twisting her up affect her performance. Tonight was too important.

"You look a little nervous," Rebecca said, standing beside her in the back room where she waited to be told to take the stage.

Lauren pushed a curled strand of hair behind her ear and wet her dry lips. "I'm just on edge. I need to get a grip. The Dovetail Lounge didn't have to let me play after being a no-show last night." She'd assumed she'd lost her chance to perform at the coveted bar. She'd almost dropped to her knees and thanked her lucky stars when she'd gotten hold of the booker. She'd explained her situation. And he had understood.

"What happened last night wasn't your fault, and you shouldn't be punished for it. Whoever's in charge here is lucky they didn't cancel your set, or they would have had to deal with me." Rebecca anchored her fists on her hips, but it was hard to find her intimidating. Her high cheekbones and long, willowy frame could probably be knocked over with a touch of a feather if her backbone weren't made of steel.

Not wanting her friend to worry any more about her, she mustered a smile. "You're right. I earned this spot, and I'll make the most of it." She smoothed a palm over her silky black tank top, hating the slight tremor that shook her hand. "And thanks for coming with me. I really need the support tonight."

"I wouldn't be anywhere else."

The booker, Stewart, opened the door. "You're up."

She sucked in a deep breath. "Thanks."

"You got this," Rebecca said.

The sounds of laughter and chatter reached her ears as she followed Stewart down a narrow hall that led to the stage. Sweat coated her palms, and she wiped them on her black dress pants before slipping in front of the curtain and heading for the piano. A bright spotlight pounded down on her, casting a glare that kept the crowd from view.

But they were there. She could hear the tinkling of glass and lull of conversation. She offered a wave as Stewart announced her name. A smattering of applause surrounded her, and she sat on the hard bench that felt so much like home. Though tonight, instead of a sense of calm that usually fell on her shoulders, the idea that people could see her—were watching her—made her heart gallop and pulse race.

What in the world was happening? She'd played in front of countless crowds, always able to take whatever emotions brewed inside her and pour them into her music.

Tonight was different. Tonight, her hands shook, and she struggled against the tears stinging the backs of her eyes. Pressure expanded her chest. Her breath hitched and a cold sweat broke out at her hairline, making her teeth chatter. The music on the sheet placed on the music stand blurred. Her memory of how to create a melody vanished, replaced with the feel of a man's hands around her throat. Fear squeezed her lungs.

She couldn't do this. Couldn't sit here and pretend like everything was all right. Pretend like the inside of her raw throat didn't sting as she struggled to take in air.

A dull murmur hummed around her. Tingling her senses. She had to get out of here. Without a word, a look, a thought, she rose on unsteady legs and ran down the three steps along the side of the stage that spilled onto the lounge floor. Square tables clustered together. Well-dressed men and women stared at her with questioning eyes and amused smirks.

She turned in a circle, her palms pressed against her churning stomach, searching for the quickest exit. Spying the red glowing sign, she pushed her way through the crowd, ignoring the comments hurled at her. She needed fresh air, needed away from the large crowd.

"Lauren!"

Someone called her name, but the ringing in her ears made it impossible to figure out who it was. Probably Rebecca, but she couldn't stop to wait for her friend. Her lungs burned, the need for air and a quiet place to rest without the presence of strangers urged her forward.

Reaching the door, she pushed through the barrier for blessed escape. A cluster of patrons huddled on the sidewalk, smoking cigarettes and vape pens. The strong smell turned her stomach. She coughed into her elbow, moving past the toxic cloud, and winced as pain shot down her esophagus.

Bright lights from the towering buildings and flashing billboards made her head spin and the angry blasts of the congested traffic pounded against her head. She stumbled toward an empty spot on the sidewalk and rushed to lean against the cool stone structure. She greedily sucked in large gulps of warm, sticky air. Filling her lungs until they threatened to burst.

A wave of drunken college students sauntered past, and she took a step to the side. Needing to be away from the noise. The strangers. The constant feel of being watched that crawled up her skin and made her twitch.

With a forearm braced against the building beside her, she leaned forward and closed her eyes. She focused on four things she could feel—the smooth stone on her arm, the slight breeze on her face, the silky top on her skin, the too-tight shoes on her feet.

Her heart rate went down—breathing became easier.

She could do this. She could call on all the tools she'd learned to keep herself from spiraling out of control when the world seemed out to get her. Her set might be ruined, but she'd go back inside with her head held high and pray like hell they'd give her another shot. Maybe not tonight, she wasn't fool enough to think she was okay to perform, but maybe another time. After she'd given herself a chance to recover from the trauma she'd pretended hadn't affected her.

With a strong resolve, she straightened and turned toward the front of the bar. The faint sound of music reached her ears, which must have drawn in the crowd from outside. At least she wouldn't have to walk through the haze of smoke to get back in. Hurried footsteps sounded behind her, and she stepped to the side to let whoever was coming at such a quick pace pass.

A strong arm latched around her waist, and a hand clamped hard over her mouth.

She screamed, but the sweaty palm stifled any sound. She thrashed against her captor, kicking backward, trying to connect with any part of him. Fear clouded her vision, all the calm she'd fought so hard to achieve out the window.

A sharp tip pressed against her side. "I've got you now. And this time, you won't get away."

Chapter 4

The stale scent of cigarette smoke hung heavy in the air directly outside the door of The Dovetail Lounge. Nolan ducked his chin and hurried through the pungent haze. He scanned each face as it passed, shuffling around him to get back into the club, the sounds of music drawing them into the bar.

Where the hell had Lauren gone? She'd run off the stage and staggered through the maze of tables as if she'd seen a ghost. But he'd interviewed enough trauma victims to understand what had really happened.

She'd had a panic attack.

Now he needed to find her and make sure she was all right. He might be the last person she'd accept help from, but he couldn't leave knowing she was struggling. Tucking the sheet music he'd brought with him under his arm, he hurried toward the subway.

After what had happened last night, he doubted she'd order another car, and no yellow taxis clogged the street. If she was headed home, maybe he could catch her before she jumped on a train.

A muffled cry from the mouth of a darkened alley slowed his steps. He reached for his sidearm hidden behind the jacket he'd paired with his dress shirt before leaving the station at the end of his shift. Peering around the corner, his heart dropped to the dirty sidewalk. A man with a baseball hat pulled low over his face pressed Lauren against the front of his body like a shield. He couldn't make out his features, but it had to be Malcom. He'd come back to clean up his mess, just as Nolan had suspected.

"Police!" Nolan yelled. "Let her go. Now."

Even through the dim light bouncing down from the smattering of windows above, he could see the fear widening Lauren's eyes. She stood still, her body stiff.

The man took a step forward, as if taunting Nolan, and kept his grip firm on Lauren. Dark shadows fell across them. "Never going to happen."

Nolan stood his ground at the opening of the alley, gun aimed in front of him. He wouldn't let this asshole escape, wouldn't let him hurt one hair on Lauren's head.

A wave of music hit his ears and the pattering of shoes on pavement sounded behind him. Shit. A crowd of people walking into a dangerous situation was the last thing he needed to worry about. Shuffling feet came closer. Anxiety settled in the pit of his stomach, but he kept his focus straight ahead. "What's your plan? You have no way to get past me. Just give up before someone else gets hurt."

He took another step forward. "No. Now step aside before I kill her right here."

Nolan hardened his jaw, calculating the best place to lodge a bullet to get Lauren away from her captor. But unfortunately, there was no good place to shoot him without risking Lauren. Needing to act quickly, he glanced around for another option.

Wishing he could warn Lauren, he locked eyes with her for a brief moment, then aimed at the window to his left. He squeezed the trigger, the deafening sound echoing off the stone walls enclosing the alley. Screams erupted behind him, stampeding footfalls announcing the chaos his gunshot had caused.

Glass rained down. The man released Lauren and covered his head with his hands.

Lauren fell to the ground and curled into a ball, a smattering of glass landing on her.

Shit.

The man landed a swift kick in Lauren's gut then bolted down the opposite end of the alley, disappearing into the shadows.

Lauren cried out, stealing his attention. Indecision split him in two. The cop in him wanted to run after the attacker, but he couldn't leave Lauren alone and injured in the alley. He dropped to her side as he fished his phone from the front pocket of his trousers. "Are you okay?"

She grasped his wrist and her red-painted nails dug into his skin. "Go after him."

"He's gone," he said, dialing 911.

"911, what's your emergency?"

"I need officers at The Dovetail Lounge in the Meat-packing District. Possible murder suspect on the run, need assistance immediately." He cupped his palm over the speaker. "Did he hurt you? Do you need an ambulance?"

She shook her head and sniffed back tears.

"This is Detective Clayman. I witnessed the crime, but the suspect fled on foot. Contact Detective Stone and tell him to meet me."

"Yes, sir."

He disconnected and slid his phone back into his pocket. "Can you stand?"

She nodded, her hand still attached to his arm.

Cupping her elbow, he helped her to her feet. "Let's get inside. Then we can talk. Okay?"

She didn't answer but stayed close as she maneuvered past the lingering crowd.

With one arm tucked around Lauren's waist, he ushered her to the door of the bar and sent a hard look over his shoulder to dissuade any gawkers from following.

A blast of cool air beat down on him. Dozens of eyes and slack-jawed mouths greeted them, but Nolan ignored every curious glance. The hushed whispers grew louder, the din bouncing off the high ceilings. He lifted an arm, signaling to the manager he'd seen hustling about after Lauren had run offstage.

A woman with a sleek blond bob approached them with her hands clasped in front of her. "Is everything all right?"

He flashed his badge. "I'm Detective Clayman. I need a quiet place to sit and talk to Ms. Mueller. She was just attacked."

The woman gave a brisk nod and turned concerned

eyes on Lauren. "Are you all right, Ms. Mueller? Do you need me to call an ambulance?"

Lauren cleared her throat. "I'm fine. Thank you, Ruby."

Ruby pressed her lips together then gestured toward a door tucked behind the glossy black bar at the back of the room. "Right this way, please."

Nolan followed the pair of women into the office. White carpet and walls stood in direct contrast to the dark palette of blacks and deep purples in the main area. A dainty glass desk with a cream-colored chair sat at the far end of the room, and a small seating area consisting of two white bucket seats and a love seat with thin cushions and a hard-ass-looking back was closer to the door.

"Make yourselves comfortable," Ruby said, lingering in the doorway. "Call if you need anything. I have to get the entertainment on schedule."

"Detective Jack Stone will be here shortly. Please send him, as well as any other officers, back here as soon as they arrive."

Ruby gave another nod, then closed the door on her way out.

Sucking in a deep breath, he faced Lauren. "Do you need anything before we dive into what happened? A glass of water? A minute to sit, or maybe call a friend?" Although he'd planned to speak with her tonight, he hadn't expected to go over another crime—another situation where she'd been targeted and nearly killed.

Realization struck him and he winced. "Dammit. I dropped your sheet music in the alley. I'll have one of the officers grab it once they get here."

Confusion wrinkled her brow. "What music?"

Shrugging, he snaked a hand through his hair, feeling like an idiot for showing up with something for her. "You mentioned the music you left in the car last night was important. I wanted to make sure you had it, so I brought it tonight. I planned to hand it over after your set."

As if his words were the last piece of information she could carry on her slender shoulders, she covered her face with her hands and a torrent of tears burst free.

Not knowing what else to do, what else to say, he crossed to her side and buried her in his arms. "You're okay. You're safe. I promise. I won't let him get to you again."

Her tears soaked his shirt, but he held her close, letting her take as much time as she needed to pull herself back together. But he meant what he said. He'd let her, and her family, down before. This time would be different.

This time, he'd do whatever it took to protect her. No matter what the cost.

Lauren allowed herself a few minutes in Nolan's arms before the door burst open and Rebecca flew in the room. "Lauren! Oh my God. What happened?"

At the sound of her name from her roommate's lips, Lauren leaped away from Nolan as if his touch was made of fire.

And, if she was being honest with herself, being in his arms had burned her skin in a way she hadn't expected or wanted.

As Lauren fumbled to get the words out, the memory

of what had just occurred crashed against her as adrenaline leaked from her system. Her body shook, her knees trembled and she staggered to the side.

"Whoa, I got ya." Nolan braced his forearm behind her back, guiding her down to the ridiculous chair covered in white fur she hoped wasn't from an animal.

She tilted her body away from him, not wanting to admit how much she appreciated his support.

Rebecca crossed the room and took the seat to her left, clasping her hands over Lauren's. "I can't believe it. What are the odds of something like this happening two nights in a row?"

"It was the same man," Lauren said, unshed tears clogging her throat.

"Are you sure?" Nolan asked, retrieving a notepad from the pocket inside of his tan jacket.

She nodded, rubbing her trembling fingers over her exposed skin that peeked out of the neckline of her dress. "Same hat. Same smell. Same timbre of his voice." An involuntary shiver shook her shoulders.

Nolan flattened his lips in a straight line, the motion squaring off his smooth jaw. "I assumed the same thing as soon as I saw him."

Fear tightened her chest, and she locked her eyes with his. "How did he know where to find me? Is he following me? Should I be scared he'll come after me again?"

"I think he read the note you had with the papers you left behind in the car. The name and location of where you were playing tonight were written on a Post-it attached to the front of your music."

She widened her eyes. "I didn't even consider I'd left something behind that would lead him to me. Am

I safe?" A million scenarios played in her mind, none of them ending well. She had a life to live. She couldn't spend every day looking over her shoulder, waiting for the next attack that could be the last.

"Well," Nolan said. "He knows your name. Knows you're a musician, and two of the clubs where you've preformed. I can't make any promises that he won't try and find you again."

Rebecca scooted to the edge of her chair so their knees touched and squeezed Lauren's hand. "So what is she supposed to do?"

A familiar resentment bubbled up her throat and threatened to choke her. "Just trust New York's finest to solve the problem for me?"

He worked his jaw back and forth, the sting of her words seeming to land exactly where she'd wanted. But this time, a stab of guilt pierced her. He'd come to see her tonight to bring something that was important to her. An act of generosity that certainly wasn't in his job description. And if he hadn't shown up, there was no telling how her night would have ended.

"Be smart," he said, cutting into her thoughts. "You used pepper spray before, carry that with you at all times. If you use social media, make sure everything is set to private. And even then, try not to post about your plans or tag friends in pictures. At least not until this guy is caught."

She nodded along with his advice, all of which sounded easy enough to follow.

"Maybe change up your routine, if you have one. I doubt he knows much about you, but better safe than sorry."

A rap at the door turned her head. A tall man with black hair and kind eyes filled the doorway. His hands rested in the front pockets of his jeans, and he met her stare head-on. "May I come in?"

Nolan gave a crisp nod. "Thanks for coming, man. Ladies," he said, turning to address her and Rebecca. "This is Detective Jack Stone. A friend of mine who's agreed to help with the case."

Surprised, Lauren reared back her head. "Are you stepping away from the investigation?" A beat of regret confused the hell out of her. As much as seeing him last night had shaken her, the thought of someone else taking over turned her stomach. Since she didn't want to examine those feelings, she'd shove them aside and focus on the two detectives in front of her.

"No, I'm still the lead detective. Just asking for as much help as I can get." He flashed her a slow, hesitant smile. "Jack, do you want to step outside for a second before we take Ms. Mueller's statement? I want to show you the crime scene, and I need to grab something I dropped."

The mention of her music warmed her, and she watched the two men walk out the door, shutting it behind them. The night before, he'd been kind and patient even in the face of her rudeness. Then showing up tonight to bring her music… Maybe she'd misjudged him, or maybe he'd changed in the years since she'd seen him.

"You want to tell me what that look was about?" Rebecca asked.

"Not really," she said, throwing herself against the back of her chair. "Not sure how I can explain something I don't understand. Besides, it's been a long night. I wish I could just forget it instead of replay it all for the police."

"I don't blame you. As soon as you're done, we'll go home and crash. Lie low and relax. Maybe you can take a few days off work."

Exhaustion weighed her down. As much as she wished she could, taking a day off wasn't an option. Not when she needed every penny for her share of the rent. But that was a problem for tomorrow. "I'm not sure what's happening to me. I lost it when he told me he brought me my music, and he comforted me when I was falling apart." She couldn't erase the feel of his strong arms around her or the steady beat of his heart.

"Sounds like a nice guy."

She squeezed her eyes shut. "No. He's the reason my brother isn't here anymore, and I can't forget that."

No matter how badly a part of her wished she could.

Chapter 5

The bright glare of the computer screen bore into Nolan's eyes. He shoved away from his desk and rubbed his fingertips over his closed eyelids, trying to grind out the grains of fatigue that refused to leave.

"Why don't we take a break?" Jack stood from the chair he'd pulled beside Nolan's so they could watch the hours of security footage. "My head is pounding, and I'd kill for a decent cup of coffee."

Nolan dropped his hand. "I'll make us some."

"Nah, man. I said a decent cup," Jack said.

Nolan cast one more desperate look at the computer then stood, shutting off the monitor. "A quick break's a good idea. I need some caffeine, and I haven't eaten in hours."

He followed Jack out of the station and onto the sidewalk. A few pedestrians staggered by. Their rumpled clothes and bloodshot eyes suggested they hadn't made it home despite the god-awful hour. The street was as quiet as it got in this part of the city, random cars or taxis streaking by, and thick metal bars kept most of the shops and restaurants locked up tight.

Burying his hands in the pockets of his pants, Nolan dipped his chin toward Sunny Side Up. "Diner?"

"Like there's any other choice?"

Nolan snorted his agreement then waited for a cab to pass before hustling across the street. A yellow neon sun was bolted high on the exterior of the old diner, a caricature of two eggs holding hands beside it. A picture that always creeped Nolan out just a little. He didn't want to put a face to anything he ate, or in this case, a weird cartoon creature. But Sunny Side Up was the only restaurant open a few hours before sunrise for blocks, and they didn't have time to be picky.

Besides, the place was usually filled with cops grabbing a quick bite or refueling, and the food was pretty good.

Opening the door, he slid inside and was greeted by the smell of bold, strong coffee. His muscles relaxed, as if the jolt of caffeine had already hit his system and set him at ease.

"Let's grab a table in the corner. The counter can get a little noisy." Jack led the way down the aisle, four-person tables on one side and booths on the other, settling on the booth in the corner.

Nolan nodded hello to a couple of officers then scooted onto the ripped vinyl seat and folded his hands on the table, waiting for the thirtysomething server to make her way to the table before diving into any discussions on the case.

A woman with strawberry blond hair secured in a low ponytail and tired brown eyes approached with a small smile. "What can I get you fellas?"

"Coffee, black," Nolan said. "Scrambled eggs and bacon."

"Same," Jack said and flashed a quick grin before the server nodded and walked away.

Scrubbing his palms over his face, Nolan let out a long sigh and leaned against the cracked cushion. "I don't know how to find this guy and it's driving me nuts. He could be out there right now planning his next attack on Lauren or finding someone new to target."

"Do you think he'll move on so easily?"

Nolan shook his head. "No, but she's not the only one who can identify him. I have his driver profile from the car service. Hell, I spoke with his family back in Cleveland after the first attack. The only reason to keep going after Lauren is to finish what he started. And if tonight proves anything, it's that he won't give up on silencing her so easily."

The server ferried over a pot of coffee. "Food will be right up," she said, flipping over the white mugs set on the table and filling them close to the top. "Holler if you need anything else."

Jack circled his hands around his mug. "People have killed over much less. We don't know this guy's motivation, but he was ballsy to go after her tonight in such a crowded area. Tells me he won't be afraid to go after her again."

"Agreed." Nolan took a sip of the scalding hot liquid and winced as it burned his tongue.

"What did his family say?"

Nolan lifted his cup and blew into it for a second before answering. "His mom hasn't spoken with him in five days. She said that's not uncommon, but Malcom usually texts at least once a day since moving to New York."

"And the first victim was killed how long ago?"

"Four days. Timeline adds up. Suspect disappears a day before he kills his first victim."

"Any priors on his record?"

"Squeaky clean." He took another long sip of coffee and fought back a sigh as the caffeine hit his bloodstream. If he was lucky, this would keep him going for another couple hours before he was forced to crash. "Not so much as a traffic ticket, which isn't surprising since At Your Service does a deep dive into all employees they hire."

Jack drummed his fingertips along the rim of his mug. "When did he move to the city?"

"Six months ago."

"Any specific reason why?"

Nolan shrugged. "He's young. Twenty-five. Wanted something different so he thought he could make easy money driving for a car-share service while figuring out what he wanted out of life. No girlfriend, no enemies I can find. I spoke with a few friends and touched base with the local police. Nothing points to a motive for wanting to strangle two innocent women."

The smell of greasy bacon and salty eggs turned his

head to the server who approached, carrying two large plates.

She slid one meal in front of him, the next to Jack, then wiped her hands on the white apron tied around her ample waist. "There's ketchup and hot sauce on the table." She nodded toward the condiments that flanked the silver napkin dispenser pressed against the wall. "Anything else I can grab for you?"

"We're good, thanks. Just bring the bill when you get a chance," Nolan said then took a bite of the crispy bacon.

"What about friends in the city?" Jack asked, steering them back to the conversation. "Maybe something set him off here. Triggered him."

"I've only found one buddy, as well as the landlord. Not much to tell me. But I agree something must have happened here that set this whole thing in motion. My gut tells me the people I spoke with back in Cleveland weren't lying, and nothing points a finger at Malcom as a violent person."

Jack scooped a forkful of eggs into his mouth. "Any connection at all to the first victim? Could be a personal thing, and that killing spurred him to do it again. Find another young woman to murder."

Nolan threw his half-eaten slice of bacon on the plate. "It's possible, though I haven't found any connections. I can look harder, but my mind keeps going back to what Malcom said to Lauren last night. That he wanted to punish her or teach her a lesson. That has to mean something."

"If I had to guess, it means someone did something to Malcom that pissed him off enough to kill. And not just once. He's tried to kill Lauren, and chances are high he'll keep going after her."

"Maybe he's connected to Lauren, and she's just not aware of it." The new idea made the bacon in his stomach turn hard as rocks. He couldn't keep Lauren safe if he couldn't find the man who wanted to hurt her. And so far, nothing he'd found had led him to Malcom. But he had to keep trying, because he needed to put a killer behind bars as much as he needed to put Lauren Mueller out of his mind.

The whoosh of a bus stopping and a door opening cut through the thin walls and interrupted Lauren's slumber, forcing her awake. Sun filtered through the thin curtains. A heavy weight of exhaustion and pain pressed between her shoulder blades, keeping her pinned to the mattress. She hugged her pillow, burrowing her face into the satiny cover.

Soft kitty paws padded over her back and curled into a purring ball of fur on her spine.

A quiet buzz turned her toward the narrow stand she'd shoved beside her bed. She grabbed her phone and winced. Her mom's name flashed across the screen and judging by the time announced on her alarm clock, it probably wasn't the first time she'd called.

Sunday mornings were her and Mom's weekly catch-up. They tried to touch base throughout the week, but busy schedules often got in the way. Popping over to her parents' house in Brooklyn didn't happen as often as she wanted due to her busy schedule, so their ritual conversations were always a touchstone she looked forward to. Now it was an hour past their call time, and dread slowed Lauren's movement toward the phone.

In the seconds it took to answer, a million thoughts spun through her tired brain. She didn't want to add more stress to her mom's already chaotic life by telling her what had happened. Her mom already spent all her time taking care of her dad, too weak to do much for himself after his heart attack.

But not telling her mom about the attacks felt like lying. Something she never did, especially with the people who meant the most to her.

Unable to put it off any longer, she accepted the call then flopped on her back. "Hey, Mom."

Sissy jumped off the bed, shooting her a hostile glare for interrupting her slumber.

"Hi, honey. Is everything all right? I've called three times." Strain tightened the tone of Brenda's voice, even if she tried to hide it with a cheerful note.

"Sorry. I slept in. Late night." Lauren decided not to dive into the reasons why she'd lain in bed last night, replaying each horrifying moment when she thought her life would end. Doing so would do nothing to help her situation and would only upset her mother.

"Oh, that's right. How was your set at that new bar?"

"Went by like a blur." The lie tasted bitter on her tongue, but the less she said the better. "Listen, Mom, I'm so sorry to do this. But can I call you back later today? I want to talk, but I just woke up and my brain's a little fuzzy. I need some coffee."

"Are you sure you're feeling okay? It's not like you to stay in bed until almost noon."

She swallowed down another lie, the motion sending

spikes of pain to erupt in her still-tender throat. Tears misted in her eyes, but she sniffed back her emotions. Her mom knew her so well it'd be hard to hide anything. Especially if she let herself get upset while still on the line. "I'm fine. Rebecca came with me last night and we had a little too much fun."

A soft laugh sounded through the speaker. "Glad you girls let loose a little. You've been so serious ever since Charlie died. He'd hate to see you holed up in your apartment all the time, never going for drinks or evenings out with friends."

Her brother's name hit her like a fist to the heart. She felt the familiar guilt at not being there to protect her little brother when he needed her most—of failing to show up and stop him from making a mistake that would end up costing him his life. She circled her wrist where she always wore the bracelet Charlie had given her—twisting the bead-covered elastic over her skin.

She cleared her throat and pushed down the familiar feelings always boiling at the surface. "Well, I made up for all the evenings staying in last night. One too many cocktails, I'm afraid, and my head is killing me. I just need to grab some pain pills and a quick shower. Then I'll call you back."

"Take your time, sweetheart. I'm home all day."

Instead of comforting her, the thought of her mom sitting in the house she'd grown up in all day brought her down even further into the pit of despair she'd been trapped in for far too long. "Okay, Mom. Tell Dad I love him, and we'll speak soon. Love you."

"Love you, too."

Lauren disconnected and swung her feet over the

side of the bed. A heaviness hung in the air that had everything to do with her energy. She could lie around and sulk all day. But that wasn't who she was, or who she wanted to be. She had one day off a week, and errands to run and things to accomplish. So it was best to just get her lazy ass out of bed and start her day.

Standing, she finger-combed her tangled hair as she made her way to the postage stamp–size kitchen. A note from Rebecca was attached to the fridge, letting Lauren know she'd gone for a run. Half a pot of coffee was in the machine, but with Rebecca's early-morning habits, the liquid was probably cold by now.

Sissy meowed by her red dish on the floor, even though it was filled to the top with cat food.

"Looks like Rebecca fed you before she left so I don't know why you're so mouthy." She smiled at her beloved pet, reaching down to scratch behind her ears.

A knock on the door straightened her spine and had her heart racing.

It's a Sunday morning. Get a grip.

She rolled her eyes at her ridiculous reaction and crossed through the living room. Her bare feet padded over the soft rugs she'd placed on top of the scarred wooden floors, and a blast of cold air from the vent sent chills skittering up her arms.

Another soft rap had her lifting onto her tiptoes and peeking through the peephole in the center of the door.

A flash of relief at the sight of Detective Clayman crashed against irritation he'd show up at her apartment unannounced. A quick call to clue her in to why he'd need to see her would have at least gotten her out of her pajamas before answering the door. But there was no time to change. Not while he waited in the hall, staring at the door as if he could actually see her standing on the other side.

Grabbing hold of her annoyance so she could keep the fear threatening to sweep in at bay, she unlocked the door and swung it open.

Detective Clayman's stern expression and worried eyes met hers and stole her breath. "I'm sorry to bother you at home, Ms. Mueller."

She leaned against the door frame, as much to appear calm as to keep her suddenly trembling limbs from failing her. "I think you can call me Lauren at this point."

A hint of amusement broke through the tense lines of his face. "Okay, Lauren. Again, sorry to disturb you but I have some information you should hear from me."

Her pulse jumped, and she braced herself for whatever news he'd brought. "What is it?"

"Malcom Carson, the driver from At Your Service, is acquainted with Ronny Boone."

Her knees buckled and she flattened herself against the wall. She brought her hand to her chest and rubbed the bare skin above the neckline of her tank top, as if the motion would calm her.

But nothing would settle her nerves after hearing the name of her brother's best friend. The friend who'd made a wrong turn in life—then taken Charlie down with him.

Chapter 6

Ronny Boone. The name of Charlie's best friend sent shock waves through her, causing a debilitating sense of vertigo to knock her off-balance. For the second time in less than twenty-four hours, Lauren leaned into Detective Clayman's comforting support as he hurried inside the apartment.

He cupped her elbow and let her lean against his tall, hard body as he led her to the sofa in the middle of her living room and guided her to a seat.

"Thank you, Detective." The words sounded hollow, as if swallowed up by the ringing in her ears.

"If I can call you Lauren, you should probably call me Nolan. As long as you're okay with that." He took three quick strides to the door and closed it before returning to stand in front of her with worried eyes.

She blinked in rapid succession, trying to put meaning behind what he'd just said, but coming up short. Instead, she nodded, agreeing to calling him by his first name. Something that days before she'd never imagined possible.

"Do you mind if I sit?" he asked, glancing around the room.

"Umm, sure." She cleared her throat but couldn't get rid of the suffocating sensation constricting her windpipe.

"How about I grab you some water first. Is that all right?"

Again, words escaped her, and she nodded.

Nolan returned with a filled glass and settled down on the petite armchair that was angled toward her beside the sofa. "Here you go. Take a drink and a few minutes to process everything."

She accepted the glass and greedily gulped the cool liquid. Setting the half-drained cup on the coffee table, her hand trembled. "How does this guy know Ronny?"

"That's a good question."

Tilting her head to the side, she studied the hard lines of his angular face. "I don't understand. You said Malcom and Ronny were acquaintances. How could you know that without knowing how they are actually acquainted?"

"Malcom has only been in New York for six months. He moved from Cleveland. So his group of friends in the city is pretty limited. Last night I dove into his social media accounts, and I found a connection to Ronny." And he'd recognized the name instantly.

Her mind spun, and she flopped back against the

cushion. "But he's been in jail for the past four years. If Malcom just moved to town, how could the two of them have crossed paths?"

Nolan tightened his jaw and dropped his gaze to the floor. "Ronny served three and a half years. Was let out early. Which means he got out of jail around the same time Malcom came to town."

The words of her attacker came back with a vengeance. "He said he wanted to teach me a lesson. Could that message be from Ronny?" An image of the smiling boy with shaggy black hair and dimpled cheeks invaded her mind's eye and made her stomach hurt.

Nolan frowned. "Did you ever do anything to hurt Ronny? Get him in trouble in any way?"

She shook her head. "Not that I can think of. He and Charlie were eight years younger, so I didn't spend a lot of time with him. He came over a lot when they were younger, and I'd keep an eye on them both from time to time. He was a good kid...until he wasn't."

"What changed?"

Sadness rippled through her as she thought back to the wild boys with toothless grins who morphed into handsome young men. Both Charlie and Ronny had had so much potential, but neither would have the future they'd envisioned.

Charlie didn't have a future at all.

Propping her elbow on the armrest, she supported her head in her palm—her fingers interweaved in the messy strands of her hair. She cringed inwardly and fought not to fidget with the shorts that hiked up on her thighs or the thin material of her tank top that left little to the imagination.

Oh God, she didn't have on a bra.

Heat scorched her cheeks, but she trained her mind on the question that lingered between her and Nolan. "I don't know a lot of the details, but from what I overheard, his mom got sick. She lost her job, and care got so expensive. His dad wasn't the best guy and things got tense at home. Ronny started hanging with a rough crowd, getting into trouble. Mom tried to keep Charlie away from him, but he thought he could help. Wanted to stand by his buddy."

"Sounds like a good guy."

She smiled and stared down at the colorful beads of her bracelet. "Charlie was the best."

Tense silence pulsed between them. Nolan shifted in the chair and cleared his throat. "Doesn't sound like Ronny has a reason to be angry with you. You played no part in the burglary, so it wouldn't make sense for him to feel as though he needed to teach you a lesson for what happened."

A familiar ping of guilt ate at her stomach. "There might be one thing."

Curiosity furrowed his brow. "What?"

"I was supposed to take Ronny and Charlie to a concert the night they were arrested but I canceled last minute. Charlie was pissed I bailed. My parents were always strict, and even though he was seventeen, they wouldn't let him go without me."

"Okay," Nolan said, drawing out the word. "But what does that have to do with Ronny wanting to teach you a lesson?"

She met his gaze head-on. "If I'd taken them to the concert, they wouldn't have met up with Ronny's other friends. Charlie wouldn't have been driving the car. He wouldn't have been arrested or died alone and scared in a jail cell." Her lungs pressed against her chest, making each breath harder and harder to drag in through her nose.

Nolan leaned forward and rested a comforting hand on hers. "What happened to Charlie is not your fault. The decision Ronny and his friends made is not on you."

She bit the inside of her cheek to keep herself from falling apart. "Do you think Ronny believes that, or has he sat in a cell for three and a half years, planning out how to teach me a lesson?"

He shrugged. "There's one way to find out, but unfortunately, he'll only agree to speak with me on one condition."

She snapped her eyebrows together. "And what's that?"

"Ronny wants to talk to you first."

Her jaw dropped, and she shot to her feet. "Me? Why?" A combination of fear and foreboding slithered down her spine.

Nolan shrugged. "I don't know, but the decision's yours. If you don't want to speak with Ronny, I won't put you in a bad position."

The frantic beat of her heart drummed against her temples. So much of her past was colliding with her present, spinning her out of control. She'd done everything she could to get over what had happened, but what was the point when the feelings she hid were always right there—when the people she'd hidden from knocked on her apartment door?

When the kid who shoved her brother's life off the

tracks demanded she talk to him in order to speak to the police.

Maybe all this was happening for a very sick and twisted reason that would help her find a tiny shred of closure. To get past the guilt and grief and anger blocking her ability to heal. And if she had to confront the man who set this whole nightmare into motion, that's what she'd do.

Sucking in a deep breath, she faced Nolan. "Fine. I'll talk to Ronny."

Unease wiggled inside Nolan…for more than one reason. The least of which was sitting beside Lauren with her teeny pajamas exposing way too much skin.

But he shouldn't be thinking about anything in regard to Lauren Mueller except the case at hand, and the other issue that didn't sit well with him. When he'd reached out to Ronny regarding Malcom Carson, the young man had been uncooperative. Once Nolan had pressed a little harder, and Ronny understood why information was so important, he'd dropped one hell of a bomb.

He wanted to speak with Lauren.

Even though Nolan wasn't sure it was a great idea, he'd given the choice to her. And now that she'd made it, there was no turning back.

"Okay, as long as you're sure you want to see him, I'll set it up."

Lauren's eyes flew wide. "See him? I thought he just wanted to talk to me. Like on the phone or something."

He winced. He hadn't been specific enough with Ronny's request. "He wants to meet with you, today if

possible. I'll be with you every second, if that's okay?"
Again, he kicked himself for not laying all the cards on
the table. Two days ago, Lauren told him she'd never
wanted to speak to him again, and now he'd intruded
on her personal space and requested to accompany her
while she met with a young man from her past.

A young man who'd played a key part in the disaster
that had swallowed her family.

Just like Nolan had.

Lauren licked her lips, uncertainty dancing in her
crystal-blue eyes. "Why does he want to see me? What
could that possibly do for anyone?"

"I wish I could tell you. All I know is when I called
to ask about the photos I saw of him and Malcom on
social media, he clammed up and wouldn't explain their
relationship. Refused to say anything until he put things
together and realized who I was. I never told him Malcom attacked you."

She pulled her brows low, the ends almost colliding
at the bridge of her slender nose. "Then how did my
name come up?"

His throat tightened on the memory. "He asked if
you or your parents had forgiven me for what I'd done."

She dropped her gaze, her hand circling her wrist
and playing with a beaded bracelet.

As hard as it was, he continued. "He said he'd tried
to contact your parents but they haven't returned any
of his calls, and that he didn't know how to get hold of
you. But if I wanted to make amends, to do something
for Charlie, I'd find a way to get you to him. Then he'd
talk to me about Malcom."

"He called my parents? My mother never mentioned

anything." She curled her hands into fists and placed them on her lap. "She's been through enough. She doesn't need to relive this."

Nolan shrugged, searching for the right thing to say. "Some people need the closure."

The fire in her eyes darkened them to the shade of cobalt. "Well, some people will never find closure. And I won't sit on my hands and let Ronny storm back into our lives just to make himself feel better or to torture us more or whatever other reason he has for wanting to speak to us. I'll meet him. Get the answers about Malcom. Then tell him to leave us the hell alone."

The venom in her voice flew at him like shrapnel, and he couldn't help but feel her message was also meant for him. It didn't matter if she'd let her guard slip a little—hell, who wouldn't? Holding her in his arms had nothing to do with her hostility lessening and everything to do with being the person around when she fell apart. He'd gladly stepped in, given her whatever she needed in the moment, but he couldn't allow himself to believe Lauren had forgiven him. That when she looked at him, she'd ever see anything more than the man who'd ruined her family.

Slapping his hands on his thighs, he rose to his feet just as a fat ball of fur slinked into the room and rubbed against his shins. He couldn't fight the smile at the cat who looked at him with round eyes and a pathetic meow.

He crouched and scratched the pretty feline under the chin. "Well, who's this?"

"That's Sissy. My fur baby," Lauren said, a hint of amusement lifting her words. "She doesn't usually come out from under my bed when strangers are here. She likes you for some reason."

Glancing up at her, he arched one brow.

She scrunched up her face. "Sorry. That's not what I meant. I just—"

He raised a hand to stop any more unwelcome sentiments then ran a palm over Sissy's head before standing. "Don't worry about it. No need to explain."

She bit into her bottom lip, as if unsure she should say more or not. "I appreciate everything you've done for me. Saving me last night. Bringing my music to the bar. Even this." She waved a hand through the air.

Pressing his lips into a firm line, he rocked back on his heels. "Just doing my job. I'll get out of your hair. I'll contact Ronny and get a meeting set up, then let you know when I have the details."

She nodded.

"Will you please make sure to keep your phone with you today?" he asked, scratching at his chin as anxiety swelled in his gut. Damn, what the hell was wrong with him? He sounded like a needy schoolboy. He just wanted to give her plenty of time to throw on some clothes so his stupid blood wouldn't hum the entire time he sat across from her.

Her brow wrinkled, which combined with her slightly upturned nose and pouty lips and made her look cute as hell. "Yes. Why wouldn't I?"

He slid his hand from his chin to the back of his neck. "My calls earlier went unanswered, that's why I stopped by this morning. I needed to tell you about Ronny, but I was worried. I don't want to just show up again, and I'm sure you'd appreciate a heads-up."

She crossed her arms over her chest as if she understood exactly where his mind was.

He cleared his throat, but it did nothing to erase the awkwardness between them. "Okay. Thanks. So, just lie low today if you can. I'll hopefully be in touch soon."

She offered a small, tight smile as he turned away. He didn't need her to walk him the three steps to the door. One more glimpse of her long legs and toned arms in those skimpy shorts and tank top would push him over the edge.

Not like it'd really matter. It was only a matter of time before he took that plunge right over the edge.

Chapter 7

Taking a detour before heading home to grab a little shut-eye, Nolan drove through the familiar wrought-iron gates of the ancient cemetery in Brooklyn. It'd been months since the last time he'd been there, but a pull in his chest had led him back to a place he'd once visited weekly.

He parked in a small lot at the front of the property instead of driving along the narrow lane that weaved through the burial plots. The summer air was warm but didn't have the stickiness that usually came along with the afternoon sun. The smell of fresh-cut grass reminded him of summers long ago. A slight breeze rustled the vibrant green leaves of the trees, the sound soothing in the otherwise quiet space.

Grabbing the flowers he'd purchased, Nolan strolled

along the path. A peacefulness settled over him that was often hard to find—especially in his line of work. Funny how meandering among the dead calmed his nerves more than traipsing along with the living.

But it didn't surprise him, or even creep him out the way it did other people. Growing up, his mom loved to take him and his sister on walks through the cemetery by their home in Jersey. They'd read the tombstones, making it a game to see who could find the oldest one. His mother, an artist, would bring paper and pencils and show them how to trace the intricate designs and old-timey names on their sheets.

Nolan had forgotten about the moments of joy from his childhood until right after Charlie died. He'd taken it hard, the turmoil of playing a part in an innocent young man's death almost too heavy to bear, and he'd shown up at Charlie's gravesite in a moment of grief and confusion. He'd returned often, talking to Charlie and seeking those peaceful moments again and again.

And now he was back.

This time, he didn't take precious seconds to admire the stone statues or impressive mausoleum that dominated the center of the cemetery. He bypassed the benches and shaded patches of grass under wispy willows, making a beeline for Charlie Mueller's grave.

A simple stone marked Charlie's final resting place. A bouquet of wilted flowers was perched in a gold urn at the base of the headstone. Nolan plucked them out and replaced them with the fresh gerbera daisies tied with a red ribbon, then he buried his hands in his pockets.

"Hi, Charlie, it's been a while," he said, speaking

as if the boy was right beside him instead of long gone from this world.

"Your sister still hates me, not that I blame her." He chuckled and scratched the scruff he needed to shave on his jawline. "She's a spitfire. A fighter. I knew that already, but seeing her now is different. She's facing something dangerous head-on, and damn, she's fearless. I promise I'll do my best to keep her safe. To protect her like I should have protected you."

He swished his lips to the side and mouthed the words he'd read a hundred times before.

Charlie Mueller. Beloved son and brother. Taken too soon. Fly high and light the world from above.

Lauren's earlier words came back to him—that sometimes people couldn't always get closure. Had she meant that Ronny didn't deserve closure, or had she lumped Nolan into the same category? The ice had thawed considerably between them, but walls were still high.

Not like it should matter. All that mattered was finding Malcom Carson and putting an end to his reign of terror. Even if the idea of never seeing Lauren again sat heavy in his chest.

His phone rang, the shrill sound slicing into the tranquility. An unknown number flashed on his screen, but he didn't have the luxury of not answering. Accepting the call, he pressed the phone to his ear. "Hello?"

"It's Ronny. Did you talk to Lauren?" The gravelly voice on the other end spoke of a man who smoked his fair share of cigarettes.

"I did," he said, unwilling to let surprise sneak into his words. He'd texted Ronny after leaving Lauren's apartment, asking for a time and place to meet. Ronny hadn't answered, and Nolan had assumed when he did, it would be via text. Not a phone call.

"And?"

"Like I explained in my message, she'll meet you, but I'll be with her the whole time."

A rough snort sounded through the line. "I'm surprised she'd agree to that. She made it clear she wasn't your biggest fan. I'd even venture to say she'd be fine seeing you as the one in the cold ground."

The idea of being buried under the hard earth sent shivers down his spine. Not much scared him like the thought of being trapped—constricted—in a cold, dark space. He'd survived that once—no way in hell he wanted to do it again.

"How Ms. Mueller feels about me isn't the issue." His gut twisted, betraying the truth of that statement. Dammit, he needed to get a grip. Lauren's beautiful face and hard blue eyes had haunted him for years. But this was different. The last couple days had shown him another side of her. A side he wanted to see more of, but he had no doubt he never would.

"Fine. Can we meet today?"

"How about Brooklyn Bridge Park in an hour?" The sooner the better, even if it meant putting off getting some rest. He was running on fumes, but he could push himself a little harder before he collapsed. Besides, he was sure Lauren would rather get this over with and not sit around all day, anxious about the impending meeting.

"I'll text you when I get there and let you know where I am. Once Lauren sits down and talks with me, I'll tell you whatever you want to know about Malcom."

A whoosh of relief blew through the knot of tension coiled around his neck. Finally, a lead that would take him somewhere and not have him smacking his head against a dead end. He just hoped he wasn't putting Lauren at risk in the process.

"Okay. See you soon." He disconnected and stared back at the hard stone in front of him. He sighed, wishing he'd known Charlie Mueller in life. But that wasn't an option. He placed his palm on top of the smooth stone. "Until next time. And don't worry. I'll do everything I can to keep your sister safe. You can trust me this time. I promise."

He turned his back on the gravesite and hurried back to his car, typing out a message for Lauren in the process. The promise he'd made to her dead brother rang in his ears, and he hoped with every fiber of his being that the words weren't empty and hollow. No way he could live with himself if he let her down again.

A subtle breeze whipped off the Hudson River and tousled the long strands of Lauren's hair. She hooked the unruly hair behind her ear, wishing she'd brought a rubber band to secure it. The scent of fried foods and sweet pastries from nearby food carts turned her stomach. She might not have eaten anything today, but no way she could have forced anything down from the time Nolan showed up at her apartment until now when she sat next to him on a bench facing the river.

"How you holding up?" Nolan kept his gaze fixed straight ahead, his aviator sunglasses making him look more like a sexy fighter pilot than a city detective.

She shrugged, the movement pushing her own shades up her nose. "Just want to get this done."

"I don't blame you." His phone buzzed in his hand. "He's here."

She glanced behind her, squinting against the harsh rays of the warm sun despite her protective eyewear. She looked past the couple with a clapping toddler sitting on a blue blanket stretched over the grass and beyond the old man walking his large black dog.

A twentysomething man with all the roundness of youth gone from his face and a buzz cut she'd never expected walked into view, and her heart lodged in her throat. "I see him."

Nolan twisted around for a better look then stood. "You okay?"

Unable to tear her gaze from Ronny, she nodded. She didn't know what she'd expected, but this hardened young man strolling toward her definitely hadn't been it. She should stand but feared her legs wouldn't hold her.

Would Charlie look so grown-up now if he would have lived? Would he have gotten out of jail and gone on with his life as carefree and happy as he'd always been? Or would faint lines and a tight jaw showcase the difficult turn his life had taken like with his friend?

Ronny kept his head down, hands deep in the front pockets of his baggy jeans, and crossed the manicured lawn to the wide pathway that stretched along the river. He stopped behind the bench and shuffled his feet. "Hi." The greeting came out low and full of insecurity.

Tears hovered over her lashes, but she blinked them back. A plethora of emotions caught in her throat. She might not have recognized Ronny if she'd passed him on the street. But standing so close, she could see the little details she remembered from his youth. His deep green eyes that broadcast his feelings, the angular edges of his face—even if his chubby cheeks were long gone—and the scar above his dark eyebrow.

But she couldn't get sucked into the past. She had to focus on the reason Ronny was here. The reason she hadn't seen him in four long years. Inhaling a deep breath of warm air, she rose to her feet and turned her back to the river so she could face him. "Hello, Ronny. I heard you wanted to speak to me."

He nodded and rubbed the back of his neck, refusing to meet her eyes. His muscular arms strained against his black T-shirt, but he didn't give off the energy of a stacked criminal fresh from prison. "I didn't know how to get ahold of you, and when Detective Clayman called me, it was like a sign or something. A perfect way to find you."

Nolan stood tall and silent beside her, lips pressed in a tight line and eyes narrowed. Lauren took a breath.

"And why would you want to find me? What do you possibly have to say to me after all this time?" Nothing he said could change the past, and she refused to give him even a tiny shred of forgiveness.

She couldn't. Because forgiving Ronny for setting up Charlie would mean forgiving herself for blowing him off that night.

Ronny finally looked at her. Sadness and grief and regret shone through his eyes. "I'm sorry. For all of it. For making a shitty decision. For being so damn self-ish. For not telling Charlie what was happening. I put him in a bad situation, and if I would have come clean from the beginning, he wouldn't have been arrested. He wouldn't have been in that jail. He wouldn't have died." His voice cracked, and he dropped his head once again.

Pressure mounted in her chest, and a million thoughts swirled in her brain. She'd imagined this moment and what she'd say. She'd condemn Ronny, insisting he leave her and her family alone. But the idea of saying those things out loud twisted her gut. Her mouth went dry, and she licked her chapped lips, searching for the right thing to do. The right thing to say. "How's your mom?"

Ronny's head shot up and confusion pinched his face. "My mom?"

Lauren nodded.

"She's okay. In remission. I live with her now. I'm working, chipping in where I can. I put her through hell at a time when she was at her lowest. I owe her everything."

She tilted her head to the side, a small smile touching her lips as she stared at the scar again. "Do you remember when you got that scar?" She tapped her finger above her own eyebrow in case he wasn't sure what she meant.

Chuckling, he nodded. "Sure do. I jumped off your couch and hit my head on the edge of the coffee table."

"You thought you were a comic book hero. Charlie told you to fly."

He sucked in a deep, shuddering breath. "I tried."

"Keep trying," she said. "Charlie loved you like a brother. He wouldn't want you to waste a second living in the past. He'd want you to live your best life right now. He'd want you to fly."

Ronny grinned and the boy he used to be shone

bright as the sun on his face. "He *was* my brother. You all were my family. I know we can't ever go back to that. But thank you for showing me what that looks like. For being there for me. I'm sorry for everything and wish like hell Charlie was here instead of me."

She might agree with him, but she couldn't say it. Instead, she glanced at Nolan. She didn't have anything else to say to Ronny. Nothing more could be done for them. But a tiny weight lifted from her shoulders. "I think the detective has some questions for you, if you wouldn't mind answering them."

"I don't know how much I can tell you about Malcom," Ronny said, shifting his weight from one foot to the other. "But I'll answer whatever I can."

Nolan took a step forward, and she wished he'd offer a comforting hand or hold her for a brief minute like he had before. "How do you know Malcom Carson?"

Ronny shrugged. "Friend of a friend. He drives a car for At Your Service. We've hung out a few times."

"Have you spoken to him in the past week?" Nolan asked.

"Nah, I don't even know that guy's number."

Disappointment crushed down on Lauren. She'd come here today hoping to get more information about the man who'd attacked her. If this was all Ronny had to tell them, they'd leave with nothing. "What about your mutual friend?"

"My friend's a driver, too. I can give you his information if it helps."

"That'd be great." Nolan snatched a notepad and pencil from the back pocket of his jeans and handed them to Ronny.

Ronny scribbled on the pad and returned it to Nolan. "Why are you so interested in this guy?"

Lauren could see the hesitation on Nolan's face as he weighed the best way to answer. She was sure he didn't want to divulge too much information to Ronny, but her instincts told her Ronny didn't want to hurt her. On the contrary, that he wanted to make things right as best he could. Being honest with him could be more beneficial than keeping him in the dark. "He attacked me."

Nolan scowled, but she ignored him.

"We need to find him before he hurts someone else. So if there is anything else you know, it's important you tell me."

"I promise, I barely know the dude. But my friend knows more. I'll tell him to be up-front. To tell you guys whatever he can. It's the least I can do."

"Thank you, Ronny."

He dipped his chin and turned to leave.

Sadness overwhelmed her as she watched him go. One bad decision had cost them all so much, and no matter how much she wanted to, she could never go back. Never be there for Ronny the way she had while they'd grown up. But facing him had shown her that she could move forward, shed the shackles of hurt and grief she'd carried for so long.

A long shadow fell across her face, and she looked up into Nolan's kind eyes. If she was going to unlock those shackles, Ronny wasn't the only person she'd have to forgive.

Chapter 8

The pad of paper with the name of Nolan's new lead burned the inside of his pocket. He wanted nothing more than to call the number and get whatever information he could from Malcom's friend. But the wounded look on Lauren's face demanded his immediate attention. "Are you okay?"

She nodded but kept her gaze on the horizon, on the spot where Ronny had disappeared moments before.

"Why don't you take a seat?" He rested a hand on the curve of her spine and guided her back down onto the bench they'd sat on before Ronny arrived.

Touching her made his skin tingle. Dammit, he needed to stop this nonsense, stop seeking out every opportunity to put his skin on her body. He was probably coming across as some creep, not a desperate man who wanted to erase her pain in any way he could.

Sitting beside her, he tilted his head and watched the water. The Brooklyn Bridge stretched across the river, the jagged peaks of Manhattan's buildings a stunning backdrop behind the famed structure. Cars crammed together on the lanes and pedestrians looked like tiny ants as they made their way from one borough to another.

Lauren sighed, drawing his attention to her. He hooked an arm over the back of the bench, the tips of his fingers dangling down and brushing against her arm.

"Want to talk about it?" He didn't want to pry, but also wanted to be here if she needed to let out what she was feeling.

She shrugged and pressed her hands to her stomach. "I feel a little sick. Partly from wrapping my mind around what just happened. Partly because I haven't eaten anything today."

He glanced over his shoulder at the line of food trucks. "I can fix one of those problems. Looks like we got tacos, chicken wings or, if you just want something sweet, fresh doughnuts."

"I don't know if I can actually eat." She wrinkled her nose. "It might make things worse."

"I doubt that." He slapped his hands on his thighs then stood, unwilling to take no for an answer. "I haven't had lunch, and I haven't stopped smelling those chicken tacos since we arrived. How about I grab a few and we share?"

The side of her mouth hitched up. "Okay."

Before she changed her mind, he hurried to wait in the short line. His turn came after a few minutes, and he placed an order for five tacos and two bottles of water, springing for a side of chips and salsa. No one in their right mind could pass up chips and salsa.

But if he had to take a guess, he'd wager Lauren wasn't in her right mind. Not after the conversation he'd just witnessed between her and Ronny. After her reaction when he'd told her Ronny wanted to speak to her, he'd expected her to be hostile. That the conversation would be tense and awkward.

Instead, Lauren had surprised the hell out of him. She'd been kind and empathetic. Giving the guy what he needed—her words of encouragement and blessing to live a good life. As he carried lunch back to her, he couldn't help but wonder if her new perspective extended to him as well. Unfortunately, there was no way to ask the question without seeming unprofessional and putting himself out on a very thin and dangerous ledge.

Shutting the thoughts from his mind, he took the spot beside her and handed her a bundle of napkins. The strong scent of cilantro mixed with garlic and poured from the plastic bag he sat on the ground by his feet.

"Oh my. That smells amazing." She peered down, and her stomach growled.

He chuckled. "Sounds like I made the right call." Scooping out a pack of aluminum foil–wrapped tacos, he handed one to her then plucked out the other and placed it on his lap. Warmth seeped through the barrier and heated the skin beneath his jeans.

Lauren pinched the foil and peeled it open. She inhaled deeply. "I hope these taste as good as they look."

Not wanting to waste time finding out, he sunk his teeth into his first taco. Fresh pico de gallo spilled over the edge and sour cream smeared onto the corner of his mouth. An explosion of flavors erupted on his tongue.

He swiped a napkin off Lauren's lap and wiped the mess from his face. "I'm so glad you were hungry."

She laughed and took a small bite from her food. "It's a nice day for a picnic. Almost makes me forget someone tried to kill me last night."

He cringed, hating the heavy cloud that hung over them. Shifting, he pulled out the paper with the name and number of Ronny and Malcom's mutual friend. "Does the name Thomas Beetle sound familiar?"

Taking another nibble from her taco, she shook her head. "Never heard of him. Will you call him now? I'd rather not wait for you to talk to him if we can help it."

"Sure." He finished off his taco, cleaned his hands with the napkin, then grabbed his cell phone. He punched in the numbers, putting the call on speaker so Lauren could listen. When voice mail picked up, he ended the call.

"Why didn't you leave a message?" she asked, frowning.

"Gives him time to come up with a story, if he needs one. Let's see if I can find more information on the guy before I ask him to call me back." He opened a popular social media platform that was big with college-aged kids. Judging by Malcom's and Ronny's ages, he assumed Thomas was early twenties. If he got lucky, he might find some bread crumbs that could lead him to the guy. If that didn't work, he'd go into the station and use his resources to find an address.

Lauren scooched over, her slim thighs nestled right

next to his. She leaned to the side, craning her neck for a better view of his screen. "What are you doing now?"

The scent of lavender wafted up his nose, mixing with the feel of her body against his, and spiked his blood pressure. "Seeing if he's posted anything today. Maybe something that could lead us to him."

He typed the name in the search bar and a public profile popped up. A smattering of photos lined the page. Nolan zeroed in on the most recent picture. Dark smudges were smeared across his cheek, his brown hair neatly parted to the side. "He just posted about twenty minutes ago. Does he look familiar?"

"Not really." She slid her sunglasses on the top of her head and squinted at the screen. "Looks like he's at work. His shirt's part of a uniform, and the caption says, 'Workin' on the Weekend, Come See Me.'"

Nolan lifted the phone for a better view of the photo. He zoomed in on the logo on Thomas's shirt. "Logo says Big Al's Autobody Shop. Must be a mechanic."

Lauren wrapped up her remaining taco then put it back in the bag, hooking the plastic handle around her forearm before standing. "I thought your engine sounded a little funny on the way here. We better get it checked out before you take me home."

"You sure you're up for this?" Nolan asked as he slid his SUV into a spot close to the door. "You've dealt with a lot today. You can wait in the car if you want while I speak with him."

She pressed her lips together and shot up her eyebrows. "Seriously? I think I can handle it."

He shut off the engine and pocketed the keys. "I

never said you couldn't. Just don't want to put you in a bad situation. I usually hit the streets with a partner, as in another homicide detective, not a victim I'm trying to protect. It's creating a different dynamic than I'm used to, and I want to respect your boundaries."

Appreciation curled her toes hidden in her white sneakers. "I'll let you know if anything is too much. But honestly, feeling like I'm a part of the action, that I'm actually doing something productive, is helping more than you can imagine."

She'd always been a doer, a go-getter. Being on the sidelines had never been for her. Which was why she'd jumped in with both feet when she *knew* the role Charlie had played in his crime wasn't his choice. She'd been a thorn in everyone's side, including Nolan's, and she didn't regret one second of being her brother's advocate.

Now she needed to be her own advocate. And the comic twist of fate that put Nolan in her corner, fighting alongside her, could only make her shake her head. When life wanted to teach a lesson, it made sure to jam someone's past down their throat in a way they couldn't spit back out. She just needed to figure out what exactly that lesson was supposed to be.

"I understand that. But I think you should sit in the waiting room while I speak with him. I promise to tell you everything that he says, but having you in the room with me while I interview someone connected to a murder investigation isn't a great idea." He held her gaze, and nerves twisted inside of her that had nothing to do with having a conversation with Thomas Beetle.

She swallowed hard, pushing down this growing and unwanted attraction to the man she'd spent so many years despising—blaming for her brother's death. Not knowing what to say, she nodded then climbed out of the car. Being away from Nolan was probably a good idea anyway. She needed to put some distance between them to screw her head on straight.

Turning toward the street, she took a second to admire the cluster of old brownstones on the opposite side of the road—the stones warped from age. A few shops interrupted the row of homes, restaurants rounding out the area to announce the ethnic melting pot of culinary tastes. It didn't matter how long she lived in Manhattan, Brooklyn would always be home. "I wonder if Thomas and Ronny were friends before he went to prison. We aren't far from where I grew up."

Nolan waited for her to join him on the sidewalk before answering. "Maybe. I hope Thomas isn't trouble. Ronny's had enough of that. Joining the wrong crowd is the worst thing he could do."

Lauren agreed but kept her comments to herself. As much as a large part of her was glad she'd confronted her past, it was time to leave it all behind her and move forward. As Nolan led the way past the open garage door that showcased the tinkering mechanics and an old sedan, a tingling sensation danced up her spine.

The skin of his arm brushed against hers and her stomach did flip-flops. So much for that space she needed. She rushed past and yanked open the door, hurrying inside and welcoming the blast of air that cooled her suddenly flaming cheeks.

Nolan's furrowed brow and amused eyes told her he'd noticed her odd behavior, but he didn't mention it.

Instead, he marched past the towers of tires for sale to the front desk.

A man worked on a computer on top of the red laminate countertop. He lifted his index finger while keeping his focus on the screen. "I'll be with you folks in one second."

Nolan flashed his badge. "One second is fine, but then I need to speak with one of your employees. Thomas Beetle."

The man's gaze shot up, mouth in a hard line. "Excuse me?"

"I need to speak to Thomas Beetle," Nolan repeated.

"Is he in some kind of trouble?" The man, Al according to the name embroidered on his shirt, folded his arms over his chest and the muscles on his dark arms bulged.

"No, sir. Just looking for some answers he might have."

Al darted his scowl from Nolan to Lauren then back to Nolan before giving a subtle nod. "Head back to my office," he said, hooking a thumb over his shoulder. "I'll send Thomas back. For what it's worth, he's a good kid, despite some hardships thrown his way. Good worker."

"Appreciate your input." Nolan surveyed the showroom. "If you sit in one of the chairs on that back wall, I'll be able to see you if I keep the door open."

She nodded and offered a smile before opting to sit in the chair in the corner. She watched Nolan walk into the office, her attention drawn to the connecting door to the work area at the far corner of the room. A broad-shouldered young man with dark brown hair wiped his palms on a red handkerchief, his head down and focused on his hands as he entered the office.

A tug of regret had her wishing she hadn't agreed so quickly to stay out of the office while Nolan questioned Thomas. She'd just have to trust Nolan would fill her in when he was finished. And the odd thing was, she did trust him. That realization scared the hell out of her.

Nolan kept on his feet as he waited for Thomas to enter the office, making sure to keep Lauren in his line of vision.

A young man with finger-length brown hair and worried blue eyes rushed inside. He carried a red handkerchief that he used to wipe oil from his hands. "Hello. I'm told the police wanted to speak to me. I'd shake your hand, but…" He lifted a grease-encrusted palm.

"Don't worry about it. I'm Detective Nolan Clayman. I have a few questions about your friend. Malcom Carson."

Thomas's round eyes grew wider. "Malcom? Is he okay? I haven't heard from him in a few days. I've been a little bit worried, but figured he just took a trip home or something."

"I'm afraid not. I need to find Malcom in connection to one murder, and one attempted murder."

Thomas laughed and stuffed his handkerchief in the back pocket of his fitted trousers. "You're joking, right? Malcom wouldn't hurt anyone. Is he pranking me or something?"

Nolan frowned. "I'm afraid not. How well do you know Malcom?"

Thomas's face fell, as if the seriousness of the situation was sinking in. "I mean, pretty well, I guess. I just met him a few months ago, but I've spent quite a bit of time with him. He's a nice dude. Driver with At Your Service, that's where we met. I drive at night for extra money."

"In the time you've spent with him, has he ever exhibited a short temper? Been violent?" Nolan asked.

"Not at all." Thomas shook his head. "This doesn't make any sense."

Nolan cycled all the information through his mind. How was it possible that someone could fool every single person in their life? Unless whatever had set Malcom down this path of destruction was a recent development. "Is there anyone from At Your Service that doesn't like Malcom? That maybe wronged him in some way, and now he may feel as though he has something to prove? Like he needs to punish someone or teach them a lesson of some kind?"

"Nothing that he mentioned. Honest, I'd tell you if I knew something. I'm sure this is a big misunderstanding. The guy I know wouldn't hurt anyone."

Al poked his head around the door frame. "We're getting slammed out here. I need Thomas back as soon as possible."

Irritation tightened Nolan's jaw. "Do you know where Malcom would go if he was in trouble? Any place he'd hide or a person he'd turn to for help?"

Thomas sighed. "No. He hasn't lived here long and doesn't know many people. If I hear anything, or get ahold of him, I'll let you know. But I'm telling you right now, you've got it wrong. Malcom isn't a killer."

Nolan passed over a business card with instructions

to call if anything else came to mind or Thomas heard from Malcom.

Disappointment sat heavy on his shoulders and mixed with defeat. Thomas was the one who was wrong, and if Nolan couldn't crack the code and find Malcom, he had no doubt he'd strike again. And next time, Lauren could be the one who wound up dead.

Chapter 9

The little bell above the door at On the Rocks, the jewelry store Lauren worked in, chimed and anxiety tightened her core. She forced a smile, making it as wide and convincing as possible. "Good morning."

A woman with shoulder-length black hair and blunt bangs offered a hip-high wave then hurried to the nearest glass counter, peering inside.

A rush of relief relaxed Lauren's muscles, and she leaned against the wall, catching her breath for a second before approaching the customer. Since her shift started an hour before, every time that stupid bell signaled someone was entering the store, her muscles stiffened, and her mind went into overdrive. Imagining all the worst-case scenarios of Malcom busting through the door and finishing what he'd failed to accomplish twice.

"Can I help you find anything?" She peeked beneath the case the woman studied, spotting glittering diamond engagement rings.

"Just looking." The woman flashed a quick smile before glancing at the rings again. "I'm hoping my boyfriend proposes soon, and I can't stop myself from looking at rings. I'll love whatever he buys, but there's something about looking at them that just makes tiny tingles of excitement burst in my stomach."

Lauren bit back a sigh. Her salary was based largely on commission, and a woman swooning over possible rings her boyfriend might buy would leave her with nothing but wasted time. "That's so exciting. If you need any help, just let me know."

She took two steps back, not wanting to crowd her but needing to keep an eye on the customer just in case her luck suddenly changed and the woman wanted to make a purchase.

Amy, her manager, emerged from the back room and made her way to Lauren with a wide smile showing off her straight white teeth. Layered chestnut brown hair fell down her back and around her shoulders, the shaggy cut showcasing her high cheekbones. "She's here again?" she asked through the side of her mouth, the words only meant for Lauren's ears.

"Not the first time, huh?"

"Not even close."

The customer took another few seconds to drool over the expensive jewels then glanced up with a faraway look in her hazel eyes. "I have to go. Hopefully one of these will be mine soon."

Lauren crossed her fingers and feigned excitement. "We'll be here when he's ready."

Once the sales floor was empty, she leaned against the counter behind her. The store boasted a circle of clear display cases that trapped her in the center, making her feel exposed from every angle. Her fingers drifted to the base of her throat, and she kept her gaze trained on the door.

"Are you going to tell me what happened?" Sincerity coated Amy's sugary-sweet voice. She furrowed her brow and dipped her chin toward Lauren's neck.

Lauren cringed. Amy was a good three inches shorter than her, at eye level with the ugly bruises. She was close with her coworker, but she was tired of poring over every single detail of her attacks. As much as she hadn't wanted to go to work today, she'd craved the distraction. The slice of normalcy and routine that would force her mind from her constant fear.

Blowing out a long breath, she dropped her hand and crossed her arms over her waist. "Will you be upset if I just give you the short version?"

Amy rested a hand on her shoulder. "Of course not. You can tell me as much or as little as you want. No pressure. I just want to make sure you're okay, and judging by those nasty marks, you're far from all right."

She shrugged. "Physically, I'm fine. I was attacked over the weekend. Now I'm trying not to dwell on it while the police search for the man responsible."

"Your attacker hasn't been caught?" Amy's eyes bulged, and her slightly square jaw dropped. "Oh my goodness. I'm so sorry. This is terrifying."

"Yes, which is why I just want to push it out of my

mind right now. The detective in charge of the case is smart and capable and I trust him to do his job."

The truth of her statement slammed against her chest. Her world had been flipped upside down in more ways than one. Not only was a murderer wandering the streets, searching for her, but she actually trusted Nolan. Trusted him to find Malcom and trusted him to keep her safe.

"What's the goofy look on your face about?" Confusion rippled across the shallow wrinkles of Amy's brow.

Lauren scrunched up her nose, unsure of how to respond. So much turmoil and unease boiled in her gut, she didn't know the best way to answer. "In all the chaos of the last few days, I met a man who has completely taken me by surprise. Well, not really met, but our paths crossed again."

"From that grin I'm assuming that's a good thing."

"It would be, if our past wasn't so difficult."

"One thing I've learned in life is that our past can only make our present difficult if we let it."

Lauren wished that was true but couldn't make herself believe she could get over all the things keeping her from opening up to a possibility of something more with Nolan. She'd be betraying her brother if she acted on her feelings. She couldn't live with herself if she let that happen.

The bell chimed again, and Lauren tightened every muscle in her body.

Amy gave her a reassuring smile. "I got this. Why don't you handle inventory?"

"Thank you," she said before slipping into the back, away from the gaze of the middle-aged man who'd entered the store. Working away from the public would keep her busy while giving her the privacy she needed. The only person she had to worry about encountering was Amy.

Bypassing the small break room where her lunch waited in the mini fridge, she stepped into the office. Inventory wasn't something she usually handled, but it wasn't difficult. All she had to do was go through recent sales and figure out what they needed to replenish, then put together an order with their distributor. Amy would double-check everything before placing the order.

Forty-five minutes later, she stretched her arms high above her head, leaning from side to side to give her muscles some relief. Stomach growling, she stood. She needed to check on Amy and make sure everything was all right on the sales floor before grabbing something to munch on. As much as she wished she could hide away in the office for the rest of her shift, it wasn't an option. Especially when she depended on commission.

She made her way to the front of the store and found Amy happily ringing up a costumer.

Glancing up after the sale was made, she slipped her hand in the line of shelves under the register. She pulled out a square box with a fancy red ribbon tied over the top. "Someone left this for you. I would have gotten it to you right away, but I got a little busy. The guy said it wasn't a rush and he had to leave. Maybe it's from the man you mentioned earlier."

Dread slowed her steps. Uneasiness vibrated her body, but she grabbed the unfamiliar box and lifted the top. The hinges groaned with the motion. "It's a pocket watch." Weird. Why would anyone bring a pocket watch to her at work?

"Is there a note?" Amy asked, peering over her shoulder at the gold watch with the intricate lines etched on the front.

Lauren lifted the watch, but no note fell out. She pushed a tiny button and the lid flipped open. An engraving inside sent chills down her spine.

Your Time Is Up.

Terror catapulted Nolan through the door of the high-end jewelry store. He searched for a glimpse of Lauren in the crowded space, but she was nowhere to be found.

The store housed glass display cases that connected at the corners, with a cash register located close to the back wall. A woman with worried eyes and brown hair approached him. "Detective Clayman?"

"Yes. And you are?"

"Amy Sanders. The manager here. Lauren mentioned you were on your way. She's in the break room. I can show you."

Appreciation squeezed his throat. "Thank you."

He'd leaped into action the second he'd received the call from Lauren explaining what'd happened. A sense of panic had grabbed hold of him as he rushed across the city. He quietly urged Amy to move faster as she led him past the cases of expensive jewels into a quiet hallway.

The first door was propped open, and she angled her head inside. "She's with the officer who took her statement. Now, if you'll excuse me, I have to get back to work. I've already turned over the security footage and spoken with an officer, but if you need anything else, please don't hesitate to ask."

He uttered his gratitude then hurried into the break room. A square table sat in the center of the room. A thin counter took up one wall, a microwave on top and a mini fridge below. A television was mounted in the corner.

Lauren sat in a chair with her elbows propped on the table and nibbled on both her thumbnails. Officer Jeffery sat across from her. Good, Officer Jeffery was damn good at her job and already had information on the case after being first on scene after the initial attack on Lauren.

"You're here." Lauren hopped to her feet then stopped, as if unsure what to do next.

He pressed his lips together and gave a brief nod toward Officer Jeffery then skirted the edge of the table to wrap his arms around Lauren. He didn't give a damn if it was unprofessional or if it was the wrong move. He hadn't been able to take a full breath since her frantic call, and now he was the one who needed a moment of comfort.

She melted against him, clueing him in that he'd made the right decision.

"Are you okay?" he asked, ignoring the young officer's curious gaze. "I got here as soon as I could."

She nodded in an exaggerated motion against his chest, the top of her head brushing against his chin. "I know it sounds stupid, but I swear when I read that inscription the watch turned to fire and burned my hand."

Anger heated his veins and he squeezed her a little tighter. "I'm so sorry."

The sound of a throat clearing had Lauren springing away from him like a snapped rubber band. His arms felt empty without her in them, his body cold without her pressed close. He pivoted to the side, catching Officer Jeffery's wide eyes.

Okay, moment over. He needed to pull down the mask of professionalism and stop getting sucked into Lauren's orbit. Even if the fact that she'd leaned into his embrace made his pulse jump. "Officer Jeffery, have you watched the security footage from the time frame in which the suspect dropped off the package?" He still couldn't believe Malcom had the audacity to stroll inside and just leave a message for Lauren. As if he hadn't a care in the whole damn world.

"Yes, sir. A man walked in wearing a baseball hat and dark clothes. His face is angled away from the camera the entire time, so we don't get a clear view. But the height and build are similar to Malcom Carson's."

"Pull the feed from all the surrounding businesses. I want a visual of this guy when he comes, and when he leaves. How did he get here? Does he have another vehicle we don't know about, or is he taking public transportation?"

Officer Jeffery jumped to her feet. "I'm on it." She dipped her chin in Lauren's direction before heading out the door.

Lauren settled back into her seat, a pasty sheen taking over her face. "He found out where I work. How? And does that mean he knows where I live?"

He dropped into the chair beside her. "There's no way to know for sure. But if he figured out where you work, it couldn't be much harder to find where you live.

He may have followed you, or who knows, could have possibly hacked into your account from At Your Service to gain more information about you. But you live in a safe building. No way to get inside without a key or being let in by one of the residents."

"True," she said, though she didn't look convinced.

"I can't promise he'll stop coming for you. He's attacked you twice, and he's tracked you down at work. This is no longer a random encounter. He has an agenda and you're a part of it." Unable to help himself, he covered her hand with his. "If you don't feel safe at home, you can stay somewhere else. Your parents' home or a friend's place. Maybe a hotel?"

She shook her head. "Not an option. I don't have the money to cover the cost of holing up in a hotel until this is over. My mom has her hands full taking care of my dad. I haven't even told her about any of this. And I don't want to bring danger to any of my friends' doorsteps. I'm already putting Rebecca at risk."

He gave her hand a reassuring squeeze before sliding his palm from her knuckles. He ached to stay by her side, to be the one standing guard until danger had passed, but that'd be crossing a line. "None of what is happening is your fault. You can't blame yourself for other people's actions. Ever."

She dropped her gaze and rubbed the pad of her index finger against the top of the table. "It's hard to believe that."

Her words pressed against his lungs. She wasn't just talking about feeling responsible for putting the people she loved in danger. She was talking about Charlie.

A sharp rap on the door turned him away from her sad eyes.

Amy stood in the doorway. "Lauren, why don't you head home? Cynthia is coming in early, so your shift is covered. There's no reason for you to be here right now."

Lauren pinched the bridge of her nose. "I need the paycheck, but I really don't want to stay."

"Don't worry about that," Amy said. "I'll make sure you're taken care of. Now you need to take care of you."

She sighed. "Okay. Thank you. But just for today. I'll be back tomorrow morning."

"I'm not sure that's the best idea," he said, hating to be the one to burst her bubble. "Malcom knows you work here. He's already come by once. There's no telling if he'll come back again, and next time he might have more than a threat for you."

Tears rimmed her dark lashes, and she blinked them away. "I need to work. I have bills to pay. I can't just sit around doing nothing and hope things go back to normal."

Determination surged through him. It didn't matter what he had to do, he'd pound the pavement and watch as many hours of video footage as he needed to nail this guy. Lauren's life had already been derailed once. He'd do everything in his power to make sure it didn't happen again.

Chapter 10

Lauren unfastened her seat belt, keeping her fingers wrapped around the nylon strap across her chest as she stared out the passenger window of Nolan's SUV. She needed to step into the afternoon sun, but trepidation kept her glued to the seat.

"You don't have to go inside and tell your mom everything about what's happened." Nolan sat beside her, his fingers draped over the bottom of the steering wheel. The engine purred as the vehicle idled in her parents' driveway.

She released a long breath and studied the redbrick house she grew up in—just a few miles uptown from her current apartment. The grass needed cutting and the flower bed around the stoop her mother used to tend with love was filled with nothing but dried-out mulch.

"Yes, I do. There's no telling how far this guy will go to get to me, and I need to make sure Mom is protected. Even if just by staying on alert and not answering the door to strangers."

A humorless laugh puffed from her mouth. "Feels like I'm the parent. Giving directives Mom and Dad gave me when I was a kid left home alone."

"People say that happens. That the kids become more like the parents as they get older. But I agree that giving your mom a heads-up is a good idea. You just don't need to do it in person if you don't want. Give her a call and fill her in."

She shook her head. "Something like this, she needs to see I'm okay. Bruises and all. Thanks for the ride. I know you have your hands full. Babysitting me is the last thing you should be focused on, but the thought of being alone and making the trip out here…" Unable to put words to her nightmares, she let her voice trail off.

"No problem at all. Besides, I had Officer Jeffery forward all the security footage to my phone. I can leave and watch the footage in my office, or if you'd rather I stay and wait, I can pull it up on my screen and start wading through it."

Nibbling on her bottom lip, she weighed her options. She should tell him to leave, to do everything within his power to track down Malcom and throw him behind bars. But the idea of him being anywhere but close to her made the hairs on the back of her neck stand on end.

"Can you wait? I won't be long. Then, if you don't mind, you can drive me home. I could take the train, but I'd rather avoid it." Clearly, she was letting fear cloud her judgment and dictate her decisions, but dammit, she had every right to be afraid.

Wanting him beside her had nothing to do with the way he made her feel—safe and protected and a little like she was taking the first step off the edge of a cliff. The only problem was that taking that step could lead to the ride of her life until she smacked so hard against reality it took everything from her.

The side of his mouth ticked up. "I'll wait as long as you need me."

Her stomach did a somersault and she catapulted herself from the SUV before she did or said anything stupid. Coming home for a quick visit to give her mom an update on what was happening was the best choice she could have made right now. Not just because she couldn't drop a bomb like this on her mom's lap through the phone line, but also seeing the destruction Nolan's actions had caused in her family was exactly what she needed to get her head on straight.

Sticky summer air slid across her face, and she could feel it frizzing her hair as she made her way up the short driveway to the front door. She turned the knob, relieved to find it locked. Not wanting to wake her dad if he was resting, she grabbed her phone and called her mom.

"Lauren! What a surprise. I didn't expect to hear from you today."

"Well, I have a bigger surprise for you. I'm standing on the stoop. Can you let me in?"

Hurried footsteps grew louder until the front door swung open, and her mom beamed as she disconnected her call and slipped her phone into the front pocket of her tailored white pants. "What in the world are you doing here? And who is that sitting in my driveway?" She leaned to the side to peer around Lauren's shoulder. "Oh my gosh! What happened to your neck?"

Lauren twisted the hem of her blouse with her index finger, unsure of which question to tackle first. Her mom wouldn't like the answer to either. "Detective Nolan Clayman is in the car. He gave me a ride from work."

Her mom's eyebrows snapped low above her milky blue eyes. "Officer Clayman? Why in the world did he give you a ride here?"

Steeling her resolve, Lauren decided to rip off the Band-Aid and get the entire mess out in the open as fast as possible. "Friday night, the man who drove the car I'd ordered after work attacked me. That's how I got the bruises." Her fingers instinctively went to the still-tender spots around her throat.

Her mom gasped and covered her mouth with a shaking hand.

Lauren winced, determined to barrel through. "Nolan was the detective who came to the crime scene and is searching for the man who did this. He also showed up Saturday night when the same man attacked me again. Nolan saved my life."

Her mom leaned against the doorjamb, her eyes growing impossibly larger beneath her bifocals.

"That same man brought a menacing gift to my job today with a threat. I'm sorry I didn't tell you any of this when we spoke yesterday, but I'd hoped to protect you. Now that things have escalated, I need to make sure you're careful—that no one comes here under some guise and uses you or Dad to get to me."

A beat of silence passed between them. The whoosh of cars and the chirping of birds filled the otherwise quiet space, and Lauren's heart lurched as her mom wiped tears from her cheeks. "Is that everything?"

Lauren nodded.

"And Nolan." She said the name with way more interest than Lauren expected to hear. "Is he dropping you off or did you plan to lay all that on the doormat and rush away?"

"He said he can work in the car while we visit. I'm scared, Mom. He makes me feel safe."

"In that case, he might as well come inside. I just made a fresh batch of lemonade, and there's no reason for him to wait out in this heat. Even if his car is on."

Anxiety churned in her gut. "Are you sure you want him in the house? You do understand who he is, right?"

"Of course I do, and it wouldn't be the first time I've invited him in. Now, come on."

Her mom's comment ignited a flame of curiosity inside her. She'd invited Nolan inside their home before? When? And why? Turning toward him, she waved him in, wondering what other secrets he held back. No matter what those secrets were, she'd do whatever it took to see each and every one of them come to light.

Curiosity had Nolan cutting the engine and stepping out of the SUV. Why in the world was Lauren motioning him to come inside? He pocketed his phone and keys and stopped in front of the stoop attached to her parents' home. She stood a few inches above him, her mother just inside the doorway offering him a wobbly smile.

"Hello, Mrs. Mueller. How are you?" He was struck by the similarities between the two women. Lauren's hair didn't have the streaks of gray weaved through the chestnut like her mother's, but their builds and delicate features were almost exact replicas.

"I was fine until I found out all this awful news," she said, squeezing Lauren's hand. "And please, call me Brenda. Come on inside, you two." She turned and retreated into the bright hall, tugging Lauren along with her.

Lauren glanced over her shoulder and shrugged. "Sorry," she mouthed.

Not seeing a way out of it, he followed them inside the house and closed the door behind him. A wall of heat greeted him, the space stuffy as if fresh air hadn't entered the house in years. The living room was right off the narrow hallway, the kitchen beyond. A set of stairs climbed to the second story as soon as he entered the home. He assumed it led to the bedrooms and possibly a second bathroom, but that was part of the house he'd never been in before.

"Come on back to the kitchen," Brenda hollered. "I have some fresh lemonade and I just bought a pack of those cookies Lauren always liked."

Lauren hesitated at the threshold to the living room, glancing in for a quick peek before continuing toward the kitchen. "Where's Dad?"

"Lying down, dear. I would have kept him up from his nap if I'd known you were stopping by. But don't worry. I'll wake him before you leave so you can say hello. It will do his heart good to see you."

Nolan cringed. Lauren had mentioned her dad's heart attack the first night he'd taken her statement back in the convenience store. He hadn't asked for details, and she hadn't provided any, but a nagging feeling in the pit of his stomach told him Mr. Mueller wasn't the intimidating mass of a man he used to be.

The hallway opened up to a bright, cheery kitchen, and Nolan's stomach sank to the linoleum floor. His lunch rebelled as memories of his previous visit assaulted him. Sitting at the white farmhouse table across from Brenda as she cried, Lauren's dad hunched over in his chair with his arms folded over his broad chest. They'd been broken and defeated as he delivered the news that Charlie had died.

As he'd sat in their lovely kitchen with lemons on the curtains and pictures of their smiling children all around them and destroyed their world.

"Have a seat," Brenda said. "Do you like cookies, Nolan? They're store-bought, but trust me, they taste much better than anything I could throw together."

"Can I help, Mom?"

"You just sit on down. I've got this."

Brenda bustled around fetching glasses and tiny plates then placing them on the cluttered table. She scooted clipped coupons and crossword puzzle books to the side and made room for a pitcher of lemonade and a tray lined with paper doilies with the cookies on top.

"This looks great, Mom."

"Yes, thank you, Mrs. Mueller."

"I won't tell you again to call me Brenda, Detec-

tive. Especially after you saved my daughter's life."
Her voice caught and she dotted her eyes with a handkerchief she plucked from her pocket. "Funny how life
works itself out. I know how much you toiled over Charlie's case—how hard you fought for the truth. Your
kindness will always be remembered by me and my
husband, even though you wouldn't accept those words
from us all those years ago. Now you have my gratitude
again for keeping this one safe."

Lauren's hand stilled on the glass handle of the
pitcher. "Wait. What are you talking about?"

Like a coward, he kept his gaze glued to the table.
Mrs. and Mr. Mueller had never held him accountable
for Charlie's untimely passing like he and Lauren did.
Until now, he wasn't sure if they'd ever told her about
the times he'd stopped by to talk about Charlie.

But after listening to Lauren's admission that a part
of her blamed herself for her brother's death, he'd gladly
play the bad guy. Her parents must have felt the same
way. Better to place the blame at his feet and not mud-
dle her mind with the fact he was actually a decent guy
who'd fought so hard for Charlie, it had taken more from
him than anyone realized.

"Nolan stopped by a few times. He wanted to know
more about Charlie to help clear his name. Then when
Charlie died, he made sure he was the one who told
us. Came to the house and shed a tear for our boy right
alongside your father and me." Brenda doled out the
cookies then eased the handle from Lauren's hand to
fill their glasses with the yellow liquid.

"I…I don't understand." Lauren's pleading tone lifted

his gaze to hers. "You visited my parents? You tried to help Charlie?"

Unease tied his insides into a hundred knots. This wasn't how he wanted her to find out—hell, he'd never wanted her to find out what he'd tried and failed to do for her family. Because in the end, it didn't matter. *He* made the arrest. *He* slapped on the handcuffs. *He* was responsible.

"Nolan did everything he could for Charlie," Brenda cut in, saving him from having to answer. "And now he's watching out for you. All I ask is that you keep her safe. That you find this man who hurt her and lock him up tight."

The raw emotion in her voice tightened his fists. "Yes, ma'am. She's my number one priority."

Something deeper pressed against his chest that had nothing to do with Lauren's mother and everything to do with the truth of his words. Yes, he wanted to take down the man that was after her. The man had killed an innocent woman and repeatedly threatened another. But beyond that, Lauren had come to mean something to him the last couple days. Something more than what a victim should mean to the officer sworn to protect her.

His phone vibrated against his thigh, and he fished the device from his pocket. "I'm sorry. But I have to take this. Excuse me."

Accepting the call, he ducked his chin and angled himself away from the two women seated with him at the table. "Detective Clayman."

"Detective, this is Officer Jeffery. A call just came through. You're going to want to come to the crime scene."

Dread had him resting his head in his hands. He was too slow. Someone else had been killed, and he hadn't been able to stop it. "Was another woman murdered?"

"No, sir. The body of Malcom Carson was discovered."

Chapter 11

A million questions raced through Nolan's mind as he sped across the city. He stole a glance at Lauren, an unhealthy sheen covering her face. He should have taken her home—should have left her with her parents—but he didn't have time. He had to get to Malcom Carson's death scene as soon as possible.

Not to mention he couldn't bring himself to drop her off alone at her apartment until he verified the body found by the river was Malcom's. It was too risky and could all be an elaborate ploy to get him away from Lauren.

"When we get there, you can stay in the car," he said, weaving through the constant congestion of vehicles on the highway.

She shook her head. "I need to see with my own eyes that he's dead. That this is all really over."

He kept his opinions to himself. He'd learned the hard way what seeing a dead body could do to a person's mind—learned that some things you could never unsee. Lauren didn't need an image of a waterlogged and bloated corpse haunting her dreams at night, but he wouldn't argue with her now. Not when the Brooklyn Bridge was in view, the crime scene just around the corner.

Lauren shuddered, and he turned down the blast of cool air blowing from the vents.

She offered him a weak smile. "Thanks, but that's not the problem."

"Then what is?" he asked as he made a turn and pulled into a parking lot with two other police vehicles. He could make out the yellow crime scene tape ahead, looped between trees and keeping away gawkers.

"We were just here yesterday." She flicked her wrist toward the windshield. "Not in this exact location. But the park we met Ronny at was by the bridge. Does that mean something?"

He scratched at the whiskers tickling his chin. "It could. Or it could be a coincidence. At this point, I don't even know what happened to Malcom yet. But you bring up a valid question." He'd had the same one, but he was impressed nonetheless at how her mind worked.

She nodded, gaze fixed out the window. "Then there's the other thing."

"What do you mean?"

She grazed the tip of her thumbnail over her wrist. "I know now isn't the time to discuss this, but I want to know more about what my mother said. About you visiting my parents. When the time is right, I'd like to hear from you what that was all about."

"Okay." He drew out the word, not really wanting to have this conversation with her and grateful he could put it off a little while longer. "Once this is done, we'll talk."

She nodded and hopped out of the car before he could tell her his opinion on her accompanying him.

He met her at the hood of the SUV and flipped his sunglasses over his eyes. "This won't be pretty. I don't think you should see Malcom. Not like this. I understand wanting to see for yourself, but some things you can't unsee."

She met his stare and set her jaw. "I can handle it."

"I have no doubt you can. But you don't have to. Walk up to the crime scene tape with me, then I'll see what's going on. Do my job. Then fill you in. You can trust me."

Her lips curved. "I thought I could until I discovered you're pals with my mom. So many secrets, Detective."

Her teasing tone caught him off guard and he sputtered out a nonsensical sound that made her laugh.

She rested a palm on his chest as if to reassure him, and her touch set his body ablaze. "I'm joking. Like we already said, we'll discuss that later. After you figure out what happened to Malcom and take me home." Unspoken was her belief that everything would be better after that.

Her plan for the evening loosened the tension coiled through his intestines. Adrenaline had flooded his veins since his phone call with Officer Jeffery, but something held him back from the typical excitement that accompanied the impending end of such a stressful case.

But why?

He'd been sure the end of Malcom Carson meant the end of time spent with Lauren. There'd be no need to be around to keep her safe, so she could stay as far away from him as she liked—and she'd made it perfectly clear no distance was too small where he was concerned.

But if she still wanted him to drive her home and have a conversation to clear up any lingering issues from the past, maybe he hadn't seen the last of her after all.

"Deal," he said, then started toward the spot on the patch of grass where a distant group of officers were clustered together.

He tucked away all thoughts centered around Lauren to the back corner of his mind and focused on his reason for being here. Stopping under the shade of a giant maple tree, he took a quick glance around. "If you don't mind, can you hang back here?" Lauren would be within his line of sight, close enough to hear if she needed him but away from the growing crowd of gawkers.

She nodded. "Okay. If you need me for any reason, just let me know. I'm stronger than I look."

He couldn't hide his smile. As much as he appreciated her determination to assist him in any way she could, he'd handled dozens of murder scenes on his own. This case might hit a little more personal than most, but he was still capable of doing his job. "Thanks. Yell if you need anything. And I don't mean to sound paranoid but be on alert just in case things aren't as they seem."

"I will."

He fought the ridiculous desire to press a kiss to her lips before leaving her and strode down the steep incline toward the river. The closer he got to the muddy bank, the wetter and slicker the grass became. He took slow, cautious steps toward his colleagues.

"Thanks for the call, Officer Jeffery. I got here as soon as I could." He dipped his chin to the other officers standing guard over the sheet-covered body. "How positive are we this is Malcom Carson?"

Officer Jeffery took a step forward, her long hair pulled back from her face with a rubber band. "Pretty damn positive, sir. Identification was found in his wallet located in the back pocket of his jeans."

He whistled low. Identifying a victim couldn't get much easier than that. Glancing over his shoulder, he made sure to position himself so none of the spectators could see the dead man at his feet, then crouched low to pull the sheet away from his face.

He hadn't seen the ID, but a cursory look confirmed he was indeed looking at Malcom Carson. "Any wounds? Signs of cause of death?"

Nothing stood out from this view. Malcom's eyes were closed, but no blood stained the sheet or visible injuries marred the smooth lines of his face. No bloating puffed out his cheeks and the skin wasn't yet ashy or waxen. "Doesn't look like he's been dead long."

A young man cleared his throat, gaining Nolan's attention. "I was first on scene, sir. No wounds that I saw.

Nothing suspicious. First guess, the guy jumped from the bridge and washed ashore."

Nolan stood, tilting his head to study Malcom's face. "A jumper?"

"Just a guess, sir."

The words smacked against his chest, leaving him slack-jawed. Not only was Malcom Carson, suspected murderer and Lauren's stalker, dead—but his death looked like a suicide.

"You think he jumped off the bridge?" Lauren asked, her gaze fixed past Nolan to the glimpses of the white sheet she could spot through the growing number of arrivals who'd come to study the crime scene.

Nolan shoved a hand through his hair. "It's hard to know for sure. But as of now, there's no other indicators of foul play. I'll ask them to rush the autopsy, but chances are it will take a while for the body to be examined."

She studied the bridge and shuddered. The idea of jumping from such a staggering height made her stomach flip. "Wouldn't someone have noticed a jumper? I mean, people usually call the police to report that sort of thing, don't they?"

He angled himself for a better look at the bridge. "Good point. There's always tons of traffic. Vehicles and people crossing constantly. The idea that no one saw him jump—no one called and reported a suspected suicide—doesn't sit well with me."

"Could someone have called and you just aren't aware?" She folded her arms over her chest, as if the barrier could shield her from whatever evil had caused Malcom to take such a dramatic plunge.

"It's possible, and I'll definitely double-check, but that type of information would usually have come through already." He grabbed the back of his neck and squinted past her.

She glanced over her shoulder and the detective from the club sauntered toward them. She hadn't spoken much to Detective Stone, but he had made an impression for sure. No way she'd forget the intensity of those blue eyes.

"Afternoon," Detective Stone said as he approached.

She shifted a little closer to Nolan and offered a small smile. "Hello, Detective."

"Call me Jack. I'd say good to see you again, but the circumstances of our meetings haven't been too pleasant." He pressed his lips into a tight line then whipped off his sunglasses. A few days' worth of dark scruff covered his jawline, making the blue of his eyes brighter than the sky. He shifted his focus to Nolan. "What's it look like?"

"Like he jumped," Nolan said, snapping into police mode.

The small transition from conversation to professional communication hardened the lines of his face and made him stand a little taller. The differences were subtle but made her blood hum.

"Any other possibility?" Jack asked.

"Nothing obvious. Officers are out looking for witnesses to the fall. And an autopsy is crucial. Would like to pull as many strings as possible to get a rush on it."

Jack frowned. "You think drugs or alcohol in his system?"

Nolan nodded. "It's possible. In the meantime, I'll take a closer look at the video footage from earlier. Pay special attention to his walk, his behavior. See if he's staggering or off-balance at all."

"You think he could have been on something when he came to the jewelry store?" She frowned, adding that possibility in with everything else spinning her mind in circles. "Amy would have smelled alcohol on his breath. Especially if he was drunk enough to accidently fall off a bridge."

"Maybe. Maybe not. I want to talk to her again," Nolan said. "See if this new context shakes anything else loose she hadn't thought important."

Lauren swished her mouth to the side as she tried to put her emotions into words. "Something doesn't sit right with me. Why drop off a threatening package to me at work, telling me my time is almost up, then jump off a bridge? It doesn't make any sense."

The pointed look Nolan and Jack exchanged set her nerves on edge.

"I've had the same questions," Nolan said. "Things don't add up, and I don't know if that means there's more to the case or we just caught a lucky break."

"Do you usually get lucky breaks?" She scrunched her nose, already knowing the answer.

Nolan cracked a smile. "Never."

She blew out a long breath, weighing her options. As much as she wanted to stay by Nolan's side, even with Malcom out of the picture, he had a job to focus on. Standing around waiting in the late-afternoon heat didn't sound appealing. "You have a lot on your plate. I think I'll take the train back home."

"I'm going to take a look at the body before the coroner gets here. Give you two a chance to talk." Jack slapped a hand on Nolan's shoulder then gave her a wave before dipping below the crime scene tape.

Nolan shifted his weight to his right foot. "I don't like the idea of you traveling home alone."

His concern heated her cheeks, warming her from the inside out, but she couldn't let him waste any more time on her. "There's no reason for me to be scared anymore. Malcom's gone. The threat is over. I'm a big girl. I can see myself home." Her words may have been true, but a tiny sliver of fear slid down her spine.

"How about a cab, then? I'll walk you to the street. Flag down a taxi and make sure everything's on the up and up."

She was a grown woman who'd lived in this city her entire life and was more than capable of hailing a cab. But his willingness to go above and beyond just showed her more of the kind of person Nolan really was. "Deal."

They fell into step beside each other. Her hand brushed against his, the contact sending sparks of electricity up her arm. She should take a step away, move her arm so her pinkie didn't collide against his with every footfall, but she couldn't bring herself to stop.

At the street, cars and buses flew by. Nolan lifted a hand in the air, snagging the attention of a taxi driver.

The car squeezed itself beside the sidewalk, and Nolan circled his finger in a motion to indicate the driver needed to roll down the window. He leaned down and flashed his badge. "Just want to see your identification."

The man frowned. "Excuse me?" he asked, accent thick and annoyed.

"Just a precaution."

She couldn't bite back her grin. She couldn't remember the last time someone had taken care of her this way. She hated to admit it, but she liked it. Even if he was just doing his job.

The driver handed over his ID, which Nolan studied for a full minute before returning it. "Thanks." He opened the back door and gestured her inside. "I'll call if I get any more information."

She slid past him, the scent of his aftershave wafting up her nose. "Thank you. For everything." A lump wedged in her throat, as if this was their last goodbye. Which was stupid. The case wasn't officially closed, and he'd agreed to speak with her about his conversations with her parents.

"Be safe." He closed the door and stepped back on the sidewalk.

After giving the driver her address, she plopped back against the cloth seat while the events of the last few days flashed in her mind. So much had happened. So much had changed. A sudden need to hash out every detail had her grabbing her phone and calling Rebecca. Her roommate should be home from work by now, but she couldn't wait to dissect every feeling swirling around inside her. The line rang until voice mail picked up.

Dang. She didn't leave a voice mail but decided to call again in five minutes. Just in case Rebecca hadn't been able to get to her phone in time.

Voice mail.

A silly sense of dread tightened her core. Rebecca was busy. There were a million possible reasons why she couldn't answer the phone. She fought the urge to call a third time during the twenty-minute ride. When the driver pulled up to her building, she paid the tab and jumped out of the cab. She ran the few feet to the door, hurling herself inside and jogging to her apartment.

She fisted her keys in her palm and hurried down the narrow hall. Reaching the door, she jammed her key into the lock and turned it. Her heart stopped.

Okay. So the lock didn't click. Rebecca must have stopped home then forgot to lock it. No reason to panic.

She swung open the door and stepped inside. "Rebecca?"

No response.

"Are you home?" Noting that the living room and kitchen were empty, she tiptoed toward Rebecca's bedroom.

Her pulse raced and an uneasy feeling puckered the skin at the back of her neck. Her knock on Rebecca's closed door went unanswered, so she opened it a crack to find it as empty as the rest of the apartment. She spun around, facing the bathroom, but no one was inside.

She swallowed the ball of fear lodged in her throat and called Rebecca again. A ringing phone sounded from the living room. She ran down the hall and found her roommate's phone glowing on the end table by the sofa.

Well, crap. Rebecca wasn't here, and she had no way to get hold of her. And if she was honest with herself, she had no real reason for the panic swelling in her gut. Rebecca was always forgetting her phone at home and loved to be out and about. Staying in was never her thing, even early evening on a Monday. Besides, Malcom was dead. There was no reason to be afraid anymore.

She disconnected the call and sank onto the couch. She needed to get a grip. Then realization struck down on her. Rebecca wasn't the only one she hadn't found in the apartment.

Sissy was gone.

Chapter 12

No! Sissy has to be here!

Lauren shot to her feet. "Sissy! Here, kitty kitty." She clucked her tongue, making the noise that always had Sissy running her way.

Crossing the room, she wiped her palm over the smooth bench tucked beneath her piano, then moved aside the boxes of music stored under the bench. Sometimes Sissy liked to slide her way through the clutter like a contortionist and sleep in the most awkward positions. Nothing but stray dust puffed out of the hiding spot.

She darted to the kitchen, swinging her gaze to every corner she passed for her beloved cat. Lunging for the drawer where she kept Sissy's treats, she yanked it open and rummaged around until she found the resealable plastic bag. She snatched it and shook it in the air. "I've got your num nums, Sissy. Come on. Come out and see Mama."

No soft padding of little feet across the floor. No quiet meow or gentle hum of Sissy's happy purr.

Panic shot her back to the living room and to the nook she claimed as a bedroom. Sissy's usual spot at the foot of the bed, bathed in streams of light through the window, was empty. Lauren dropped to her knees and searched under her bed. A pair of running shoes, a discarded sock and too many dust bunnies were scattered in the shadows, but no cat.

Unshed tears pressed against the backs of her eyes and pressure built in her sinus cavity. She sprang back onto her feet and grabbed her phone as she retraced her steps back to Rebecca's room. Maybe she'd accidently locked Sissy in the closet. Ducking inside the room, she flipped on the lights and pushed open the sliding door. "Sissy? Here, kitty. Where are you?"

Not knowing what else to do, she found Nolan's number in her phone and pressed Call. She looked under Rebecca's bed as the phone rang in her ear.

"Lauren? Are you all right? Did you make it home safe?" The rapid-fire questions made Nolan's anxiousness all but shine through the phone line.

She stood and turned a circle, spying any crevice her cat could have holed up or gotten stuck in. "I'm sorry to call. I'm sure it's nothing, but I don't know what else to do and I have this sinking feeling in the pit of my stomach."

"Okay. Just slow down and tell me what happened." The calmness of his voice settled her nerves.

"When I got home, the door wasn't locked, which

was odd, but I figured Rebecca left in a hurry and forgot." She crossed the room and shook out the curtains, hoping the motion would send Sissy scattering across the floor.

"Did you go inside?"

The trepidation in his question had her doubting her decision to enter her home. "Yes. I mean, Malcom's dead, right? No need to worry. I got in and Rebecca isn't here. I called her number, but her phone is on the end table." She jogged out of the room and entered the bathroom. She peeked into the shower then in the slim strip of space between the cabinet and the wall. The emptiness made her heart thunder in her ears.

"Is that uncommon? I mean, most people are practically glued to their phones."

"Rebecca's a little scatterbrained and isn't one to stay home. So the fact her phone is here and she isn't home doesn't alarm me too much. But Sissy's gone." She hated the slight crack in her voice but the idea her cat was in trouble made her palms sweat.

"Has she ever gotten out before?" Nolan asked. "Does she like to sneak out when someone leaves? Maybe she's in the building, walking around the halls."

"I never thought of that. I'll look." She'd wander the halls, but as much as she wanted to look for Sissy, it didn't do anything to calm her anxiousness over Rebecca. "Should I be afraid for my roommate? I mean, I'm just being silly, right?"

"Maybe, but I'm always an advocate for instincts having a lot to tell us. Do you have the number of some of her friends you could call? Can you find out if anyone has seen or spoken with her?"

She nodded, flipping through her memory of mutual friends Rebecca may be with.

"Umm, do you want me to stop by? I left the crime scene and I'm not too far from your place. I can help you look for your cat or brainstorm where your friend might be."

Relief sagged her shoulders, and a little bit of the turmoil boiling in her gut floated away. "Really? You'd do that?"

"Sit tight and make those calls. We'll search the building for your cat together."

"Okay. Thanks. I'll see you soon." She disconnected and held the phone close to her chest for a beat while she tried to control the erratic racing of her pulse. Nolan was coming over, taking time out of his day yet again to help her. Just because she was shaken by two things that most likely didn't mean a darn thing. Sissy was probably begging for treats from unsuspecting tenants, and Rebecca was probably out for a drink after a quick stop by the apartment to change out of her work clothes.

And here she was, sitting alone and still worrying over everything after the danger had passed. Or maybe she'd built the situation up in her head as an excuse to call Nolan, ask for help and hope he made the offer to come to her aid.

Not wanting to give that too much thought, she pulled up her contact list and found the information of one of the teachers from Rebecca's school, where she taught seventh grade. Lauren licked her dry lips as she waited for someone to answer the phone.

"Hello?"

"Hi, Bailey. It's Lauren. Have you seen Rebecca?"

Bailey, a close friend of Rebecca's who'd taught with her for the past five years, made a little humming noise as though trying to recall the answer to such a simple question. "I saw her at school today but not since. She planned to meet me and Sue for happy hour, but she hasn't shown yet. I assumed she was running late. If you catch her before she heads this way, you should come with her. I haven't seen you in way too long."

"Thanks for the invite," she said, not wanting to go into all the reasons that wouldn't be happening. "Any chance you know of someone else Rebecca could be with? She's not home, and she left her phone here. I really need to get ahold of her."

Bailey chuckled. "It amazes me how someone who is so organized at work can be so frazzled and forgetful."

Lauren smiled at the description, wholeheartedly agreeing.

"But no," Bailey continued. "She didn't mention meeting anyone else. Try her mom or sister. She tells them everything."

"Okay, thanks. If she shows up, tell her to give me a call." She disconnected, wondering who else to try. She and Rebecca didn't have a lot of mutual friends, and no way she'd alarm her family over a nagging feeling that was unwarranted at this time.

She scrolled through her contacts, searching for anyone else to call and coming up blank. Frustration tightened her fist around her phone.

A buzz sounded on the intercom that connected to the outside of the building. She hurried to the panel by the door and pressed the button. "Hello?"

"It's Nolan. Can you let me in?"

She granted him access, keeping her finger pressed on the button long enough to ensure he'd entered the building, then tapped her toe against the floor as she waited for him to get to her apartment. Seconds ticked by like hours, anticipation heightening her awareness of everything around her.

A soft knock sounded. A quick peek in the peephole showed her Nolan's concerned face. She opened the door and launched herself into his arms. To hell with the past and the questions and the contradiction of feelings playing tug-of-war with her heart. She needed to feel safety and comfort right now.

She needed Nolan.

Nolan held Lauren tight and breathed her in, her hair tickling his nose. The feel of her in his arms was becoming way too familiar—way too enticing.

He allowed himself one more second to inhale the scent of her lavender shampoo then took a step in retreat, keeping his loose grip on her biceps. Her hair was messy, as though she'd shoved her hand through the long strands a few times. She still wore her nice blouse and black trousers from work, which were a direct contrast to the wild worry in her eyes. "Have you heard anything?"

She shook her head and wiped at her eyes with the backs of her hands. "I spoke with a friend who said Rebecca was supposed to meet her for a drink and hasn't shown yet. I told her to call if Rebecca shows up."

"Okay, that's good. We know she had plans. Hopefully she's just running late." He skimmed his hands up and down her bare arms, hating the way she shook from the new fear coming into her life. "And Sissy?"

"No," she said, sniffing. "She's not in the apartment. I waited for you to search the building."

The muscles in his stomach tightened at the look of anguish on her face. He'd never had a pet, but Lauren's cat obviously meant a lot to her. Knowing something she loved was lost and possibly scared did all sorts of unwelcome things to his insides. "I made sure to keep an eye out for her while I was driving. I didn't notice any cats on the sidewalk or by the building. Grab your keys and we'll walk every hall of every floor. Knock on as many doors as we need to until we find her."

Lauren nodded and broke away from him to gather her things and meet him in the hallway. After she shut and locked the door, he walked beside her as she searched every possible space her cat could be and spoke to as many neighbors as were willing to open their doors and chat. Twenty minutes later, they were back in her apartment with no cat and no sign of her roommate.

"What now?" Lauren asked, raising her arms in the air then dropping down into the sofa.

Nolan scooted the piano bench out and sat, hunching over to brace his forearms on his knees. He wanted to sit next to Lauren, hook an arm over her shoulder and offer his reassurances, but being too close wasn't a good idea right now. Especially when her worry was rubbing off on him.

When she'd first called, he'd assumed it was an excuse to get him to her apartment without having to ask. A roommate she hadn't spoken with in a couple hours and a cat who was probably fast asleep in some unknown hiding spot didn't seem like good reasons to call the police. Now his gut told him otherwise.

Combine that with the odd sensation he couldn't let go of that Malcom's death wasn't as cut-and-dried as it appeared, and he needed to pop an antacid.

"Call her friend again. The one who she was supposed to get a drink with. Maybe she forgot to call."

Lauren made the call then pressed her phone to her ear. "Bailey, hi. It's Lauren again. Has Rebecca showed up?"

He couldn't hear the other woman's response, but the way Lauren's face fell told him everything he needed to know.

"Okay. Thanks. Yes, please have her call if she stops by." She disconnected and hung her head. "Am I crazy for worrying?"

"Never. I hate to say it, but there's not much I can do right now. She's not technically missing, and we have no evidence there's been foul play. From an outsider's perspective, this looks like your roommate left in a hurry, forgot her phone and to lock up, and accidently let your cat out when she left. For all we know, she's outside searching for Sissy right now."

"And from your perspective?" She twisted the bracelet around her wrist, avoiding eye contact.

Unable to stay away any longer, he crossed the small room and took the seat beside her. He rested a hand on top of her knuckles, stilling her nervous movement over the childish-looking piece of jewelry before it rubbed a hole in her skin. "I think that when a lot of bad things happen to the same person, they're usually connected. I don't want to jump to conclusions, but there are a whole lot of things that are off."

She stared at him with wide, terror-filled eyes. "You don't think Malcom is really still out there, do you?"

He bit back a soft chuckle. "No, of that I'm one hundred percent certain. But something else isn't right and I can't put my finger on it."

Sighing, she leaned to the side and rested her head on his shoulder. "I'm still scared. My brain is telling me that the threat is gone. That there's no real reason to be fearful anymore. But my gut doesn't believe it."

Shifting his arm to rest behind her back, he skimmed his knuckles over her soft skin. He understood what she meant because he felt it, too. Not fear, but something else. Something sinister with the promise of more violence, more death.

But if that destruction wasn't coming at the hands of Malcom, then who?

"Nolan?" She said his name in a hushed whisper that sent shivers up his spine.

"Yes?"

"Will you stay with me? Until I know what happened to Rebecca? I'm sure she'll come home and tell me how silly I was for overreacting. But until then, I don't want to be alone."

He pressed a simple kiss against the top of her head, needing to reassure her in any way that he could. "I'm not going anywhere."

He had a million things to do, a million questions to answer. But right now, all that mattered was keeping Lauren safe from whatever threat still waited for her. And in the end, there was one thing he was sure of.

Rebecca wouldn't be walking through the door anytime soon.

Chapter 13

Lauren flipped the lid of the pizza box closed and squeezed the hardly touched dinner in the cramped refrigerator. Nolan had insisted they eat something.

Funny how she wouldn't have eaten anything today if it hadn't been for Nolan keeping an eye on her.

The few bites she'd consumed at lunch and dinner would have to be enough. No way she could force down any more. Not when hours had passed, she hadn't heard a word from Rebecca and Sissy was still nowhere to be found.

With the leftover pizza sufficiently shoved into place, she made sure the fridge was latched before returning to the living room.

Nolan stood facing the wall, phone pressed to his ear and a tight set to his shoulders. She studied his broad back and the way the fabric of his dress shirt strained just a smidge around his biceps. His hair was mussed, as though he'd been running his hand through it. He'd unbuttoned his shirtsleeves at the wrists and shoved the material to his forearms, the result sexy as hell.

Her core tingled, and she winced. Now was not the time to fall victim to some ridiculous fantasy with the handsome detective. Not when her roommate was missing, and her world was tilted on its axis. She couldn't trust these feelings bubbling up every time she laid eyes on Nolan. Couldn't trust the rush of excitement that flooded her system when he held her.

No, too much had happened in too little time. Playing tricks with her mind and leaving her on unstable ground. Nothing she felt for Nolan was real.

He disconnected his call and shoved the phone back in the front pocket of his trousers then turned toward her. His eyes met hers, and all the moisture evaporated from her mouth.

Well, damn, maybe these stupid feelings brewing inside her were real after all.

"That was Jack. Not much to report. He's spoken with the coroner about speeding up the autopsy for Malcom, but there's no way to know if that will happen or not. I told him about your roommate."

She held her breath. She *knew* something wasn't right, but having Nolan discuss Rebecca with another homicide detective made it even scarier. "And?"

"He agrees with us. None of this sits well with him, but there's not much we can do. You talked to her family, alerted her friends. Now all we can do is wait and hope we're wrong and she comes home soon."

"And if she doesn't?"

"We can file a missing persons report and get more eyes looking for her."

Blowing out the air she'd held in her cheeks, she ran her fingers through her long tangle of hair. The messy strands had to look as unkempt as his. The day had been long and frustrating and full of ups and downs—mostly downs. She couldn't make heads or tails of anything and didn't have the energy to try.

She hung her head, searching for the next right step. She'd already posted pictures of Sissy on all her social media pages and neighborhood watch sites. Rebecca's family and friends were called, all now as worried as she was, and the police were looped in on everything that was going on. She should tell Nolan to leave. Then she could finally get out of her work clothes, into her pajamas, and try to sleep.

But sleep likely wouldn't come, and she'd lie in bed for hours, anxious at every creak and groan of the old building. And the thought of being alone, of Nolan being gone, made her wrap her arms around her middle.

The pluck of a piano key lifted her head.

Nolan stood in front of the piano, one hand in his pocket with the other settled on the ivory keys. He ran his fingers along the instrument, creating a choppy melody she'd learned as a child.

Smiling, she crossed the room to stand at his side. "You play?"

The corner of his mouth ticked up in a smirk. "A little."

"Show me what you got." As much as she loved sitting down and pounding out the music building up inside her, she always enjoyed watching others. She even gave lessons when she had time. Teaching children to play and discover their own passion for the piano was almost more fulfilling than sitting onstage, getting lost in the music while captivating an audience.

He slid his fingers off the keys. "I'm pretty rusty. I'll pass."

"Please," she said, resting a hand on his arm. "I could use a distraction right now."

Sighing, he moved to the center of the piano and positioned both hands on the keys. He moved his fingers, slowly at first, creating a slow, hesitant song. He picked up the speed as his confidence must have grown, connecting melodies and creating a beautiful sound that filled her apartment. When he was done, he shoved his hands back in his pockets and twisted his lips to the side.

Her jaw dropped. "That was beautiful. Why didn't you mention you could play so well?"

He shrugged, inching up his gaze to meet hers. "You never asked."

Such a simple statement with so much power. So much meaning. How often had she made assumptions about this man simply because she'd been blinded by circumstances? Caught up in her own drama and unwilling to see what was in front of her?

She squirmed beneath his gaze but refused to look away. "Like how I never asked if you visited my parents? I mean, that'd be a pretty random thing to just assume happened, don't you think?"

He ran a palm over his face then let his hand fall to his side. "Speaking with your parents was part of me chasing my own demons. Trying to right wrongs. It started out with wanting more information about your brother. Your mom was so welcoming, so happy to sit in the kitchen and tell me everything about him. So I kept going. Kept learning more. And every time I left, I had more motivation to help Charlie. To prove his innocence and get him out of that hellhole of a jail cell."

His admission had her stumbling back to the couch. After seeing her mom, she'd already known most of this, but hearing it from his lips broke something loose inside her. The backs of her knees hit the cushions and she sank down. "You told them in person that he died. Why?"

He followed her to the sofa and sat beside her. "I owed them that much. They didn't deserve to hear their son had been killed from a stranger. They deserved to hear it from me, the person who put him in that cell to begin with."

For the first time in four long years, the truth all but smacked her in the face. "You might have made the arrest, but you aren't responsible for his death."

Shock widened the planes of his face. "I might not have thrown the grenade, but I'm the one who pulled out the pin."

She took his hands in hers. The warmth of his skin encased her, spurring her on. "You acted with kindness and compassion toward two scared and grieving parents. You did what you could to help. No one can ask for more than that."

Before she lost her nerve, she leaned forward and placed a small kiss on his soft lips then rested her head on his shoulder. She threaded her fingers through his and sat in the silence. His shallow breaths combined with hers the only sound, the steady rise and fall of his chest the only movement.

The vise that had tightened her insides for so damn long loosened. Letting go of her anger toward Nolan freed her in ways she'd never thought possible. If only she could forgive herself as easily.

The blast of the television met Nolan at the doorway of his apartment the next morning. He groaned, shutting and locking the door behind him. Since there didn't appear to be a burglary in progress, only two people had a key to his apartment and could be inside his home right now.

Jack or Madi.

Since he'd already spoken with Jack, who was still at his place with his girlfriend, Olivia, that left only one real possibility. His baby sister, Madi must have stumbled in at some point the night before and, chances were, was still fast asleep.

Sighing, he made his way deeper into his apartment. He didn't have the energy to deal with Madi. Not after an uncomfortable night on Lauren's couch.

A night where he would have killed to reciprocate the simple kiss she'd given him after they'd talked about her brother. Instead, he sat while she'd leaned against him and fallen into a deep sleep. He hadn't wanted to move—to wake her—and the rest of their evening could only be described with one word.

Torture.

But at least she'd slept. Something she claimed she hadn't been able to do since the first night she was attacked. And chances were she wouldn't have been able to if he'd left her alone for the night, worried about her roommate who still hadn't come home.

Dropping his keys on the counter in the small kitchen, he stepped into the living room. A bundle of blankets hid Madi's slim frame on the couch, nothing but her face poking through the mound of material. He shut off the television, and she shifted to her side, stretching her arms over her head.

He rolled his eyes, a small part of him wishing he could just be waking up. But he'd never been the type to stay in bed much past daybreak, even when he'd been Madi's age. She'd always soaked up the baby status, choosing not to take much too seriously. Even her college classes.

That wasn't his problem. What was his problem was the mess of empty beer cans and half-eaten pizza left in an open box on the floor.

"Madi." He shook her arm, jostling her awake.

She groaned and scrunched up her nose. "What do you want?"

"I want you to get off my couch and clean this place up." He crossed his arms over his chest, mentally counting to ten to keep his temper in check. He had too much on his plate to deal with this right now. "I don't mind you crashing here from time to time but show a little respect. I don't like living in squalor like some people."

"Oh my God, who uses the word *squalor*?" She hugged the navy blanket over her shoulders and dragged herself to a seated position. Her blue eyes were bloodshot and her strawberry blond hair stuck out like she'd put her finger in the light socket.

He bit back a smile at the seriousness of her question. "Why are you in my apartment, anyway? You have a perfectly good dorm room where you can leave your trash all over the floor if you want."

"I was at a party last night a few blocks away. It was cheaper for the car to drop me off here," she said, finger-combing her short strands. "I didn't think you'd mind."

Her statement set him on edge. "Car? Where did you order from?"

She shrugged. "I don't know. Some app. At Your Service, I think. Sounds so prim and proper, like the driver would bring me tea if I asked."

The name scattered goose bumps up his arms. "You always double-check you're in the right car, right? Match the license plate to what the app gives you, make sure it's the right driver?"

Madi pressed together her lips and narrowed her eyes. "Yes, big brother. I'm not an idiot. Besides, the drivers are vetted. It's no big deal. Nothing's going to happen to me."

He bit his tongue, not wanting to dive into another lecture with too many details that Madi refused to hear. "Just be careful, okay?"

"Okay." She kicked off her covers and rose to her feet. Last night's clothes were wrinkled and way too small for his liking. "Where were you last night, anyway? You're always home, unless you caught a case."

"None of your business." He bent down, scooped up the pizza box and carried it to the kitchen.

The sound of footsteps padded after him. "Why won't you tell me? Big date?" She leaned against the doorway and wiggled her eyebrows.

He clenched his jaw, not wanting to disclose anything about his evening. "No date."

Madi made the same pouty face she'd used as a child to get her way. "Come on. Tell me. You have that dazed look of running on no sleep but also being exhilarated because it was one hell of a night."

He couldn't stop his laugh at her ability to read him so well, even if her correct assessment wasn't for the reason she probably assumed. He was exhilarated by the time he'd spent with Lauren, even if it hadn't gone beyond a quick peck on the lips. But she'd forgiven him, had shown him that she'd moved past her resentment and hard feelings. He just needed to figure out if her kiss was just a way to show him the depth of her gratitude, or an indication she was open to something more.

The idea of more with Lauren made his chest ache in a way that had him reeling. Damn, he had it bad. Maybe talking things over with Madi wasn't the worst idea. "I spent the night with Lauren Mueller, but nothing happened."

Madi's jaw dropped. "You what? No! No, no, no. That woman made your life a living hell. Why were you with her in the first place? After everything she said about you? After what happened because of her?"

He winced. Okay, maybe talking about this with Madi was a bad idea. He rubbed a palm over his face, needing a shave and a shower even more than a cup of coffee. "I'm not getting into this with you. You wanted to know where I was, I told you. Now leave it be."

Lifting her chin, she folded her arms over her chest. "All those interviews she did back then, claiming you were incompetent and killed her brother—all the social media posts that were blasted across the city—she nearly destroyed your career. She nearly destroyed *you*."

"She had a point, you know. I never should have arrested Charlie. He was innocent." He nearly yelled the words, the same sentiment that had replayed on repeat in his head over and over, year after year. Driving him to the brink of insanity, which led to keeping his concentration off his job.

Which led him to not pay attention that night on the highway. When he'd drifted left of center and flipped his car—trapping himself in the confining vehicle for hours.

Dammit to hell and back. Maybe Madi had a point. It had taken years to erase the smear campaign against him from his mind. To keep his focus where it needed to be at all times—on the job.

And all it had taken was a few days with Lauren back in his life to keep his head turned only in her direction. He couldn't go back to that. Lauren wasn't the only one whose past was filled with demons she couldn't forget, and the truth of the matter was, there was only one thing from his own past that still haunted him.

Lauren.

Chapter 14

Lauren stepped out of the shower and dried herself off with the white cotton towel she'd hung on the back of the door. She drew in a deep breath of the steamy air trapped inside the bathroom. She'd managed to have a more sound night of sleep last night than in more years than she could remember.

Even if her muscles were a little stiff and a hint of embarrassment remained from the image she'd presented of herself to Nolan first thing in the morning.

But damn, he'd looked good. With sleep in his eyes and his hair a mess… A shiver ran down her spine at the memory of waking in his arms. His hesitant smile the first thing she'd seen before she'd jumped to her feet, making apologies for falling asleep.

He'd been kind and sweet and all the things she'd

never thought he could be. A perfect gentleman, at a time when she'd been perfectly okay with him not being one at all. He'd left her alone with the rising sun and a promise to call as soon as he could.

After drying off, she slipped on her gray terrycloth robe and padded down the hall and into her room. The bright shafts of sunlight streaming onto her bed cast a blinding glare on the harsh reality awaiting her. Sissy was gone, and she still hadn't heard a word from Rebecca. Each passing minute heightened her fear to a new level. There had to be something she could do, anything to help find her roommate.

While calculating a plan, she rummaged through her dresser drawer until she found her favorite pair of lilac joggers and a fitted black tank top. The day would be warm, but she didn't plan on stepping out of her apartment unless necessary. Too many unanswered questions, too many lingering feelings of terror and unease awaited her outside.

Dressed and with a comb run through her wet hair, she made her way to the kitchen to start the coffee. The empty pot pulled at her heartstrings. Rebecca was the early riser and usually had coffee waiting for her. She blinked away tears. She'd be no help to anyone if she couldn't pull herself together.

When the steady drips fell into the pot, she took a deep breath. After she had a mug in hand, she'd try to figure out Rebecca's password for her phone and maybe she'd find a clue as to where her friend was. Last night, hacking her device seemed like an invasion of privacy she wasn't ready to commit. But this morning, with no word from her, privacy was the last thing Lauren was worried about.

The shrill ring of her phone cut into the quiet apartment and sent her pulse racing. She ran into the living room where she'd left her device on the end table and scooped it up. Nolan's information popped up on the screen, and her stomach did a clumsy cartwheel.

"Hello." She winced at the breathy quality of her voice. "I'm so glad you called. I was thinking I should try to access Rebecca's phone. Maybe there's something I'm missing."

As she spoke, she rounded the end of the sofa and grabbed Rebecca's phone. She swiped the screen to life and typed in the first thought that came into her mind for a password—one, two, three, four. Of course, it didn't work.

"Lauren, you don't need to mess with her phone," Nolan said, his voice eerily calm, as if talking to a child who was about to throw an epic tantrum.

"Why not? Do you think we'd have better luck if I brought it to the police station? I'm sure you have all kinds of people who are trained on how to hack into one of these things. I can come right now." She searched for her keys and purse, wanting to get started on an actual plan to find Rebecca as soon as possible. She'd been a fool to think she could stay hidden inside her apartment all day. Not when she had to do whatever was possible to help find Rebecca and bring her home.

"You don't need to come to the station, but I would like you to meet me at the hospital."

Fear dropped like a bowling ball in her stomach, stretching it all the way down to the floor. She squeezed her eyes closed, dreading asking the question she needed to have an answer to, but not wanting to know what waited at the hospital. "Why? Who is at the hospital?"

"Rebecca's here. She was brought in early this morning. She'd like you to come. Bring some things for her. Clothes, toiletries, her phone."

The words fell into the room with explosive power and knocked her off-balance. She gripped the back of the sofa to keep herself upright. Relief swept through her, and her hands trembled. "She's there? At the hospital? Oh my God. What happened? Is she all right?"

"She's a little banged up, but she'll be fine. At least physically. She was taken from your apartment, Lauren. She managed to escape. I'll tell you everything when you get here."

Realization struck down on her. "Is her kidnapper still out there? Was it Malcom? Am I safe to come down there on my own?" The sensation of being watched made her shiver even though the curtains were drawn. But if someone had grabbed Rebecca from their home, was that person still out there? Or was he lying on a cold, hard slab in the morgue?

"The timeline is murky," Nolan said, cutting into her spiraling thoughts. "We'll go over everything once you're here. Just be careful. Stay on alert." He said what hospital he was at and a room number.

She nodded along with his words as she ran back to Rebecca's room and yanked what she'd need from her closet. "Okay. That's close. I should be there soon."

Disconnecting, she found a bag at the bottom of Rebecca's closet and threw her things inside then sprinted for her own room. She quickly braided her still-wet hair, shoved her feet into a pair of sandals and scooped up her purse. After leaving and locking up behind her, she secured her pepper spray in her hand. If the timeline of yesterday's events was muddled, there was a chance that someone who wanted to hurt her was out there—and knew where she lived. The thought tightened her grip on the cylinder can. She wouldn't be caught off guard again.

Nolan sat in the waiting room, waiting for Lauren. Anxiety pitched high in his gut as he checked the clock hanging on the wall for the tenth time since they'd hung up.

He should have gone to her apartment and delivered the news about Rebecca in person. Then he could have seen her safely to the hospital. But as much as he wanted to keep a constant eye on her, he had a job to do. Not to mention the nagging voice of his sister in the back of his head warning him to keep his distance from Lauren.

A voice that made too much sense to ignore.

The automatic doors whooshed open, and Lauren sprinted inside. Her long hair was thrown over one shoulder in a simple braid and her eyes were wide and haunted. She carried a large duffel bag along with a purse strapped across her body and something in her clenched fist.

Pepper spray.

Guilt chomped down on him. She was afraid, as she should be, and he hadn't been there when she needed him.

Jumping to his feet, he lifted a palm in the air. "Lauren," he yelled through the chaos. Nurses bustled about, wheeling injured patients from one place to another. Annoyed people waited to be seen, grumbling about lack of care in their chairs or slumped over their phones.

She turned his way then weaved through the obstacles to make her way to his side. "How is she? Can I go up to her room?"

"She's okay, but it will do her good to see a familiar face." He cupped a hand under her elbow and led her to the bank of elevators on the other side of the nurse's station.

"I can't believe this happened," she said, shaking her head as if to showcase her disbelief. "I never imaged she'd be in danger. Especially in our apartment. How did she escape? Where did he keep her?"

The elevator door slid open, and he ushered her inside before pushing the button for Rebecca's floor. The smattering of people inside kept his mouth closed until they reached their stop and stepped under the bright fluorescent lights. "I'll let her share those details."

He hadn't taken her official statement yet. She'd been in too much shock to put her through that. With her family out of state, Rebecca needed a close friend to calm her nerves and make her feel secure. Once that was accomplished, he'd see if she was ready to tell him everything she remembered about the terrible ordeal she'd survived.

Approaching Rebecca's room, he nodded toward the open door. "Do you want me to wait in the hallway and give you ladies a few minutes alone?"

She sucked in a shuddering breath. "I'd rather you were in there with me. I'd hate if she mentioned something when you weren't inside that could be helpful to the case."

Madi's voice might still be in his head, but he hated seeing the agony flickering across Lauren's face. Reaching out, he wrapped his hand around her fist still clenching the pepper spray. "She's fine. She's safe. And so are you. You can put the pepper spray away. I won't let anything happen to you."

A flicker of a smile rewarded him, and she tapped lightly on the door before she crossed over the threshold while putting away her chemical weapon. "Hello? Rebecca? Can I come in?"

He followed, making sure no one else was in the room before he closed the door behind him.

Rebecca lay in the bed with the blanket up to her chin. Her long auburn hair tumbled around her shoulders, her eyes wide and filled with terror. She pushed a button on the little control beside her, which lifted her into a sitting position.

The stiff white blanket fell to her lap. Her frame was so small, so frail, hidden under the boxy hospital gown. Tears filled her eyes. "Lauren. You're here. Thank God."

Lauren rushed to the side of the bed and threw her arms around Rebecca. "I'm so sorry this happened to you. I can't believe someone would break into the apartment and just take you. You must have been so scared."

Nolan slipped farther inside and sat on one of two hard chairs shoved against the wall. He'd let the women talk and comfort each other before he asked any questions.

A choked sob poured from Rebecca's mouth.

Lauren sat back and smoothed a piece of hair from her face.

Nolan noted Rebecca's injuries. Red skin circled her mouth, and stitches lined her temple where she'd been hit on the head. Her right foot and calf were hidden behind a white cast. Her other scars would lie beneath the surface.

"It all happened so fast," Rebecca said, voice shaking. "I got home from work and changed. When I opened the door to leave, a man rushed through the doorway. He had a gun, a mask pulled over his face, and he told me he'd shoot me if I made a noise or tried to run. Sissy hissed and leaped at him, but he kicked her out the door."

Lauren's face crumpled, and she covered her mouth with her knuckles.

Anger heated Nolan's blood as he listened to how Rebecca had been ambushed in her own home, but curiosity kept him tuned in to the conversation. He didn't have a time of death on Malcom yet, but he could have gone to the apartment after leaving the watch for Lauren. Waiting for her return but choosing to attack her roommate instead.

But could he have made it back to Brooklyn? Jumping or being pushed from the bridge or whatever had happened to end his life? Those answers would be impossible to know until he knew exactly what had happened to Malcom.

"How did you get away? Where were you all night?" Lauren asked. She sat on the edge of the bed and took Rebecca's hand in hers.

Rebecca swallowed hard, as if the memories were too

painful to recall. "He put me in the trunk of a car. Muttered about teaching you a lesson. He bound my wrists and ankles and put duct tape over my mouth then hit me on the head with the gun. I passed out."

He leaned forward, a fact sticking out amidst the horror she'd just described. Malcom didn't have another vehicle registered to his name.

Rebecca wet her lips with her tongue. "Can you pass me my water, please?"

Lauren reached over to the little side table wheeled next to the bed and handed the plastic cup to Rebecca.

Rebecca took a long sip then handed the cup back. The skin around her wrists was an angry red. "I don't know how much time passed before I woke up. I realized he wasn't coming back for me. The car hadn't moved in hours. It was so hot. I thought I would die in that trunk. Something snapped inside me. I started thrashing around, kicking my legs. My foot smashed through one of the taillights. I messed up my foot pretty bad. Someone saw and called the police. He talked to me, kept me calm and assured me help was on the way. When the police showed up, they broke me out and brought me here. I was in that trunk all night." Her voice cracked, as if that realization was the last straw.

With her hand back in Rebecca's, Lauren glanced over her shoulder at him. "Was it Malcom? Did he grab her before he died?"

Rebecca's eyes flew wide. "He's dead?"

Nolan nodded. "His body was found yesterday. Early evening, which means it's possible your attacker was Malcom. That could explain why he never came back for you." Though Nolan still didn't understand why

Malcom didn't kill Rebecca right away like the first woman and like he'd tried to do with Lauren.

"Where did he park the car?" Lauren asked.

"Outside a park in Brooklyn."

Nolan stood, needing to make a call that Rebecca and Lauren shouldn't hear. "I'm going to step out in the hall for a second. Rebecca, do you know how long they plan to keep you here?"

"The doctor said at least overnight."

"I'll make sure to post an officer at your door until we know exactly what's going on." He offered the ladies a grim smile and walked out of the room.

In the wide hallway, the light bounced off the shiny linoleum floor and the harsh scent of stale air and disinfectant stung his nostrils. He'd call Jack and see if they could meet in Brooklyn. Another car waited to be combed through, and he had to know who was listed on the registration.

Because until they found out who had taken Rebecca, neither one of the women were safe.

Chapter 15

"Hey, man. How's Rebecca doing?" Jack asked as soon as he answered.

Nolan scratched the back of his neck, the image of Rebecca's scared face ingrained in his mind. "She's better now that Lauren's here. Went through quite the ordeal last night. She's lucky she made it out alive."

"I got the highlights from Officer Jeffery."

"Glad to hear it. She does good work. Has she found out who the vehicle is registered to?" He rubbed the sole of his shoe against the floor.

"A guy named Timothy Troth. Claims the car was stolen yesterday morning, or at least that's when he noticed it was missing."

A dull thud pulsed against the center of Nolan's forehead. Another name to add to the mix. "Where had he parked his car?"

"A garage a few blocks from his place, which was pretty damn close to Lauren's apartment."

Nolan blew out a long breath. "Probably swiped the car while casing the building. Had a plan for grabbing Lauren but changed his mind and took her roommate when the opportunity presented itself. Any connections between Troth and Malcom Carson?"

"None that I've found. I might be missing something, but I already asked for security footage from the garage to check Timothy's story. Let's see if Malcom makes an appearance."

Guilt tightened his shoulders. He should have been the one to talk to Officer Jeffery about the vehicle registration. He should have known about the stolen car and requested the footage. Instead, he was sitting at the hospital. He could spin the story in his mind that he needed Rebecca's statement and was working to get an officer stationed at her door in case her kidnapper was still out there. But he'd be lying.

He was here because of Lauren. She drew him to her like a magnet. One of those heavy-duty ones that was useless to fight against. He had to do something to sever that connection, to get out of range of this hold she had over him.

"Learning the key to Malcom's death is crucial to every other piece of this puzzle. It's possible he grabbed Rebecca and died before he finished whatever he intended to do with her. If that's the case, searching for any other criminal is just chasing our own damn tails."

"Agreed," Jack said. "But we both know how long autopsies can take."

"Then I might have to pay the morgue a little visit.

See who's in charge of Malcom's examination and find out if there's any way to grease the wheels a little."

"Good luck. If you need me there, just ask."

"You've done plenty, but I'll be in touch." He disconnected then called the station to secure an officer for the night outside Rebecca's room. Too many questions remained unanswered. He couldn't risk Rebecca's safety if the man who'd almost killed her was still out there, pissed that the woman he'd taken had escaped.

With everything in place, he ventured inside the room.

Lauren swiveled to face him, her blue eyes bloodshot and nose red. She sniffed back tears and forced a smile. "Hear anything?"

He stood in the doorway, not wanting to intrude or get sucked into the hum of energy that surrounded Lauren. Energy that made it impossible for him to think of anything except her. "Got a name for the owner of the car. Timothy Troth. Sound familiar to either one of you?"

"Not to me. What about you?" Lauren shifted toward Rebecca, who shook her head, then faced him again. "Is he the man who took Rebecca?" She slid her hand into her roommate's, offering comfort as they each braced for his answer.

"Timothy claims the car was stolen, and Jack is poring over the security footage from the parking garage—as well as the police report for the stolen vehicle—to verify he's not involved in any of this."

Lauren screwed her lips to the side. "I don't know if that's good news or not. I mean, it'd be nice if the man was caught right away and thrown behind bars. But it'd be nicer if Malcom was responsible for everything, and we know he'll never hurt anyone else again. Does that make me a bad person?"

"Not at all," Nolan said. "And hopefully I'm going to find the answers we need once and for all."

"How?" Lauren asked, brow raised high and hope pouring off her in waves.

"I'm going to do everything I can to rush Malcom's autopsy. I have to go to the morgue."

"Now?" Lauren widened her eyes.

He nodded. "An officer is on the way. She'll stand by the door until either Rebecca is released or I know for sure the threat to both of you is gone."

She pinched the bridge of her nose. "I need this to be over. I can't keep looking over my shoulder, jumping at every noise like a scared little mouse. I lost out on two days' work, and there's no way I can bail on my standing gig tonight. They won't care why I cancel. They'll replace me in a heartbeat, and I've worked too hard to get where I am. I can't throw it all away."

A battle clashed inside him. There were only so many hours in the day, and he needed to use most of them to solve this case once and for all, but he couldn't let Lauren suffer. Couldn't let the things she loved crumble around her because he hadn't done his job. No matter how conflicted he was about what he felt for her. "Where are you playing tonight?"

"The Songbird. 8:00 p.m."

He glanced down at his watch. It was still morning, which gave him plenty of time to work before sparing a few hours to see Lauren safely through her set. Besides, if he hadn't gotten the answers he needed by then, it wouldn't be smart for her to be alone. Not after what happened the last time.

"Can you stay here until you need to get ready?" he asked, trying not to squirm under the intensity of her stare.

She nodded. "I don't want to leave Rebecca."

"Good. Then I'll know you're both safe. I'll swing by to accompany you home to change then to the bar. Rebecca will have an officer here to protect her, and I'm sure by that point will need her rest."

Rebecca remained solemn and quiet but managed a small tip of her lips as if in agreement.

He bid his goodbyes, along with a promise to be in touch about when to expect him and hurried toward the exit. He had a lot to figure out or he'd have an even bigger problem—how to leave her side at nightfall with a possible killer still on the loose.

Lauren watched Nolan leave the room, and she physically ached at his absence. But now wasn't the time to do a deep dive of her feelings. Not when her roommate sat in a hospital bed, scared and shaken after managing to survive a terrifying kidnapping.

Shifting off the mattress, she grabbed the wooden arm of one of the two chairs and dragged it close to the bed. "Now that it's just the two of us, tell me how you're really doing."

Rebecca flopped back against the mattress and tilted her chin toward the ceiling. "Horrible. Every time I close my eyes, I see that mask. I feel his hands on my skin. I hear the harshness of his voice." Shuddering, she pulled the blanket tighter around her.

Something shifted inside of Lauren. Being a victim sucked, but witnessing her friend experience the pain and horror and understanding exactly how she felt unleashed a torrent of anger like she hadn't experienced in years. "I'm so sorry this happened to you. I never imagined this guy would come to the apartment. I should have found a way to warn you, to tell you about the threat he made against me at work. I mean, if he found my job, it was only a matter of time before he figured out where I lived. I put you in the direct line of danger. Now you've been through hell and Sissy's gone."

"She hasn't come home?" Rebecca asked, worry shining bright in her tired eyes.

Lauren shook her head. "I'm sure she ran and just hasn't made her way back yet. I just hope she's not hungry or scared." It seemed almost silly to be so worried about her cat after everything Rebecca had endured, but she loved her pet like Sissy was her own child.

Rebecca sighed. "This all sucks. Hopefully Detective Clayman can figure out this whole mess quickly and we can put it all behind us. Unless you don't want to put *him* behind you."

She rolled her eyes. "What I do or do not want to do with Nolan isn't important right now."

"Oh, come on. If you're going to sit here and babysit me all day, I'm going to need the dirt. Something to take my mind off things." Rebecca cracked the first smile Lauren had seen since arriving at the hospital.

A smile Lauren couldn't resist. "First, I'm not babysitting anyone. I'm hanging out with my best friend while you're a guest in these lovely accommodations." She waved a hand through the air in a grand gesture as if pale green walls and a line of cabinets on the far wall was a five-star resort.

Rebecca snorted out a laugh.

"Second," she continued. "I don't know what I want to do about Nolan once this nightmare is over."

"Well, have things changed since the last time we talked? You looked like quite the smitten kitten when he was in here."

Embarrassment heated her cheeks. Was she that obvious? Hopefully only to someone who knew her so well. She hadn't wanted Nolan to notice how excited she'd been to see him again, especially after he'd seemed a little distant. "I've learned a lot about him the last few days. Things that have opened my eyes to the kind of person he is. Shown me that I acted out of anger and grief all those years ago when I went full-out offensive blitz on him after Charlie died."

"Did you tell him that?" Rebecca asked, curiosity lifting her words.

Lauren winced as memories of the previous night flickered in her mind. "We talked about Nolan and the ways he'd tried to help Charlie. All the things he did to console my parents. But I never apologized for the things I said—the things I did. Honestly, I don't even know if he was aware of the posts and interviews that I put out there. Most of it was just me blowing off steam and yelling into the void, trying to get anyone to listen."

"You yelled loud enough to be heard across the Hudson River," Rebecca said. "He had to have heard, read, been told about some of it. If you have any interest in keeping him in your life, you need to clear the air. All of it."

She slipped off her sandals and tucked her feet under her. Maybe that's why Nolan had been a little cold. She'd spent the whole night wanting to know his part in things then kissed him before falling asleep on his shoulder. She hadn't opened herself up completely. Hadn't apologized for any hurt she'd inflicted on him. No matter what happened from here, she needed to do as Rebecca suggested. She had to get everything off her chest.

A soft knock sounded at the door, and a middle-aged woman with a gentle smile and blue scrubs entered the room. "Hello, you two. The shift changed and I'm your new nurse, so I just wanted to introduce myself. I'm Emma. Just press that button beside the bed if you need me."

She ventured farther inside and checked the machines showcasing Rebecca's health stats. "Everything looks good. Are you hungry?"

Rebecca wrinkled her nose. "Not really."

Emma shot her a reassuring smile. "I understand, dear. I'll send in the lunch menu when the time comes. And the officer has arrived, so don't worry about a thing. We've got you covered."

Lauren waited for the nurse to leave before studying her friend. Dark circles hung low under her eyes, and she shrunk against the bed, as if wishing to disappear. Gone was the strong-willed badass who always had her back. In her place was a terrified woman who looked more like a frail child.

"I brought you some stuff," she said, wanting to change the subject and hoping to bring a little life back to her roommate's face. "Some of your clothes if you want to change. Toiletries. I even managed to squeeze a comfortable blanket in the bag."

Leaning forward, she scooted the bag her way and unzipped it. The red fleece blanket sprang from the opening. Lauren pulled it out and handed it to Rebecca.

"And if you don't want that gross hospital food, I can run out and get whatever you want. The reason you're here is awful, but we'll look at it as a chance to play hooky. Eat greasy food. Maybe find a good chick flick on TV."

A tear slid over Rebecca's cheek, and she snuggled the blanket close to her chest. "Thank you for being here. I'd be lost without you."

A lump of emotion pressed against the base of Lauren's neck. "I wouldn't be anywhere else. Do you need anything?"

"I think I'll try to sleep. I'm so tired."

"Get your rest. I'll be here when you wake." She settled against the chair and watched Rebecca's eyes drift closed.

A shadow shifted outside the door, and she spied the officer standing near the wall. A tiny sense of relief waded through the fear flooding her system. She was safe, Rebecca was safe, and soon Nolan would make sure no one would hurt them again.

She just hoped she hadn't hurt Nolan enough in the past to ensure they never stood a chance of a future.

Chapter 16

Hunger gnawed at Lauren's stomach. The call from Nolan earlier that morning had come before she'd managed to grab breakfast, and now the time was just before noon. Rebecca still slept in her hospital bed, and Lauren's muscles ached from sitting in the same position in the uncomfortable chair.

She needed to walk, get her blood flowing again and find something to eat. Securing her sandals back on her feet, she stood and stretched her arms over her head. Her back cracked as she leaned from side to side. She scooped up her phone, hating the tug of disappointment that Nolan hadn't contacted her in the last two hours, then made sure Rebecca was still asleep before slipping into the hallway.

Bright lights shone down from the ceiling, and she blinked to adjust to the harshness against her eyes.

"Is everything all right?" the young officer asked. Her dark hair was pulled in a low bun at the nape of her neck, and she stood with hands clasped behind her back. Unquestioned authority rolled off her in waves, but kindness was clear in her light brown eyes.

Lauren offered her a smile. "Just a little hungry. My friend is still asleep so I'm going to sneak down to the cafeteria. Maybe bring up something for her when she wakes up. Can I get you anything?"

"I'm fine, but thanks."

"Are you sure? I can try and find something covered in chocolate or a cup of coffee."

The officer cracked a grin. "I appreciate the offer, but I'm good."

Lauren made a mental note to buy an extra protein bar at the very least for the woman standing guard. "If you hear my friend wake up, will you let her know I'll be right back?"

"Sure."

Lauren waved a goodbye and hustled down the wide hall. She kept her eyes out for signs to point the way toward the cafeteria. The hospital was like a maze, so many floors and halls jutting in different directions. She could ask for directions, but she'd hate to interrupt a busy nurse or doctor who already had so much on their overcrowded plates. She could figure it out, hopefully before the lunch rush.

Ten minutes and a dizzying amount of turns later, an increase of chatter reached her ears. The mouth of the hallway opened up and led into the seating area for the patients, visitors and staff to relax and eat. The cafete-

More to Read.
More to Love.

More to Love.
More to Explore.

With more to explore, we'd love to send you up to 4 BOOKS, absolutely FREE when you try the Harlequin Reader Service.

They say that "less is more" — but not when it comes to reading your favorite books!

We know that readers like you can't wait to open their newest book and settle down reading.

We feel the same way. That's why today, you can say "YES" to MORE of the great reading you love — absolutely FREE!

Try **Harlequin® Romantic Suspense** books featuring heart-racing page-turners with unexpected plot twists and irresistible chemistry that will keep you guessing to the very end.

Try **Harlequin Intrigue® Larger-Print** books featuring action-packed stories that will keep you on the edge of your seat. Solve the crime and deliver justice at all costs.

Or **TRY BOTH** and get 2 books from each series!

Your free books are completely free, even the shipping! If you continue with your subscription, you can look forward to curated monthly shipments of brand-new books from your selected series, always at a discount off the cover price! Plus you can cancel any time.

So don't miss out, return your Free Books Claim Card today to get your Free books.

Pam Powers

Free Books Claim Card
Say "Yes" to More Books!

YES! I love reading, please send me more books from the series I'd like to explore and a free gift from each series I select.
Get MORE to read, MORE to love, MORE to explore!

Just write in "**YES**" on the dotted line below then select your series and return this Claim Card today and we'll send your free books & gift asap!

YES

Which do you prefer?

☐ Harlequin® Romantic Suspense	☐ Harlequin Intrigue® Larger-Print	☐ BOTH
240/340 HDL GRSA	199/399 HDL GRSA	240/340 & 199/399 HDL GRSX

FIRST NAME   LAST NAME

ADDRESS

APT.#   CITY

STATE/PROV.   ZIP/POSTAL CODE

EMAIL ☐ Please check this box if you would like to receive newsletters and promotional emails from Harlequin Enterprises ULC and its affiliates. You can unsubscribe anytime.

HI/HRS-622-LR_MMM22

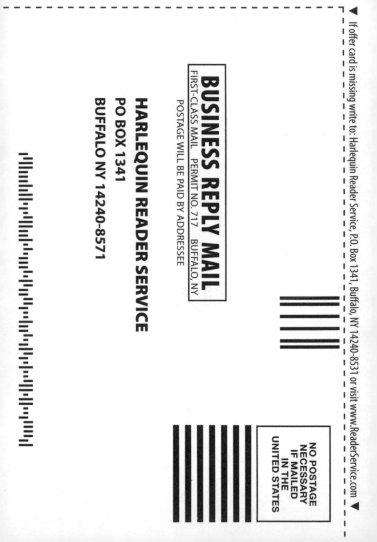

ria lay just beyond, a mecca of multiple food stands and displays of fresh fruits and bagged snacks.

Her mouth watered as an assault of delicious smells combined and swarmed around her. Okay, so she'd been dead wrong when she'd described hospital food as crappy. At least here. She had her choice of pizza, subs, Chinese, or something sizzling on a grill connected to a counter where patrons could watch their food being made.

She went straight for the salad bar. She might be hungry, but her nerves were still shot. And if she was on edge, Rebecca definitely would be. The best chance of getting her friend to eat was to bring her something light and healthy. Grabbing a brown tray, she freed two white containers and filled them with lettuce, tomatoes, cucumbers, grilled chicken and whatever else looked appetizing—multiple dressings on the side.

Satisfied by her choices, she closed the lids and picked up three bottles of water and a candy bar. She understood the policewoman needing to be on her feet and alert, but there was no reason she had to suffer while keeping a lookout.

An older man with bushy white eyebrows, liver spots and a comb-over raised a hand in the air at a nearby register. No one waited in his line, so she carried her selection over to him. Smiling, she balanced the full tray on one palm while freeing her wallet from her back pocket. "Hello, sir. How are you today?"

"I'm great," he said. "What about you?"

"As good as can be expected." No need to go into detail with some stranger about everything she'd been through leading up to this moment, but she wouldn't lie and say she was great either. She set the tray on the silver counter attached to the front of the register.

"You're about to be a whole lot better."

She flipped open her wallet, confused by his words. "What do you mean?"

"Your meal's been paid for." He waved a wad of cash in the air.

"I don't understand. How is that possible?" She frowned.

The man beamed as though the unsuspecting gesture made his day. "A guy stopped by when you got here. He pointed you out to me and said he wanted to pay for your meal. Handed me money and said it should cover your food and to keep the rest. Can you believe it? He must have given me one hundred dollars!"

Her heart pounded in her ears, and she searched the growing crowd for someone, anyone, who looked familiar. An old friend she hadn't seen in a while, an acquaintance who happened to be here and wished to do a good deed, hell, even an ex making amends by throwing around some cash.

Or Nolan. Maybe he'd struck out at the morgue and come back to the hospital. If the cop told him she'd come down for some food, maybe he followed her and paid for her meal.

No one stood out. No one she knew. No one she recognized.

The feeling of being watched crept up her spine and made nausea pitch in her stomach. No longer hungry and needing to leave this spot where she suddenly felt so vulnerable, she shoved her wallet back into her pocket and ran.

* * *

The air inside the morgue was set to a constant state of frigid. For once, Nolan was grateful for the long sleeves of his button-down shirt on a hot summer day. But even the extra fabric wasn't enough to keep goose bumps from lining his skin. Not when he stood in the stark room lined with silver cabinets that were filled with death.

"Thanks for letting me take another look at the body," he said to the technician who checked the names on the doors.

"No problem. Hope it helps. The medical examiner is so backed up, it could be over a month before the body is given a proper examination." Lloyd, the overworked employee, crouched low to study the bottom row. "Here he is. Malcom Carson, right?"

"That's the one." Nolan rubbed the stinging patch of skin under his nose. The smells in the morgue usually ranged between not very pleasant and downright disgusting. He'd dabbed some peppermint oil beneath his nostrils to combat whatever might come his way.

Lloyd slid out the drawer, revealing Malcom. "Anything in particular you're looking for?"

"Cause of death would be nice."

Lloyd snorted. "Wish I could help you. I mostly clean the bodies and the rooms for the medical examiner. But if you need a sounding board, I can stick around. I've seen my fair share of autopsies. Can't take my opinions as gospel, but they may hold some merit."

Intrigued by what the man had to say, Nolan shrugged. "Go ahead and stay. Not sure what all you know about this guy, but preliminary findings indicate he jumped from the Brooklyn Bridge. Something I doubt due to the lack of witnesses. If he jumped, someone would have seen. Someone would have called it in."

"I agree with that. It's not like the Brooklyn Bridge is notoriously empty."

Nolan chuckled, appreciating the guy's joke despite the grim surroundings. "Mind if I look closer?"

"That's why you're here, isn't it?" Lloyd crossed the room to a cabinet above a sink and grabbed a box of gloves. "Put these on first."

Nolan hid his hands in the gloves then unzipped the black bag that contained Malcom, stopping just below his belly button. "No bruising on the chest. I'd expect to find that if he jumped."

"Usually the case," Lloyd said. "Internal organs don't take kindly to being slammed against water when it feels like concrete."

Nolan cringed and continued his study of the body. "No blunt force trauma. The skin doesn't appear as though it was waterlogged at all. If the water is what killed him, he wasn't in there for long."

"Which doesn't support the no-call-from-a-witness thing you mentioned."

"You ever think about working for law enforcement? You're a quick thinker."

"Nah. I know it's weird to most folks, but I like it here. It's quiet and not many people around to bug me."

Nolan turned toward him, eyebrows raised. "Fair point."

"Could he have drowned?" Lloyd asked, dipping his chin toward the body.

"Possibly. Hard to tell without the medical examiner

studying the lungs. But if he jumped and didn't land with enough force to seriously mess with his organs, he could have knocked himself out. Became unconscious and drowned as a result."

A thought occurred to him. Could he have drowned without jumping? That would explain why no one saw him jump.

"Can you help me roll him? I want to take a closer look on the other side."

Lloyd rounded the table and gripped Malcom's shoulder then tilted him over, exposing his back.

Nolan studied the skin, noting moles and scratches. Nothing out of the ordinary. He brushed aside his blond hair that hid the top of his neck and froze.

"What is it?" Lloyd asked, peering over the top of Malcom for a better view.

"You see these marks?" He pointed to two sets of two perfectly round indents in the skin. "Look like Taser burns."

"Can you tell how long he had them?"

"This set looks older than the other one, but I don't know how far apart." Dammit, how had he missed this at the scene? If he hadn't been so caught up in his feelings for Lauren, he would have taken more time. Been more careful to search every single inch of Malcom before letting the coroner drive him away. He might not have been able to discern how long ago the Taser marks had been there, but he could have known if they were fresh.

"You think someone tased him then put him in the river? Made it look like he jumped or drowned?" Lloyd carefully rested Malcom on his back.

Straightening, Nolan stripped off the gloves and tossed them in a nearby trash can. "It's possible. Even if I don't like the theory."

"Why not?"

"Because that would mean Malcom didn't kill himself. It would mean he was murdered." Which meant his killer was still out there and Nolan had no clue who it was.

The harsh sound of his phone rang into the quiet room. He pulled it out and Lauren's name on his screen made his heart stop. "Sorry, I've got to answer this. You can go ahead and put him back. I'm done here. Thanks for the help, man."

Lloyd nodded and zipped the bag back to the top, covering Malcom's face.

Nolan answered the phone. "Hey, Lauren. What's up?"

"I need someone to tell me I'm paranoid."

The frantic pace of her words had him hurrying toward the exit. "What happened?"

"I went to grab some food down in the cafeteria. A man paid for my meal. He pointed me out to the guy at the register and gave him cash. But when I looked around, I didn't see anyone I knew, and no one came forward. I felt like I was being watched. Like someone was hiding in the wings, waiting to see my reaction. Am I just being silly?"

Fear gripped his gut and he pushed the silver bar of the door, spilling him out into the warm air in the parking lot. "Go back to Rebecca's room. Tell the officer what you just told me. Let her know that nobody goes in Rebecca's room except the nurse and the doctor. I'll be there as soon as I can."

He hung up and barreled into his car. Lauren was anything but paranoid, and the tightness in his chest told him that this nightmare was far from over. A nagging feeling in the back of his mind told him this game was just beginning.

Chapter 17

Anxiety tightened Lauren's chest as she slid the diamond studs into her ears. A slight tremor shook her hands. She tightened them into fists then shook them out in front of her. The last thing she wanted to do was make herself presentable for her performance at The Songbird, but she had to push her hesitation aside and be a professional.

Or else lose everything she'd worked so hard for.

She smoothed a hand over the simple black dress she'd chosen. Buttons ran down the front and a thin belt wrapped around the waist. Plus, it had pockets. If that didn't put a little bit of a pep in her step, not much would. Her shiny brown hair fell in a straight sheet over her shoulders. How she could look so put together when her life was falling apart was beyond her.

Pulling in a large gulp of air, she shoved aside the curtains blocking off her room and found Nolan sitting on the couch. He still wore the light blue button-down shirt and black trousers he had on earlier, but now a light stubble stretched across his jaw.

His eyes met hers, and he rose to his feet, mouth agape. "You look beautiful."

His words heated her cheeks. "Thanks. I know it's a wonderful opportunity, but I really don't want to play tonight. Leaving Rebecca in the hospital was harder than I thought it'd be."

After she'd run back to the hospital room following the cafeteria debacle, she'd refused to leave Rebecca's side. Even with a guard posted at the door and Nolan coming to her rescue, fear had kept her firmly rooted inside. Nolan had made calls, spoken with as many people as he could, and even searched the limited security video. But no one saw anything and the footage of the hall outside the seating area showed nothing out of the ordinary. Hours later, unease still rattled around inside her, but she couldn't keep her life on pause any longer.

"Her mom is with her now. She's not alone," Nolan said then winced. "Which reminds me..."

"What is it?" She passed by him to the narrow closet by the front door where she and Rebecca kept their shoes. She selected a pair of black flats and slipped them on her bare feet.

"I don't think it's wise for you to stay here tonight. Rebecca's in the hospital for another night, so you'd be here by yourself. And I still can't say with full confidence that Malcom is the one who took her. If the person who paid for your meal was playing tricks with your mind, then Malcom isn't the one we're after. At least not the only one."

She swallowed the ball of anxiety expanding in her throat. "And he knows where I live."

"Exactly." Nolan took a step toward her. "You mentioned before not having somewhere else to stay, or not wanting to put anyone else in danger, but I think it'd be smart if you didn't come back here tonight."

"I don't know where else to go." She ran her palm over her face as the reality of her situation crashed against her. "Rebecca was almost killed because of me. I can't do that to someone else."

He ran his tongue over his top lip, making her body give an involuntary shiver. "You could stay with me." Hesitation slowed his words, and he dropped his gaze to the floor as if he didn't want to see how she'd respond to his suggestion.

Her core caught fire. His proposal might be only to offer her shelter—protection—for the night, but she couldn't stop her body's reaction to spending another evening alone with him. Last night, falling asleep beside him on the couch, had been more magical than something so innocent should have been. And that had been an accident. If she agreed to sleep at his place, maybe it could lead to something even better.

Something even more special.

Tense silence sizzled in the air between them as her earlier conversation with Rebecca came back with a vengeance. If she wanted a chance of something more with Nolan, it was time to knock down all her walls. "Before I make a decision, I need to say something to you."

He cocked his head slightly to the side, eyes narrowed. "Okay. Should I be scared?"

A nervous laugh came out high-pitched and choppy. "No, but I am." She pinched the beads on her ever-present bracelet.

He tipped up one corner of his mouth. "You must be if you're playing with your bracelet. What's the deal with that thing? I don't think I've ever seen you without it, and you always mess with it when you're upset or nervous."

She dropped her gaze to the bracelet, surprised he'd noticed. "Charlie made it for me when he was a kid. I kept it tucked away until he died. After he was killed, it made me feel closer to him. Like a part of him is always with me."

"That's really special. A great way to feel his presence."

She gave a green bead one more pinch then faced him. Determination straightened her shoulders. "I owe you an apology."

He frowned. "For what?"

"I was horrible to you after Charlie died." She blurted it out, not sure exactly how to voice her feelings.

"We already discussed this," he said. "There's no reason to rehash it again."

"We never talked about what *I* did to *you*."

The tight set of his jaw told her that he knew exactly what she meant. Before she lost her nerve, she pressed on. "I was hurt and wanted to hurt you, because in my mind, you were the reason Charlie was dead. Now I know I blamed you because I didn't want to deal with the unfairness of it. Didn't want to shoulder the burden of blame all on my own. Because if you were the reason he was killed in that jail cell, I didn't have to think about how my actions resulted in him being in that car. It was easier to hate you than myself, and I needed everyone else to hate you, too. That was wrong, and I'm sorry."

He dipped his chin, his gaze cast over her shoulder as if searching for the right thing to say, before pinning her with his tender stare. "I appreciate that. I won't lie, your words and smear campaign against me caused a lot of damage. Both personally and to my career—mostly because of my reaction. My internalizing your accusations then throwing myself into Charlie's case in my free time. My choices regarding what you put out there about me. But I've moved on, just like you need to."

She pinched together her brows. "I can't move on from the pain of losing my brother."

He pressed his lips into a thin line. "Not the pain—the guilt. The blame. You forgave me for my part, now it's time you do the same for yourself. Just like you told Ronny, Charlie would have wanted you to fly without anything unnecessary weighing down your wings."

Squeezing her eyes closed, she absorbed his words. She'd needed to hear them for so damn long. The pressure in her chest fizzled away, replaced with hope. With peace. With love.

A soft caress against her cheek made her open her eyes. Nolan stood in front of her, worry creasing his forehead.

She dropped her gaze to his mouth and held her breath, hoping he'd kiss her. Hoping he'd put all the pain she'd inflicted behind them so they could step forward into a fresh beginning.

"Now that we have that settled, will you stay with me tonight? Please? I have a spare room. I promise to behave." He smirked, sucking the air from her lungs, then all traces of flirtation fled. "I just want you safe."

She nodded, leaning gently into his palm. "Okay."

He dropped his hand to his side and took a step backward. "Go ahead and pack a bag before we head out. You don't want to be late."

Disappointment crushed down on her, but she forced a smile and disappeared into her room. What had she expected? That once she'd apologized for everything she'd done, he'd take her in his arms and kiss the hell out of her?

She cringed as she stuffed her things in a duffel. Yes, that's exactly what she'd expected, but she couldn't be upset. He'd accepted her apology and encouraged her in exactly the way she needed to hear. If only she could silence the little voice inside her that told her she wanted a hell of a lot more than Nolan's protection and encouragement. She wanted his heart.

Soft music played out of the speakers flanking the stage in the center of the upscale bar. Nolan leaned back in his chair, wishing he had a better view of the entrance. Dim lights cast long shadows around the crowded room, a bright light beaming on the vacant piano.

Lauren perched on the edge of her seat, eyes wide and hands gripped on her music.

"You doing okay?"

She nodded, but kept her focus fixed straight ahead. Shit. He wasn't great at reading women, and he couldn't tell if she was nervous about playing in front of the crowded room or upset with how their conversation had gone earlier. After making a conscious decision to reestablish boundaries between them, she'd caught him completely off guard with her candor. He'd never imagined she'd bring up the way she'd treated him all those years ago, and now that she had, those boundaries had vanished.

The question was, what was he supposed to do about it? He couldn't deny he had feelings for her, and he really didn't want to hold on to bitterness from the past. Especially now when he'd seen exactly who Lauren was. But for all intents and purposes, she was under his protection. At least for the night. He didn't want to abuse his power and put her in a shitty situation.

Dammit. He just didn't want to mess this up before it even started.

She shifted toward him, and tears glimmered in her eyes. "What if I have another panic attack? Maybe this isn't a good idea."

Screw professionalism. Reaching across the small circular table, he rested his hand on hers and squeezed. "You'll be great. This time will be different."

"How do you know?"

"Because this time you know I'm here." He dipped his chin, forcing her to meet his eyes. "I'm front and center, watching out for you. I won't let anything happen."

She drew in a shuddering breath. "Last time I thought the first attack was a onetime thing. There wasn't even the possibility someone was still out there, waiting to get me alone. Wanting to hurt me. But now…" She shrugged. "We still don't know for sure if I'm safe. Whoever hurt me, attacked Rebecca and ran Sissy off, he might be here. Watching."

Nolan stood and dragged his chair next to hers then settled their clasped hands in his lap. He skimmed the pads of his thumbs over her skin, doing all he could to soothe her. "Why do you play the piano?"

Confusion knitted her brow. "What?"

He couldn't help but grin at the cute way her nose wrinkled, and her mouth pushed into a pout. "What is it about playing the piano that drives you to work so hard? What makes all the time and energy worth it?"

The tightness left the lines of her face and her lips tipped up at the corners. "I don't know if I can explain it."

"Try," he said, attempting to ignore the gaggle of women at the table beside him that were louder than a pack of hyenas.

"It's just this feeling in the pit of my stomach. A tingle of excitement I get when I put my fingers on the keys. Even as a child, I'd close my eyes and it was like the music just flowed through me. All my worries and cares left my body, even if just for a minute, and I got lost in the melody. Transported to this place that existed only in my mind, where all is right with the world. The piano is a part of who I am, a piece of my soul. Performing is a way to show that part of me to people."

The emotion behind her explanation fisted his heart. She had so much passion, so much love for her music. "You can't ever lose that, Lauren. That feeling. You need to go up on the stage, close your eyes and forget all the other bullshit going on right now. You can't let any-one take away what you love—take away who you are."

A man with close-cropped hair and black-framed glasses approached the table. "Hey, Lauren. You're up."

Nolan gave her hands a final squeeze. "You got this. I'm right here."

She nodded, slid off her seat and followed the bar employee up the three black steps to the stage. While he strolled to the microphone with a wide smile, she slinked behind him and settled onto the piano bench.

Nolan's nerves tightened. Hell, this must be what a worried parent felt like as they watched their child per-form for the first time. He had no doubt she could push past her fear and play her heart out, but if she couldn't hold it together, he'd sweep her off that stage and right back to his apartment. Making sure she understood that her reaction was normal and nothing to be ashamed of.

"Ladies and gentlemen," the man said with a touch too much dramatic flair. "Please join me and welcome the always fabulous, Lauren Mueller."

A smattering of claps and hoots echoed around the room.

Nolan shifted his chair so he could keep his focus on Lauren and still be aware of the room at large.

The spotlight highlighted Lauren. She sat ramrod straight with her fingers splayed along the ivory keys. Her chest heaved in and out. Silence hung in the room, followed by dull murmurs.

Come on, Lauren. You can do this.

As if reading his thoughts, she sought him out and their eyes met. He gave a tiny nod.

Smiling, she shimmied her shoulders, closed her eyes, then slowly brought the glistening instrument to life.

He recognized the notes as they practically poured from her hands. She swayed along with the melody, her face a picture of serene beauty. A tear leaked from one closed eye and rolled down her cheek as her fingers flew over the keys. The music was slow and sweet, then fast and steady, before morphing into a combination of notes that left him breathless.

She left him breathless.

The ache from earlier came back into his chest, and he rubbed at the weird sensation as if to make it go away. But watching Laruen as she continued to captivate the room only made the ache grow—his breath harder to catch.

Realization knocked him back in his seat. Lauren was magnificent and there was no way he could walk away from her.

No way he could ignore his feelings and forget her.

Chapter 18

Adrenaline leaked from Lauren's system, replaced with a bundle of nerves as she followed Nolan into his apartment building. The stone on the outside was gray and weathered, the sidewalk in front of it filled with people enjoying the city on a pleasant summer night. With the subtle breeze and the sun long gone, the air outside was almost as cool as in the lobby, where a cluster of mailboxes and a well-kept, intimate seating area took up most of the space.

Moving up the stairs, Nolan stayed close behind her.

His presence caused a slight tremor throughout her body. She clenched her jaw to keep herself in check. The silence in the narrow stairwell was awkward and she was distinctly aware her backside was in his view while climbing to the fourth floor.

At the landing, he placed his hand on the small of her back and ushered her down the hall to his apartment. He snatched his keys from his pocket and pushed open the door. "Here we are. It's nothing fancy, but it's home." He flipped the switch on the wall and light illuminated the space.

She hiked her overnight bag higher on her shoulder and preceded him inside. Wooden floors ran the length of the hall in front of her and spread into the kitchen and living room. The area was open and airy, something she envied.

"I have two bedrooms, but I only have furniture in my room." Nolan led her down the hall, casting a sheepish grin over his shoulder before continuing to the first door on the left. "Jack lived here before moving in with his girlfriend. He took his things with him, and I haven't bothered to replace anything. You can stay in my room, and I'll take the couch."

A wave of heat slammed against her at the thought of sleeping in Nolan's room—in his bed. She hesitated in the hall beside him instead of entering his bedroom. "Don't be silly. I'm sure I'll fit on the couch better than you."

He shrugged. "I don't mind. Besides, I'm usually up late. Especially when working a case. Please," he said, nodding toward the doorway. "I insist."

Not seeing a way out of it, she stepped past him to enter his room.

From his place in the hallway, he turned on the light and leaned against the doorjamb.

She studied his private space, impressed by his cleanliness. A sea green blanket covered the bed, and all the dresser drawers were closed. No dirty clothes scattered on the floor or dust settled along the tops of the furniture. She set her stuff on the edge of the bed then faced him with wide eyes. "Thanks. What now?"

Shoving his hands into his pockets, he rocked back on his heels. "I don't have much food in the fridge, but if you want, we can order something."

"I'm not really hungry." After abandoning lunch earlier at the hospital, she'd snacked the rest of the day. Nibbling on what was brought up to Rebecca's room. And after Rebecca's mother had arrived, Shelly had made sure to stuff whatever food she could in both her and Rebecca. With the anxiety tightening every muscle in her body, eating was the last thing she wanted to do right now.

He blew out a long breath, as if at a loss for what to do. What to say. "Listen, I know this is kind of weird. But I want you to be comfortable here. I don't want you to feel awkward and like you can't just do whatever it is that you'd normally do."

She considered his words, appreciating that he wanted to make her feel welcome in his home. "Have any wine?"

He wrinkled his nose. "I've got a couple beers in the fridge. Maybe a bottle of tequila."

"Beer it is. I need to unwind a little after a show. Being in front of everyone hypes me up and it can take a while to come down off that high. A drink always helps."

"Makes sense," he said, turning for the kitchen.

She fell in step behind him, studying the living room as she passed through. A single beige sofa sat in front of a flat-screen television nestled inside an entertainment stand. Shades were pulled over the two windows that looked out onto the street, and the sounds of passing cars penetrated the wall. It was just as clean as the bedroom, but there was no doubt Nolan lived in a bachelor pad. No framed photographs or meaningful mementos on display. No cozy blankets or throw pillows on the sofa.

Nolan reached into the refrigerator and pulled out two bottles of beer by their brown necks. "Watching you up on that stage was impressive as hell, by the way." He handed her a cold bottle then leaned against the counter. "No way I could ever do that. Be up there in front of everyone. Playing the way you do…" He shook his head as if unable to find the words to finish his thought.

His compliment heated her cheeks. "Thanks, but tonight I owe to you." She screwed the top off her beer and took a sip of the cool, bitter ale.

"Me? No way. I didn't do a damn thing."

She smiled at his modesty. "I froze. My body started shaking. Then I saw you and everything you'd said came floating back. With you there, I didn't need to be afraid. I could just lose myself in the music."

She pinched the bottle cap, needing to tell Nolan exactly what tonight meant to her. What *he* meant to her. "Tonight was special. Something came over me when I played, and I have you to thank for that."

He brought the bottle to his lips and lifted one shoulder. "I didn't say anything that wasn't true. I wanted you to know I had your back. You did the rest."

She erased the distance between them and set her beer and the top on the counter beside him. Her heart thundered and a different kind of terror expanded her chest. But she couldn't let that stop her. Not with something so important. "That's the thing. You had my back, and not just while I was on that stage. You've had my back since the night you walked into the convenience store, even when I was awful to you, and you've been there for me ever since. By my side, when I know that's not part of the job. I appreciate all you've done for me, and for my family. But it's more than that. I care about you. Deeply."

Sighing, he dropped his gaze to the floor.

His silence beat against her like a hammer. Okay, maybe she should have been more afraid of his rejection. Because now, not only had a dark well of turmoil opened up inside her, but she also had to stay the night in his apartment knowing he didn't feel the same way about her.

"Forget I said anything. It's been a long couple of days. I'm just going to go to bed for the night."

She turned away, but a tug on her hand spun her back to face him.

He linked his fingers in hers, pulling her even closer. "I don't want to forget you said anything, I just don't know the right thing to do. You've become important to me. More important than I ever thought possible. But I don't want to move too fast when your life is being threatened. I want nothing more than to show you what you mean to me, but I don't want to cross any lines."

"From where I'm standing, there aren't any lines to cross." If he needed her to make the first move so he wouldn't feel as though he'd broken some code, so be it. She rested her free palm on his chest, rose to her tiptoes and pressed her lips to his.

Nolan buried his hand in her hair, deepening the kiss, and fireworks exploded behind her closed eyelids. All her guilt and fear and questions melted away. Happiness was finally within reach, and tonight, she'd grab hold of it as tight as she could.

Every nerve ending inside Nolan's body sparked to life. He'd held Lauren in his arms a number of times— hell, she'd even kissed him last night. None of that compared to this. She slid her tongue inside his mouth and his core burst into flames. He wanted her, all of her, and dammit, he wanted her now.

Needing to feel her curves, he ran his hands along the sides of her body. He knotted the dress in his fists, cursing the barrier to her soft skin.

She sighed and looped her arms around his neck.

Her full breasts rubbed against his chest, and he moved his mouth over hers, soaking in her taste. Lust swirled inside him and all he wanted to do was strip her naked and worship her body.

"Mmm," she moaned. "Something tells me we need to take this out of the kitchen and into the bedroom."

His breath caught, and he cradled her jaw in his hands. She stared at him with such intensity pouring from her deep blue eyes, her hair puffing out in tangles around her face, and he lost himself in the idea that she could be his.

Forever.

"Are you sure?" he asked, searching for any signs that she didn't really mean it. He couldn't blame her if she wanted to slow down. "I want to stick around for a while. No need to move too fast."

A wicked grin lifted her lips. "I've never been more sure of anything in my life." She turned and walked toward his room, casting him a quick glance before disappearing inside.

He rubbed the heel of his hand over his chest. Oh, hell. He was a goner.

Needing to be close to her, he hurried to his room, securing the door behind him.

She stood by the end of the bed, watching him, while her hand played with the thin belt around her waist. Slowly, she untied the knot, then walked her fingers to the top button on the front of her dress.

Desire coated his throat and made it hard to swallow. His hands itched to take over, but if she wanted to put on a show, who was he to stop her?

She freed the top button, then trailed her fingers down to the next, then the next. Smooth skin peeked out, highlighted by the black dress. He took special note of all the places he wanted to kiss. The spot just above her collarbone, the hollow dent at the base of her throat, the cleavage poking out above the whisper of lace, the rest of the bra still hidden from view.

Her fingers dipped to the button at the center of her chest. She loosened it, exposing the rest of the black lace. Her breasts barely concealed behind the thin material.

His composure snapped. He stormed across the room and wrapped one arm around her back while he plunged his free hand into her bra. He found her nipple, and he worked his fingers around the hard nub, filling his hand with her breast. He ducked his head, swirling his tongue around her flesh.

She arched her back, as if she needed to find a way to be closer.

He flattened his palm between her breasts, then brought his mouth to all the places he'd wanted to kiss on his way back up to meet her mouth. "I think we need to get rid of the rest of this."

Her moan was all the answer he needed. He moved his lips over hers as he sprang her free from her dress, leaving it in a pool of material at her feet, then unhooked her bra.

She slipped her finger under the strap and guided it off her body, then shimmied out of her panties.

She stood in front of him, her satiny skin glowing under the streams of moonlight pouring through the window, and the pressure in his chest almost had him doubting his ability to continue. "You do the craziest things to me, Lauren. You've gotten under my skin, into my head, and I can't escape you. I don't want to escape you."

"What do you want, then?" She arched one eyebrow high.

She played the coy vixen to perfection, and it was time to show her exactly what he wanted. With a lot less tact than her, he unbuttoned his shirt as quickly as possible and threw it on the floor.

She laughed then hooked her fingers into the front of his trousers, yanking him close. "You didn't answer my question."

He fisted her hair in his hands and brought her mouth to his, unleashing all the emotions she stirred inside him. As he kissed her, she undid his pants. "I want you. I want you so damn bad I just might burst."

She lowered his pants and boxers to the ground. "I can see that," she said, her voice husky and low.

Unable to keep his hands off her a second more, he scooped her up and tossed her on the bed.

Her smile melted away, replaced by a tenderness that took away his breath. She was so beautiful. So perfect, his heart constricted, pressing against his chest.

"How did I get so damn lucky?" he asked, awe thickening his voice.

She cupped his cheek in her palm. "I'm the lucky one. Fate brought you back into my life. This time, I'm not going to ruin it. I won't get bogged down with fear and guilt. My heart is open to you."

He grinned, feeling like a teenager about to experience his first time, then kissed the hell out of her. He reached between her legs and dipped one finger inside her slippery folds. Hot moisture coated his skin, and he teased her with slow, easy strokes before adding another.

She gripped his biceps, and her breaths came out in ragged gasps.

He watched her face, her eyes wide and focused on him. Hair matted around her forehead as she moved in rhythm to his fingers inside her. He wanted to remember the soft lines of her face, the affection in her eyes. Every moment was perfection. Every second pure and raw and creating a flurry of emotions he'd never experienced before. He wanted to make every moment count—longed to bring her to pleasure over and over.

Her hold on his arms tightened, her nails digging into his skin, as she cried out her pleasure. A sigh puffed from her open mouth, and she stared up at him with complete trust in her eyes. "The things you do to me, Nolan."

"We're not done yet, baby." Leaning to the side, he rummaged through the drawer of his nightstand until he found a condom. He ripped it open and rolled it into place before pinning Lauren beneath him. He pressed her knees apart and sunk into her. Her heat surrounded him. His muscles tight, hot need consumed him.

Circling her arms around his neck, she wrapped her legs around his waist, hooking her ankles together. The action pushed him deeper into her center. Her heart beat against his, fast and steady. Pleasure spasmed through his body. Shifting his weight to one arm, he loosened her hold and captured her palm in his, pressing it to the mattress. Squeezing her hand as joy and happiness and desire pushed his hips harder and faster.

Her eyes locked on his. A smile curved her lips and she panted, keeping rhythm with his frantic pace. She ran her knuckles along his jawline. The sweet and simple gesture was almost his undoing. She stretched to meet his mouth with hers then trailed her lips to his ear. "You're everything I've ever dreamed of."

He thrust into her until her cries of pleasure erupted into the room. She kept her lips to his ear, her hot, sticky breath like a damn aphrodisiac. "Let yourself go, Nolan. I want to give you what you need. I want to be the one you can lose yourself in."

Pleasure built inside him, and he entered her again and again until every muscle in his body tightened in anticipation of his release. He came inside her, groaning out her name. He braced his weight on his forearms, not wanting to smother her but unable to hold his body up as he fought to catch his breath.

Lauren sighed and smiled up at him.

He quickly removed and disposed of the condom before falling back into bed and tucking her into the crook of his arm. "Are you okay?" He pressed a kiss to the side of her head, her damp hair sticking to his lips.

She laughed and rested her hand on his chest. "I've never been better."

"Me, too. You're amazing." The ringing of his phone interrupted his next thought, and he groaned. "Whoever it is can wait. I don't want either of us to move from this bed for the next twelve hours."

"As lovely as that sounds, someone might be calling about the case. How about I grab us some water so we can rehydrate and do that all over while you answer?"

"Deal."

She stood and slipped her dress back on, leaving most of the buttons undone, as he hurried to find his pants and the phone left inside. Whoever was calling was in for one short conversation. Now that he had a taste of Lauren, he only wanted more.

Locating his phone, he hurried to accept the call before the ringing stopped. "Hello?"

"Detective Clayman, this is dispatch. You're needed at a crime scene immediately. Another young woman's been murdered."

Chapter 19

Lauren's body hummed as she braced herself against the wall in the hallway for a beat before heading into the kitchen. She'd never understand how her knees hadn't turned to Jell-O after making love to Nolan. Her nerve endings were frayed, giving off spastic jolts of excitement and giddiness she'd never experienced before. If all he needed was a glass of water for a repeat performance, she was in for one hell of a night.

Her bare feet padded across the floor to the oak cabinets, and a distinct rattling sound made her skin crawl. Someone was trying to get into the apartment. "Nolan!" she yelled, fear turning her limbs to lead.

The door swung open, and a young woman wearing a short black skirt and white crop top stood in the doorway. A loaded-down key chain that looked like it belonged

to a janitor dangled in her hand, and beachy waves surrounded her stunning face. "Well, who do we have here?"
she asked, a smirk playing on her red-painted lips.

Indignation swept through Lauren. She clenched her
jaw, weighing her words. She'd just had sex with a man
she trusted, who she cared about, and some woman had
keys to his apartment? And she'd just shown up in the
middle of the night for what? A booty call?

"I could ask you the same question," Lauren said,
standing tall and ignoring the gaping material of her
dress where she hadn't bothered to secure the buttons.

The young woman tilted her head to the side, amusement lifting the lines of her face. "I'm Nolan's sister,
Madi."

Embarrassment replaced the indignation. "Oh, I'm
sorry. Hi, I'm Lauren. Nolan's…friend." She rubbed one
foot over the top of the other, unsure of how to proceed.
Shaking Madi's hand seemed a bit formal, but standing in the kitchen staring at her, while barely dressed,
didn't feel appropriate either.

Madi arched her well-groomed brows so high they
almost touched her hairline. "Oh, I know exactly who
you are."

Nolan emerged from his room with shoes and socks
on his feet, his trousers fastened, and buttoning his shirt
as he walked. A pronounced frown pulled down his lips.

"Hey, big brother." Madi beamed, her grin lacking
sincerity.

His head popped up. "Madi, what are you doing
here?"

Shrugging, she swung the door closed. "My roommate took a guy back to our dorm, so I thought I'd crash here. So glad I did." She aimed her false smile at Lauren.

Lauren bristled. Meeting Nolan's family wasn't something she expected to do tonight, even though she welcomed the opportunity. But his sister's obvious hostility raised her hackles.

"I don't have time to deal with you right now," he said, hurrying to Lauren's side. He took her hands. "I just got a call. There's been another murder."

She swayed, grateful for Nolan anchoring her. She tightened her grip in his. "Oh my God. Is the killer the same man who attacked me? Does that mean it wasn't Malcom?"

"I don't have many details right now, but I have to get to the crime scene. I want you to stay here. With Madi." He cast a gaze over his shoulder then focused on her again. "If it is the same man, he doesn't know where I live, and if he killed another woman tonight, that means he didn't follow you here."

She winced.

"I don't want to leave you like this, but I have to run. I'll be in touch." He landed a kiss on her lips then rushed toward the door, shooing Madi away. "Lock up behind me and be nice."

She crossed her arms over her chest and rolled her eyes.

Lauren watched Nolan disappear into the hallway and wished she could be anywhere but here. Tension sizzled between her and Madi, who secured the locks, then plopped onto the couch.

"You coming in here or going to hang out in the kitchen by yourself all night?" Madi asked.

Lauren bit back a groan. Dread slowed each step into the living room. With Madi on the couch, there was no other place to sit so she stood in front of the television, trying to think of the right thing to say to diffuse the unease hovering over the room like a dark cloud.

"I'll wait for you to put yourself together before we get into things," Madi said, roaming her gaze down Lauren's body.

Keeping her chin held high, she fastened all her buttons and retied the thin string around her waist. She refused to run her fingers through her hair. They were all adults, and there was no mistaking what had just happened between her and Nolan. She had nothing to apologize for, nothing to hide. "And what exactly do we have to get into?"

"The fact that you almost destroyed my brother."

Her heart fell to the floor, but she wouldn't let Madi see how her words affected her. "What happened was between Nolan and me, and we've already discussed it."

Madi snorted. "You think it was between you and my brother when he almost lost his job because he was so obsessed with clearing your brother's name? Or what about when he was so absorbed in following a new lead that he crashed his car and almost died? I didn't see you in the hospital. Standing with me and my parents while we listened to the doctor explain all his injuries."

The image of Nolan hurt and scared knocked her off-balance. "I…I didn't know any of that. He never mentioned it."

"Sounds like *you* might have discussed things, but Nolan spared you the details of the destruction you caused. So like him. Always more concerned with everyone else's feelings at the cost of his own. And now what? You sucked him back into your drama. Do you think his head's on straight after what you two just did? What kind of damage will you cause this time?"

She absorbed each question like a physical blow. "I'd never want Nolan to get hurt. To go into a situation with his focus on anything other than his job. I care about him."

"Then don't get in his head again—twist him all up then leave me and my parents to pick up the pieces. It's not fair to him and it's not fair to us. He deserves better." Grabbing the remote from the coffee table, she turned on the television and stared through Lauren as if she didn't exist.

Lauren stood for a second, grappling for a reply or response that wouldn't leave her standing around like a fool. When nothing came to mind, she fled to the privacy of Nolan's bedroom. The room smelled like his woodsy cologne mixed with the remnants of their lovemaking. The rumpled sheets on the bed mocked her, and unshed tears pressed against the backs of her eyes.

Maybe she was an idiot to think she and Nolan could put the past behind them. There was too much hurt, too much pain. Madi was right, she'd sucked Nolan into her drama. Another innocent woman had died tonight and all she could think about was herself. Nolan deserved better, and she needed to make sure he got it.

Even if that meant walking away.

The grungy alley in the Lower East Side reminded Nolan of the same street where Lauren was initially attacked. For a split second his mind pasted Lauren's face on the dead woman's body, and nausea rolled through him. He blinked, forcing away the image until he saw the scene exactly how it really was.

Officer Jeffery stepped away from two older policemen who stood guard in front of the victim.

"Thanks for looping me in," he said.

Grim-faced, she nodded. "My fellow officer was first on scene with his partner but contacted me after he spoke to a witness who saw a man dump the body from the back of the car. An At Your Service sign in the windshield. Figured you'd want to be here."

"Where's the witness the officer spoke with?" he asked.

Jeffery signaled for the other cops to join them. "This is Detective Clayman. He's in charge of this investigation and has been working this case for over a week now."

"How do you know the cases are connected?" the older of the two men asked, his energy screaming he wasn't happy for someone else to swoop in and take the reins.

Nolan peered past the small group toward the young woman. "I can see the bruising around her neck from here. And her clothes indicate she was out for the night, probably at a club or bar. Given the age, the location in which her body was dumped and the fact a driver for At Your Service appears to be responsible, I'd say the odds are pretty high the cases are connected."

"But Malcom Carson is dead," Jeffery said, a scowl on her round face. "Do you think he had an accomplice?"

"I don't know what I think."

"I'm Officer Richards," the younger man said, hand extended. His blond hair stood in spikey disarray and eagerness shone from his pale eyes. "My partner, Officer Gandee, and I were first on scene. How can we help?"

Nolan took his hand and shook it once before side-stepping him and approaching the body. "Tell me about this witness while I take a look at the victim."

Gandee positioned himself so his thick legs were hip width apart and his fisted hands anchored on his wide waist. Wrinkles lined his face, and he kept his eyes narrowed. "When Officer Richards and I arrived, we found a squatter hiding around the side of the building down there." He flicked his wrist toward the far end of the alley.

"Is he still around?" Nolan secured his hands in a pair of gloves he'd shoved into his pocket before exiting his SUV. He crouched beside the victim, studying her hunched-over form leaning against the rusted door.

"Not sure," Gandee said. "We can take a look if you want to talk to him again."

"No need to look for him now." If the man already shared everything he saw, there was no reason to waste time tracking him down again. "Any identification on the victim?" A brown purse was strapped across her body. Hopefully it held information on who she was.

Richards nodded. "Found her driver's license in her purse. Name's Alicia Lokie. Age twenty-two. Address listed is in Queens."

"Was there a phone in the bag?" He gave the body a cursory exam, not surprised there weren't any other wounds on Alicia. Nothing else at the scene that would identify a killer.

"Already placed in an evidence bag in the back of the cruiser," Richards said.

Nolan stood. "Did you access it? If your witness saw an At Your Service sign in the car window, I'd like to know if she scheduled a pickup tonight, and if so, who the driver was."

"We haven't attempted to unlock the screen." Gandee swished his pinched lips to the side, either annoyed to be asked the question or upset he hadn't thought to try.

"I'll grab it." Richards jogged to the vehicle and ducked inside the front passenger-side door, emerging with an orange-tinted plastic bag. He handed it over.

"Thanks." Nolan rummaged through the limited evidence they'd collected until he located the smartphone. He handed the bag back to Richards and pressed the button on the bottom of the device that brought up the home screen. "Locked."

"Does it have face recognition?" Jeffery asked.

He double-checked the lock screen. "Sure does. Good thinking, Jeffery." He'd assumed the same thing but loved the initiative Jeffery showed. Carrying the phone to the body, he couldn't help but compare the poor soul in front of him to the smiling young woman on the lock screen. Her red hair piled high on her head as she hugged a black puppy close to her face.

Crouching low, he pressed the button on the phone again, and when facial recognition was requested, he held the phone in front of Alicia's face. The photo changed and a handful of apps littered the screen. He stood and found the car service app. He brought it to life and navigated the features until he found what he needed.

Sonofabitch.

"Jeffery. Come here and tell me what you see."

Jeffery joined him and glanced over his shoulder. Her subtle intake of breath told him she saw exactly the same thing he did.

"This might not be Malcom, but it sure as hell looks like him," he said. "Get an APB out on Kevin Simpson ASAP."

The sinking feeling in his stomach told him that when they found Kevin, he'd have met the same fate as the woman on the street—the same fate as Malcom.

Chapter 20

The sound of creaking floorboards roused Lauren from a restless sleep. After hiding in Nolan's room, she'd tossed and turned for hours, wishing for sleep to come. But the trauma of the last few days, combined with the increasing regret for jeopardizing Nolan's safety, kept her awake until early morning.

She sat up in the bed that still smelled like Nolan and clutched the top sheet to her chest. She'd drawn the curtains, so no light floated in from outside, but there was no mistaking the silhouette that crept into the room and quietly disrobed.

"Hey," she said, the word sounding so lame in her ears after everything they'd shared earlier.

After everything she'd reevaluated.

But now was not the time to dive into that. Not when the digital clock on Nolan's nightstand read 3:42 a.m.

Down to his boxers, he crawled into bed beside her and pulled her into his arms. "Hey, yourself."

Her mind screamed to fight against his embrace, but her body didn't listen. She melted into him, loving the way the bristly stubble on his cheek tickled her when he leaned in for a quick kiss.

"Sorry I had to leave you with Madi. She can be a little rough around the edges. Hope she wasn't too horrible."

Lauren stiffened, not wanting to discuss his sister or the things she'd said. Mostly because Madi might not have been the friendliest, but she'd been honest. "No need to worry about me. What did you find at the crime scene?"

Sighing, he rolled onto his back, slipping one arm under her shoulders to pull her close while he rested his other arm above his head. "The cases are connected. Poor woman was left out on the curb, just like the one who was killed before you were attacked."

She curled against his side, resting a palm on his muscular chest. That could have so easily been her. Could still be if the person responsible wasn't caught soon. "What does that mean as far as Malcom is concerned?"

"I can't know for sure, but my gut says I was chasing a ghost. I saw the photo of the driver who was supposed to pick up the victim. Blond hair. Light skin. Similar build, as far as one could tell from a quick glance at a picture."

Alarm had her sitting up. "So, what? Some guy is out there finding drivers he resembles, killing them, then stealing their cars so he can attack women?"

Nolan slid up and leaned against the wooden head-board. Exhaustion seemed to weigh him down. He tunneled a hand through his hair, leaving it stand on end, before letting it come down on her shoulder. "That's what it looks like. I did all I could tonight to find the driver, but he's nowhere. If I'm right, it's already too late for him."

Bile coated her throat, and she swallowed it down. "That's awful. Why would someone do that?"

He shrugged. "I've seen a lot of bad shit in my job. Some people don't have a reason—others have twisted things so much in their minds, they think their justification for murder makes sense to everyone. It's figuring out the motive that usually leads to the killer. Something I haven't been able to do yet."

She let that thought circle her brain for a beat. "I wonder if he wanted to punish this woman, too." A shiver ran down her spine, and she pulled the sheet tighter around her.

Nolan frowned. "There's no way to know for sure, but she was picked up at a bar. Same as you, and the first victim. Rebecca was taken from home, and he told her that he was using her to teach you a lesson, not be punished."

"It has to mean something," she said. "Maybe he was punished harshly as a child?"

"Or someone in his life was abusive, and he picked up on those tendencies. The theory plays with all the victims being women. Maybe a history of domestic abuse in his family." He let his hand fall to her bicep, skimming his knuckles up and down her skin.

She shivered again, but this time it had nothing to do

with calculating the inner workings of a criminal and everything to do with her physical response she couldn't control. She yearned to snuggle under the covers with him, maybe even have round two and satisfy the growing desire burning in her belly, but after her conversation with Madi, she had to resist.

So instead, she focused on how to catch a murderer.

"What about Thomas Beetle?"

"What about him?"

"Do you think he'd know the missing driver?"

Nolan scratched his chin. "Maybe. Paying him another visit might be beneficial. If he's connected to both drivers, he might be connected to the killer. Even if he doesn't realize it."

She settled back against the mattress, resting her head in the crook of his shoulder. "Whoever did this must understand how the whole driving service thing works. I mean, if I was hell-bent on killing someone and stole a car to do it, I would need to know how to access the database or whatever the drivers use to find their next client."

He pressed a kiss to her temple. "I agree. I plan to speak to someone in management tomorrow about just that. Get a list of drivers based on their physical descriptions and locations. This guy has shown up in the Lower East Side twice, as well as Brooklyn. There has to be a reason."

Silence weaved between them. Nolan went back to brushing his hand over her arm. An intimacy that had nothing to do with sex bonded her to him in a way she never expected.

She squeezed her eyes closed and soaked in the moment. This was pure heaven, but it wasn't real. It couldn't be. Not with his sister's earlier accusations—which hit too close to home—playing in her mind on an endless loop. She'd spend this one night with Nolan, then put distance between them. His family hated her. She couldn't be the reason he was hurt again.

"If I can find Thomas tomorrow, I want you to come with me to talk to him. I don't want you alone. Not with so much unknown. I need to protect you." He lay down and turned on his side, wrapping her up tight.

She shifted, fitting her backside against him like a puzzle piece. Being in his arms felt so good, so right. She sighed, not knowing how to respond. "We'll figure it all out in the morning. We both need to get some sleep."

Her eyes stayed wide open as Nolan's breathing slowed then fell into a steady rhythm on the back of her neck. If this was the only night she'd spend in his arms, she didn't want to sleep. She wanted to remember every single second until the sun came up and reality forced her to walk away.

Hot water sprayed down on Nolan. He closed his eyes and lifted his face toward the steady drips as they cascaded from the showerhead. He'd managed to squeeze in three hours of sleep, but he didn't have the luxury of lounging in bed with Lauren all day. He'd have to save that for another time.

He allowed himself one more second to enjoy the pulsing heat on his tired shoulders then shut off the shower. He snagged the towel draped on the rack attached to the wall and dried himself off before hooking the towel around his waist.

Steam covered the mirror. Lifting the end of the white cotton, he wiped a streak of moisture away then brushed his teeth and shaved. Fatigue made his movements slow. Damn, he needed coffee more than he needed air if he was going to make it through the day.

He quickly threw on the clothes he'd brought with him to the bathroom and hurried to the kitchen.

Madi stood at the sink, filling a glass with water.

"What are you doing awake?" he asked as he grabbed the pot and waited for her to finish.

She rubbed sleep from her eyes. "Someone was making a bunch of noise at the crack of dawn and woke me. Just getting some water before I try to go back to sleep."

Once the pot was full, he dumped it in the machine's reservoir and piled bitter grounds into the filter. He inhaled deeply, the aroma of the crushed beans almost enough to give him a boost of energy. "You'll need to head back to your dorm soon, and I don't want you to come back until I say it's okay."

Her mouth dropped open and she slammed the glass on the granite counter, spilling water all over. "Seriously? What, your new girlfriend tattled on me, and now I'm banished from your apartment? You've got to be kidding me. What kind of a brother are you?"

His temper flared hotter than the steam puffing from the top of the coffee machine. He turned toward her, hands fisted at his sides. "First of all, adults don't 'tattle.' Second, what exactly did you say to Lauren when I wasn't here?"

She shrugged. "Just the truth. Something you didn't bother to mention."

"Dammit, Madi, I'm not playing games with you. What did you tell her?"

Her bottom lip trembled until she locked her jaw. A sign she was upset by his outburst but refused to show it. "That she already caused enough damage and didn't need to come waltzing along and do it again. That because she threw a hissy fit and tossed around accusations and falsehoods, you almost died. She might have apologized to you with those big blue eyes and flashed her perky boobs, but that doesn't mean shit, Nolan. Not after the pain she caused." Tears rimmed the edges of her black-smudged eyelids.

He pinched the bridge of his nose. Yelling wouldn't help anything, and as much as he hated what Madi had said to Lauren, she was being protective. Her approach was sloppy and misguided, but her intentions were good. Typical Madi.

"Listen, I appreciate you looking out for me, but I don't need you to. I'm a grown man who makes my own decisions."

She snorted. "Oh, I know what part of your body you made a decision with last night."

"Madi," he growled, struggling to keep a lid on his escalating irritation.

"Fine. Forget it." She swiped her glass off the counter and marched past him to the living room.

He followed, waiting for her to make herself comfortable in the cocoon of blankets that had become her signature on his couch. He studied the blankets he kept stored for her in his hall closet.

"Why are you here so much?" he asked, keeping his voice low and gentle. He'd always taken her reasons for showing up at face value, never spending time to question why a college student would choose to stay so many nights at her older brother's apartment all the way across town.

She fiddled with the tag at the edge of the blanket. "You know, things come up. Too far from the dorm after a night out. My roommate has a guest over I don't like. Whatever. I didn't think you minded."

Realization crushed down on his insides. He sat beside her and rested his forearms on his knees. "Madi, do you come here to make sure I'm okay?"

She lifted a shoulder.

"You know that's not your job, right? You have a life to live. Standing guard over me isn't your responsibility. Besides. I'm fine. Have been for a while. The accident. My obsession with that case. That was years ago. A lot of time and therapy has helped me heal. I know how to cope with my problems better—how to create the boundaries I need to do my job safe and do it well."

"I don't think you understand what that time in your life was like for *me*," she said, wrapping her arms around her knees. "Watching you fall into such a dark place. Listening to Mom and Dad talk and worry about you. Standing in the hospital by your bed and not knowing if you'd make it through the night. I don't ever want that to happen again. And then of all people, Lauren shows up? Bang. You're going to be right back in that place. *We're* going to be back in that place."

Scooting closer, he looped an arm over her shoulders. "Sometimes I just see you as the little sister and forget that things from the past affected you, too. I'm sorry for that. I wish I could have explained to you before why I fell apart. It didn't have anything to do with Lauren and her crusade."

Madi stiffened. "But she was so mean. Said so many horrible things."

"She did exactly what you would have done if you blamed someone else for my death. You would raise hell to see my name cleared of any wrongdoing. That's what she did. Did those things upset me? Yes. Were they what drove me so hard? No."

She frowned. "What do you mean?"

"Charlie Mueller's arrest was the first arrest I made that had me questioning if I should be an officer. It was the first time what I saw in front of my face didn't line up with my gut. I didn't have a choice but to slap those cuffs on him. I was supposed to just let the legal system take over from there and forget it, but I couldn't. I couldn't forget the fear in his eyes—the confusion and absolute refusal to believe his guilt from his family. I needed to know I hadn't made a mistake."

"But you didn't. You did your job. Everyone said so."

He smiled, loving his sister's unfaltering faith in him. "You're right, but I learned that things aren't always so black-and-white. It was a lesson I learned the hard way, but I'm a better detective because of it. Honestly, I think I'm a better person. I just wish Charlie wouldn't have lost his life to get me where I am."

She rested her head on his shoulder. "I'm sorry I was mean to your girlfriend."

He chuckled. "She's not my girlfriend, but I think

you owe her that apology. Not me. Now, for the love of God, can we stop talking so I can get some coffee?"

She bumped against him then straightened before he stood.

"Is Lauren the reason you don't want me to come back?" she asked, tucking her bottom lip between her teeth.

Her question fisted his heart. "Never. But the case I'm working on is heating up. Someone is after Lauren. I don't think they know where I live, but I can't be too careful. I don't want you to get hurt. Stay in your dorm until this is all over, okay? Then you're welcome here anytime, no matter who my girlfriend is."

She grinned up at him. "Okay. Now get your coffee and let me go back to sleep. No one should be up at this ungodly hour."

He chuckled as he made his way to the kitchen and found a mug. He had things settled with one woman in his life. He just hoped that whatever Madi had said to Lauren hadn't driven a wedge between them he couldn't remove.

Chapter 21

The scent of savory bacon pulled Lauren from a deep sleep. Her stomach growled. Groaning, she turned to her side and blinked a few times to orient herself to her surroundings. The soft sea green comforter wasn't hers, and the window faced the east, not the north like her own room.

Flickers of the previous evening played in her mind. Nolan kissing her, touching her, making her feel ways she'd never felt before.

Then the phone call and her horrible conversation with his sister.

If ever there was a sign sent from the heavens that being with Nolan wasn't the right decision, it was being interrupted by the announcement of murder and a meddling relative.

The truth of what she had to do made her burrow

back under the blanket, until she caught the glaring red numbers staring back at her on the alarm clock.

She bolted upright. She couldn't remember the last time she'd slept until close to eleven o'clock in the morning. And with Nolan nowhere in sight, he must have woken up hours before while she'd spent half the day in bed. She scurried to her feet, found the clothes she'd packed and quickly dressed.

She studied the room. Damn, no mirror. Vanity wasn't usually an issue, but she didn't want to step out of the room looking like an electrocuted squirrel. Grabbing her toiletry kit, she snuck out of the room and tiptoed down the hall to the bathroom. She put herself together as best she could, borrowing a dollop of toothpaste to brush her teeth, then left the kit in his room before making her way to the kitchen.

Nolan stood in front of the stove with a spatula in one hand and his phone pressed to his ear. He was dressed in his usual slacks and dress shirt, his feet bare. Bacon sizzled on a skillet and a pan of scrambled eggs was on the stove.

Her heart fluttered. She'd never had a man cook for her before.

As if sensing her presence, he turned and grinned, holding up a finger to indicate he needed a second. "Great. Thanks. I appreciate your cooperation. If you can send that to the email address I gave you earlier, that'd be a big help."

He nodded along with whatever was being said on the other end of the line.

"Perfect. I'll be in touch if I need anything else. Have

a good day." He ended the call and tucked his phone in his front pocket. "Morning. Looks like my plan worked."

She frowned. "What plan?"

"To get you out of bed."

Heat rushed into her cheeks, and she wrinkled her nose. "Sorry. I'm not used to staying up so late."

He chuckled. "No need to apologize. I'm glad you got some rest. But I talked to Thomas, and he can meet us in thirty minutes during his break at work. I figured waking you with the smell of bacon and eggs would be the best way to go."

"Very clever," she said, spying the pile of cooked bacon on a plate beside the stove. "Who were you talking to?"

"Person in charge of hiring with At Your Service. She was very helpful. She's putting a filter on a spreadsheet she has of all her male drivers in the area and will send me the results as soon as she gets them. I'm hoping to find someone with a connection to either the Lower East Side or Brooklyn." The snapping of grease turned him back to the skillet. He picked up a pair of tongs and placed the cooked meat on the plate then switched off the burner.

"That's going to be a hell of a list."

"True," he said, giving a final stir to the eggs before sliding them into a silver bowl waiting by the bacon. "But I can weed out drivers based on physical descriptions."

"I can help with that. It'll be easier with two people." She'd spent hours awake last night considering his words. He was right. She couldn't be alone with a killer on the loose—a killer who had targeted her repeatedly. But she also didn't want Nolan to lose focus and have his head wrapped up somewhere it shouldn't be. The best way to guarantee she wasn't a distraction that could get him injured was by doing whatever she could to help.

"That'd be great," he said. "You can help right now by filling up a plate and eating quickly so we can leave." He gestured toward a cabinet beside the fridge.

She found two white plates and handed one to him before choosing a few strips of bacon and scooping up some eggs.

Nolan did the same. "I usually eat on the sofa. Not enough space for a table in here."

She hesitated, not wanting to go toe-to-toe with his sister again this morning. "What about Madi? Is she still asleep?"

"She left about an hour ago." He led the way to the living room then set his plate on the coffee table. "Want some juice? Water? Coffee?"

"Coffee'd be great." She took a seat beside the folded-up blankets left on the arm of the couch and balanced her plate on her lap. Relief loosened the knotted tension at the back of her neck. Madi might have made some valid points last night, but that didn't mean she wanted to rehash it all in the harsh light of day. Once had been enough.

Nolan returned with two full mugs and set them down before taking a seat beside her. "I'm sorry about her, by the way."

Not knowing what to say, she took a bite of the crispy breakfast meat. Salty goodness coated her taste buds.

"She's a little overprotective and has the worst delivery of anyone I know."

Sighing, Lauren decided to just dive right in. No matter how badly it hurt. "I'm glad she said what she did."

Puzzlement caused a deep line to run between his eyebrows. "You are?"

"You left out a lot of details when we spoke."

He winced. "I told you, I want to move forward, not keep looking behind us."

She took a second to consider her words. "I agree, but when our past doesn't just include us, I need to know."

"What do you mean?"

She laid her plate next to her untouched coffee. "I hurt your family. Your parents. Your sister. My actions didn't just affect you negatively. They affected them. Family is too important to just gloss over that. To pretend like their feelings don't matter. If I can't make things right with them, you and I don't stand a chance. And if I'm the reason you're ever hurt again, I could never live with myself." Emotion stung her nose, tears threatening.

Facing her, he tucked his thumb under her chin. "My family will love you. And like I explained to Madi, I can take care of myself. My actions are on me, not on you or anyone else. Yes, I was in a dark place before, but I've come out stronger and smarter. We both walked an ugly path to get to where we are—to find each other again. I don't want to blow this."

He pressed his lips to hers long enough for butterflies to erupt inside her, then broke away. "We better get ready to head out. Thomas doesn't have a big window of time to talk. I don't want to be late. I'll pour your coffee in a travel mug."

"Thanks." She flashed him a quick smile then hurried to his room to finish getting ready. His words played on repeat in her ears. Could they really move past all the baggage weighing them down, or were they destined to do nothing but destroy each other?

Nolan parked in the same spot he'd occupied a couple days before in front of Big Al's Autobody Shop. He'd hoped to continue the conversation with Lauren about their future. He wanted her to feel secure in their new relationship without adding pressure or making her feel as though he was getting too serious too fast. But he'd spent the whole ride to Brooklyn on the phone, discussing theories with Jack and getting updated by Officer Jeffery.

Maybe it was better the subject hadn't been broached again. Better to not appear too needy and let things play out naturally. That had worked so far.

Stepping into the sticky summer air, he met Lauren on the sidewalk then walked her to the door, ushering her through the entrance.

Al stood behind the counter, a scowl on his bulldog face. He glanced up from the computer, his frown growing impossibly bigger. "Thomas is in the office. I told him to wait in there so he could have some privacy."

"Thanks," Nolan said.

"I hope this is the last time you come by. I know you have a job to do, but I don't need you troubling that boy. He's upset by what's going on, and he's been through enough in his life."

"I understand, and trust me, I hope this is the last time I have to speak to Thomas as well. I'll make this as quick as possible. Just have a couple questions."

Al nodded then disappeared through a glass door that led out to the garage.

"That guy's a little scary," Lauren said.

He arched his brows. "Little bit, but he strikes me as a lot softer than he wants people to realize. He's just looking out for his employees. I respect that." He stepped behind the counter and knocked twice on the office door. "Do you mind sitting out here like you did last time? I'll leave the door open so I can see you at all times."

She nodded and took the chair tucked into the corner of the waiting room.

Opening the door, he stepped inside the office.

Thomas sat hunched over in the chair across from the desk. His eyes were bloodshot, and his light brown hair was messier than the last time Nolan had seen him. He drummed his fingers against his thigh, barely looking up as Nolan entered the room.

"Hi, Thomas," he said. "How are you?"

He shrugged. "Not great. I heard about Malcom. I can't believe it. I mean, how can he be dead?"

"I'm really sorry about your friend." Nolan walked around to the other side of the desk and dragged the chair so he could sit right across from Thomas. If he glanced out to the waiting room, Lauren remained in his sight line, yet hidden in the corner from anyone else. "Do you know Kevin Simpson?"

"Yeah, he's a buddy of mine. Me, Kev and another friend all started driving at the same time. Thought it'd be cool if we all worked for the same company to bring in some extra cash." Thomas's eyes widened. "What about Kev? You don't think he killed Malcom, do you?"

He dipped his chin, forcing the young man to meet his eyes. "I don't know, but the person driving Kevin's car last night while he was working for At Your Service is suspected of murdering a young woman. Do you have any information about that?"

Thomas shot to his feet and rubbed the back of his neck. "No. It's not possible. I knew Malcom couldn't have hurt anyone just like I know it wasn't Kevin. He wouldn't do that. Couldn't."

"Okay," Nolan said, raising his palms to signal Thomas to calm down. "Have you spoken with Kevin? If I could talk to him, maybe he could clear up what happened last night."

"You can't find him? Oh God. What if he's dead like Malcom? What the hell is going on? Should I be worried? Is someone going after the drivers?"

"That's what I'm trying to figure out. Now, I know I asked you this before, but I really need you to think hard. Is there anyone you know, who was friends with Malcom and Kevin, who has acted strange lately? Who has been upset or isolated? Someone who would understand how being a driver with At Your Service works?"

Thomas let his hand drop to his side, fear filling his eyes. "You think it's one of the drivers?"

"It could be. Or maybe not. Can you explain how the job works? How you know who to pick up and where?"

Thomas blew out a long breath. "Each driver has an account that can be accessed with an app. I get a notification when someone in the area needs a ride, and I choose if I want to accept that ride or not."

"Are you always logged in to your account?" Nolan asked. "Or do you need to log in every time you start a shift?"

"On the app, it's always logged on. But someone would need to gain access to a driver's phone to get to the app," Thomas said, moving across the room as if needing to expel pent-up energy, his head facing the tiled floor as he walked. "Your account has to be approved by the company. So not just anyone can log on and get information."

Tired of tipping back his head to keep his eyes on the pacing man, Nolan rose. "So as long as the killer is aware that a driver has the app, all he would need is to unlock the phone. Something that's pretty easy nowadays with facial recognition or a thumbprint." Or with someone the driver knew, he could just unlock the phone and hand it over—maybe the killer would ask to make a phone call?—before things went south.

"No." Thomas ran a palm over his face. "That can't be. No one can be that messed up. Not someone Malcom and Kevin both trust. Not someone *I* trust."

"Can I get the name of your other friend who joined At Your Service at the same time as you?"

Thomas faced him with defeat in his eyes. "Jim Pearl, but he's a good dude. I swear. No way he's involved in this."

Al stood in the doorway and cleared his throat. "Break's over, Thomas. I need you back in the garage."

"Yes, sir."

"Thomas," Nolan said before the young man got too far. "Be careful."

He nodded then walked out of the room, leaving a tense silence in his wake.

After returning the chair he'd used behind the desk, he joined Lauren in the waiting room.

She glanced up from her phone. "How'd it go?"

He shrugged. "I've got a better understanding of how things work for the drivers. And there's no doubt the killer knows both drivers at the center of this, possibly Thomas as well. That should help narrow down that list when it comes through."

Lauren stood and shoved her phone back in her purse. "That's something."

"Let's get out of here." He took three steps before his phone rang in his pocket. He grabbed it, noticing Officer Jeffery's number. "Hey, Jeffery. What's going on?"

"Kevin Simpson was found, sir. We need you at the crime scene."

Chapter 22

An eerie sense of déjà vu settled over Lauren as she leaned against the wall outside Rebecca's hospital room. Another phone call. Another murder. Another instance when dread weighed her down, knowing Nolan would leave while she waited and hoped for his safe return.

Nolan stood in front of her and braced his forearm above her head, boxing her in. "Rebecca won't be discharged for another hour or two, so you should be all right to stay here until I'm done at the crime scene. I'll swing by and pick you up when I'm done."

"You don't have to worry about me."

He lowered his forehead to hers and breathed in deeply. "I'll always worry about you. Especially when I know there's someone out there who wants to hurt you. I won't rest until he's off the streets and behind bars where he belongs."

As much as his words warmed her heart, they also frightened her. He couldn't afford to get sucked back into a case where he lost focus of everything else but his single goal. Last time, it had ended with him barely escaping alive. She couldn't let that happen again.

She rested her palm on his chest. The feel of his heart beat against her hand. "Please. Don't think about me. Just figure out what happened to Kevin. That's your priority right now."

"You're my priority." He pressed his lips to hers, deepening the kiss until her blood pressure shot through the roof.

Flames consumed her core, but she broke away, aware of the curious eyes of nurses walking past, and the rigid stance of the new officer standing guard outside the room. "My priority is making sure you come back to me safely."

He grinned. "I like having someone who wants me to come home."

She rolled her eyes at his teasing tone but couldn't hide her smile. "You have plenty of people who want that. But you need to go now."

He groaned then gave her one more kiss before taking a step away.

An idea struck her. "Can you send me the spreadsheet of the drivers?"

Frowning, he scratched his now clean-shaven jawline. "I can forward it to your email if you send me your address. Why?"

She shrugged. "I planned to help you whittle down the list. Might as well start now. I can even ask for Rebecca's help. I'm sure being productive will be good for her. I know it is for me."

"That'd be great. Maybe by the time I pick you up, we'll have some serious suspects to start digging into. I'll send you the email as soon as I get to my car." He pressed one more kiss to her cheek then turned for the exit.

She watched him go, waiting until he was out of sight before ducking into Rebecca's room.

Rebecca sat on the bed with her auburn hair piled in a messy bun on the top of her head. The bright red skin around her mouth had dulled, and her casted leg was stretched out in front of her. Bags hung under her eyes, an air of defeat and terror heavy in the air around her.

Her mother, Shelly, sat in a chair pulled next to the bed. The same auburn-colored hair was cut in a shoulder-length bob and the same circles darkened the thin skin under her tired eyes.

Lauren offered them a weak smile, her heart aching at the sight of mother and daughter. "How are you two holding up?"

Rebecca drew in a shuddering breath. "Honestly, I was doing a little bit better until Nolan gave us an update. I'd convinced myself Malcom was responsible for all of this, and since he was dead, we were safe. But now…" She shrugged. "It's clear the killer could be anywhere. The man who locked me in a trunk and stole my sense of security is still out there."

"You're going to be okay," Shelly said, capturing Rebecca's hand. She stared hard at her daughter then aimed her protective glance at Lauren. "You both are."

Appreciation caused tears to hover over Lauren's

lashes, and she blinked them away. Her mother was just as supportive, but she couldn't lean on her the same way Rebecca could Shelly. At least not in this situation, when she could easily bring a killer's attention to her parents' home. "Thanks, Shelly. I know it will take time, but at least we have each other."

Shelly reached out and hooked her other hand with Lauren's. "Rebecca is going to come home and stay with me and her father."

Lauren's jaw dropped, and the tears she tried to stop tumbled down her cheeks. She bounced her gaze between Shelly and Rebecca. "What do you mean? You're moving back home?"

"I can't go back to our apartment right now. Not with the memories so fresh. I talked to the school, and they're letting me take some time off to heal and process everything that's happened. Spending that time with my parents makes sense."

Lauren swallowed hard, understanding Rebecca's logic but not wanting to be apart from her best friend. "I get it."

"We want you to come, too," Shelly said, giving her hand a squeeze. "At least until the danger has passed. You're not safe here. If you come to Pennsylvania, the detective doesn't have to worry about keeping you from harm's way while trying to do his job."

She weighed the words, her stomach rebelling at the idea of putting so much distance between her and Nolan. But maybe that's exactly what she needed. Space and time to sort out her feelings without all the heightened emotions and stress of the past few days. She could come back to the city when the threat to her life was over, and she could really focus on what was best for the future.

"Are you sure you don't mind?"

Shelly pressed her lips together in an are-you-kidding-me look. "You're always welcome in our home, and we understand why you don't want to stay with your own parents. It wouldn't be wise to draw this criminal's attention to them or anyone else. Steve and I are positive we live far enough away to ensure your safety. And if not…" She shrugged, lightning flashing in her eyes. "I'd like to see this asshole get past me."

Lauren couldn't help but smile at the fierce protectiveness rolling off Shelly in waves. "Then all right. I'll take you up on your offer, but just until this guy is caught."

"Good," Rebecca said, sinking against the mattress as if the conversation had zapped all her energy. "I'll feel so much better with you by my side."

Lauren remembered the spreadsheet probably waiting in her inbox. "While we wait for you to get sprung, do you want to do something else to help the investigation?"

Rebecca frowned. "What can I do?"

"Nolan sent me a list of drivers and employee photos he received from At Your Service. He needs the list trimmed to a more manageable size. I told him I'd go through the names and weed out anyone who doesn't fit the physical description of our attacker. Do you want to help?"

Rebecca straightened, a look of renewed determination taking over her face. "Yes. I'll take half the list."

"No, you'll take a third," Shelly said. "I want the other third. I want to do whatever I can to find this guy."

Lauren couldn't help but laugh, hope blossoming inside her. She and Rebecca were taking back their power, then they'd lean on each other until it was safe to return home. She just hoped Nolan wouldn't view her decision as choosing to run away from him.

The stench of death combined with the muggy heat was like a fist to the face. Nolan fought not to gag as he studied the body of Kevin Simpson. Flies buzzed around the corpse, blood splattered on the brick building of the quiet side street close to the bar where Alicia Lokie had been picked up the night before.

"Do you think the killer's escalating?" Officer Jeffery asked. "Or just getting sloppy?"

Unlike with Malcom, the killer hadn't even tried to make Kevin's death look like anything other than what it was…murder. A bullet hole was dead center in his chest. His wallet was still in his pants and a look of surprise frozen on his face.

"He knows we're onto his scheme so why bother to hide it?" With his hands in gloves, he repositioned the body to gain a better view of the back of his neck. No marks like the ones he'd found on Malcom, but who needed a Taser when the blast of a gun was so much more efficient?

"Makes sense." Jeffery pivoted to block the view of a handful of pedestrians who slowed for a better look behind the yellow crime scene tape. "I requested security footage from the surrounding buildings."

He appreciated her forethought, although he didn't

hold out much hope the video feed would provide them with more information than they already had. Based on his theory, they were looking for a male who was the same size and build as both Malcom and Kevin. Blond hair, blue eyes, light skin—all information the media had gotten ahold of and had blasted across the city. Unless the killer had a distinguishing feature that was caught on camera, a shot angled from on top of one of the buildings would just tell him what he already knew.

Or contradict everything he'd based his theory on.

"Good thinking, Jeffery. I know watching the footage is mindless work, but at least we have an approximate time for when the victim was killed. Look up the ride request by Alicia Lokie and match the time stamp to that. Should help."

Placing the body back in the position he found it, he searched the man's arms and hands. "There appears to be fresh bruising on his arms, and streaks of dirt or mud. He might have fought back. Maybe realized what was happening and tried to stop it."

Jeffery waited for the street to clear then joined him, crouching low for a better look. "Could be why the suspect used a gun. Mr. Simpson gave him too much of a fight and he was afraid the Taser wouldn't be enough. Shoved him out of the car, put a bullet in him, then drove away."

"Makes sense," he said, impressed again with the young officer's train of thought. "We'll make sure the coroner checks under the nails for any tissue that isn't his. Usually a female victim will scratch or claw to get away from an attacker, and with his back against the wall, Kevin might have done the same."

He finished his study of the body, the street, the bloodstained building and pulled off his gloves. An urgency to return to Lauren rushed through his veins, but he pushed it aside. While he was done here, he had one more stop to make before heading back to the hospital.

"Will you stay and guard the scene until the coroner's van arrives? Let him know everything we discussed. I want to walk to the bar where Alicia was picked up. See if there's anyone around to speak with."

"Yes, sir."

He nodded his goodbye and hurried around the corner. The bustling streets of Midtown didn't slow in the afternoon. Vendors hawked their wares on sidewalks and umbrella-covered food carts sold steamed hot dogs and beverages. He pushed his way past slow-moving tourists and hurried over the crosswalk, raising a palm to a honking cabbie who wanted to turn right.

He picked up his pace so he wouldn't get run over, then stopped under the stretched-out red awning with two-person high-top tables huddled around the sidewalk. Windows rose from floor to ceiling, showing off a gleaming bar with a wall of liquor bottles behind it and an empty, scarred dance floor in front of an intimate stage.

A man with tattoos circling his biceps and a thick beard stood behind the bar.

Nolan yanked on the door, but it wouldn't budge. He knocked on the glass until he got the bartender's attention.

The man glanced up, irritation clear in every step he took to the front of the room. He twisted the lock and pushed open the door. "Can I help you?"

Nolan flashed his badge. "I was hoping to speak with a manager."

"That's me. What's this about?" He kept a firm grip on the edge of the door, refusing to open it any farther.

"A woman who left your bar last night was murdered. She was picked up by a car service. Where do your patrons usually get picked up? Right out front?"

"Well, shit," he said, rubbing the back of his short black hair. "Come on in and take a seat. I'm Mac." After letting Nolan in, he let the door swing shut then removed two chairs from the top of a nearby table.

Nolan sat. "Thanks."

Mac sat across from him. "Man. That sucks. Sorry, that wasn't what I expected to hear."

"Yeah, it's sad as hell, but where's the pickup spot?"

Mac ran his fingers through his beard. "Out front gets pretty congested. Lots of traffic day and night. Some people head down a block or two, especially if trying to hail a cab. Some just cram together on the sidewalk or run out to the cars while they idle in the road."

"You have security footage aimed outside?" He almost groaned at his own question, the hours of feed adding up in his mind.

"Yeah, I'll get it for you right away. Is there anything else I can do?"

Nolan slapped his hands on his thighs then stood. "Don't think so."

"Can I ask who was killed? We're pretty close-knit around here." Mac rose but braced a fist on the top of the wooden table.

He hesitated, but there was no point in keeping her identity a secret. He'd already notified her family and spoken with friends. Besides, Mac could have some insight. "A young woman named Alicia Lokie."

Mac sucked in a deep breath and fell back to his seat. "Dear God. Not Alicia. She was so young. So sweet."

"You knew her well?"

He nodded, then glanced up with confusion knitting his brow. "She was here last night, but she left with her boyfriend. Kev. He picked her up when her friends headed home. He'd never hurt her. He loved her, man."

The statement knocked the air from Nolan's lungs and scrambled everything about the case he thought he knew.

Chapter 23

Lauren's eyes burned from staring at her phone screen so long. She blinked, hoping to get rid of the little floating dots swimming in her vision. "All these names are starting to blur together," she said, tossing her phone on her lap.

"I know what you mean. It feels like we've been at this for days instead of an hour, and I'm still on the *B*s." Rebecca lowered her tablet and rubbed her eyes.

"I'm still on the *R*s," Shelly said. "Do you know how many drivers in Brooklyn and the Lower East Side have last names that start with the letter *R*?"

Lauren snorted. "I'm guessing a lot."

Once she'd opened the spreadsheet of names and employee photos from Nolan, she'd forwarded them to Rebecca and Shelly—along with clear instructions of what types of physical characteristics needed to stay on the list. They'd decided the best approach was to divide the last names by groups of letters. Rebecca got the start of the alphabet, Lauren the middle and Shelly the end. Not an exact science, but it was the best they could come up with.

Little did they know the process of cross-checking names with pictures, some provided and others they had to search for online, would be incredibly monotonous. "I've gotten through a few letters, but I need a break. We've made enough progress to earn a reward. Maybe some ice cream?"

Rebecca tossed her tablet on the foot of the bed. "Sounds good to me."

A soft knock on the door drew their attention to the sweet nurse with gray hair and brown eyes. "I'm here with some paperwork. I need to go over your care before the doctor pays one last visit then signs the discharge forms. Are you up for that?"

"As long as I don't have to read anything," Rebecca said.

Lauren stood and rolled back her shoulders. "Do you want me to wait in the hall? I can stretch my legs a little and make a mental list of everything we'll need to grab at the apartment before we head to your parents' house."

Rebecca's face paled. "I can't go back there. Please, don't make me go inside yet."

Lauren's heart splintered.

Shelly rushed to her side and rubbed a soothing palm over her forehead. "Shh. You're okay. You don't need to go anywhere you don't want. What if Lauren and I head back there while you speak with the nurse and doctor? We'll grab anything you want and be back before you're discharged. Then we can go straight home from the hospital. Does that sound good?"

Eyes wide and filled with tears, Rebecca nodded.

"Is that all right with you?" Shelly asked, turning toward Lauren.

She forced a smile, not wanting either of them to see how uncomfortable she was walking into her apartment. Someone had to get their things, and she couldn't expect Shelly to do it alone. That would put a red target on her back and make her vulnerable. If they were together, they could watch out for one another and do the job in half the time. "Sure."

"Let's get going then." Shelly pressed a kiss to Rebecca's cheek then hooked her purse over her shoulder. "We won't be long, and you have all these lovely people watching over you. You're safe, honey, okay?"

Rebecca nodded.

Lauren secured her own bag across her chest, making sure she'd grabbed her phone, then hugged Rebecca. "We'll be back soon."

She led the way to the hall, nodding hello to the guard, and found the stairs that spit them out the exit. Harsh rays of sun beamed between the towering buildings and glinted off the glass walls. People hurried along the sidewalk like a school of fish, weaving together to avoid obstacles in their path.

Shelly clutched her purse strap as if afraid someone would steal her things as they passed by.

Lauren resisted the urge to tell her how to carry her purse in the crowd, dipping her hand in her own bag to pluck out the pepper spray that made her feel a little safer. "We're only a couple blocks from the apartment. The idea of getting in any kind of car right now scares the crap out of me and the train isn't an option. Are you okay to walk?"

"Sure." Shelly cast a steely-eyed glance over her shoulder. Nervous energy crackled the air.

Not wanting to spend another second just standing around, Lauren started off toward home at a brisk pace. Shelly stayed glued to her side, annoying pedestrians who tried to pass. Goose bumps puckered the skin at the back of Lauren's neck, as if someone watched her. She pressed forward. The sooner they got what they needed, the sooner they'd return to the hospital.

Her building came into view and a little knot of tension between her shoulder blades loosened. She scooped her keys from her bag, keeping her other fist securely around the pepper spray. When she opened the door, she made sure to let Shelly in before quickly latching it closed.

No one lingered in the lobby, and she kept her body tuned to any sounds or movements that were out of the norm. Once at her door, she made sure the hall was clear before letting them inside then locking the door behind her.

"There's a suitcase in Rebecca's closet," she said. "She's pretty organized so you should find everything you need in her room. I already took all her toiletries to the hospital yesterday, but there may be some things she'll want in the bathroom for an extended stay. If you need help finding anything, just holler. The apartment is small enough I can hear you from anywhere." She forced a little laugh then grabbed a large tote bag from the hall closet before heading toward her bedroom.

A stab of pain pierced her heart at the neatly made bed. She hadn't allowed herself a second to think about Sissy but looking at her cat's favorite spot made grief wash over her. It had been forty-eight hours since Sissy had vanished, forced from her home after trying to protect Rebecca. If she hadn't returned by now, chances were slim that she ever would.

The thought brought fresh tears to Lauren's eyes. Sissy had been her best friend for the past six years. Being without her seemed impossible, but she couldn't dwell on that now. She needed to pack her things and get the hell out of here. Rummaging through her drawers, she yanked out enough clothes to get her through five days and stuffed them in the bag.

The loud meow of a cat made her pulse jump. Okay, she must really miss her cat if she was hearing her in her head.

The sound grew more persistent, and Lauren flew to the window.

Sissy sat on the sidewalk and stared up at her. Dirt was matted in her fur and her eyes appeared twice their normal size. She stood on her hind legs and leaned her two front paws against the stone, meows growing louder and more frantic, as if begging to be let inside.

"Sissy!" Lauren gasped, joy exploding in her chest. So much bad had happened in the past few days, she never imagined something so wonderful would just show up in her world. She ran for the door. "Shelly, I have to run outside!"

Shelly's head peeked around the side of the door, eyes wide. "What?"

"Lock the door behind me!" She waited for Shelly to rush forward before running into the hallway.

Without another thought, she dashed down the hall, nearly tripping over her feet as she ran through the lobby. She bolted for the door, excitement spurring her on, pushing her forward as she stepped into the warm afternoon. She couldn't wait to get her arms around Sissy. To feel her silky fur and hold her close, making sure she was healthy and happy.

Sissy padded toward her, meows louder than ever.

Lauren reached for her, snagging her hand around her chubby middle.

A hard grip tightened on her bicep and halted her motion. The harsh smell of chemicals turned her stomach. A muscled body that felt all too familiar pressed against her back. Something hard pushed against her spine. "Don't think about doing something stupid or I'll kill you and your damn cat before finishing what I started with your roommate."

Bile sloshed in her stomach as her options dwindled to none. She couldn't do anything that would turn his wrath on Rebecca and Sissy. Not again. She licked her lips and kept her body still as she tried to catch the eye of a passerby. But the few people who strolled by were either focused on their phones or too busy to notice a panicked woman in danger.

"Put down the cat. Now." He barked the order directly in her ear.

She winced, fear pulsing through her with every frantic beat of her heart. Maybe if she did what he said, she could buy herself enough time to form a plan. Moisture misted in her eyes and she hugged Sissy close, slipping the bracelet from her wrist around her neck like a little collar. She let her loose and prayed someone close to the building found her.

Staying behind her, the man steered her toward a car parked at the curb.

Panic pressed down on her lungs, making each breath more difficult than the last with every step she took. He opened the back door and pushed her inside then slammed the butt of a gun against the back of her head. The man shut door, the sound vibrating against her skull as her world went black.

The constant traffic clogging the streets, making each mile crawl by, added to Nolan's irritation. He tapped his finger on top of the steering wheel and fought the urge to shake his fist at the driver in front of him who wouldn't stop stomping on his damn breaks.

He bit back a growl and pressed the button on his wheel to connect to his phone. "Call Jack."

The sound of ringing poured through the speakers before the line picked up. "Hey, man. What's up?"

"Just leaving the bar where Alicia Lokie spent the evening. Manager dropped a bomb, and I want to pick your brain."

"Go ahead. I've got a few minutes."

"I've got two victims. Turns out they were dating, and the manager saw the female victim leave the bar with the male victim. I assumed the killer stole Kevin's car with him in it, murdered him, then picked up the female while pretending to be the driver." He finally reached the light and made a right turn, heading toward the hospital. He'd spent more time than he'd planned away and hoped Rebecca's discharge hadn't come through. He'd hate if Lauren was waiting around for him.

"Was the male victim alone when he picked up his girlfriend?" Jack asked, slightly winded as if moving quickly.

"Good question. The manager didn't mention. Just said he knew she went home with her boyfriend, who drove for At Your Service. My gut says the guy's friends, or at least acquaintances, with the drivers he's targeting. If that's true, it wouldn't be out of the realm of possibility if he tagged along for the drive. Neither victim would find that suspicious."

"If you can get a good image of the car around the time she left the bar, it might give you the answer."

He snorted. "To one question, but then it'll just lead to more."

"True," Jack said. "But at least it gives you more insight into what you're working with. Listen, sorry to do this, but I've got to go. Max and I are about to do an interview. I can call you back when we're done if you need to talk it over more."

"Appreciate it." He disconnected as he pulled into the parking garage attached to the hospital. He slid into the closest spot and hurried inside. Being away from Lauren had caused an actual ache to spread through his body. All he wanted was to see her, be near her, and know she was safe.

Hopping on the elevator, he rode to Rebecca's floor and refrained from jogging to her room. He waved hello to the guard and knocked on the door frame, peering inside to seek permission to enter.

Rebecca sat on the bed, dressed in a loose T-shirt and pair of jogging shorts. She smiled and waved him in. "You're right on time. Discharge papers came in, and I'm good to go. Just waiting on my mom and Lauren to get back so we can all head to Pennsylvania."

He stopped short, not sure which part of that sentence alarmed him more. "What are you talking about?"

She cringed as though she'd just spilled a secret. "Sorry. Lauren must not have told you yet. I'm staying with my parents for a while, and we all felt it would be best for her to come, too. At least until you close the case. That way she's safe and you don't have to worry about watching out for her. It's a double win."

All the moisture evaporated from his mouth, making it hard to swallow. Lauren wanted to get away from him? After their talk, he'd assumed they'd ironed out all the issues Madi had stirred up between them. "Umm, okay. Whatever Lauren feels comfortable with. And where did Lauren and your mom go?"

"To pack some things for us. The nurse came in to get the process of my discharge started. They said they'd be quick so they could make it back before all the paperwork went through and we could take off from here."

He frowned, uneasiness festering in his stomach. "And how long ago did they leave?"

Rebecca glanced up at the clock mounted on the wall. "About forty minutes ago. I figured they'd be back by now. I was about to call and find out what's keeping them."

He grabbed his phone and called Lauren. The line

rang in his ear, each second that ticked by making his unease grow until it nearly consumed him. Her voice mail picked up and he disconnected, his hand shaking. "Lauren didn't answer. Can you call your mom?"

"Sure," she said, pinching her face together as if picking up on his anxiety. She made the call then pressed the speaker button and held the phone out so he could hear. "Hi, Mom," she said when Shelly answered. "You guys almost here? I'm good to leave at any time."

"I don't know where Lauren is." Her voice was higher than Nolan remembered, panic clear in her tone. "I was in your room grabbing your things while she was getting her stuff ready. I heard her yell something. I came out and she told me she had to run outside and to lock up behind her. I waited for her to return, and she hasn't yet. What could she need outside? Why isn't she back yet?"

Rebecca's eyes widened and she locked her gaze with his.

Terror twisted Nolan up inside. He had to get to Lauren's apartment. He had to find her now.

Chapter 24

Nolan didn't bother to get his vehicle. He ran all the way to Lauren's apartment. His lungs burned, but the pain didn't slow him down. It only pushed him harder as he shoved past anyone who got in his way.

Rebecca had told her mom to stay put and open the door to no one. He'd call when he arrived so she could grant him access into the building. Hopefully by the time he got there, Lauren would have returned, and her disappearance would be one big misunderstanding.

But Nolan knew better. Something bad had happened, and he hadn't been around to keep her safe.

As he turned the corner, he shook his head to rid himself of that mindset. Now wasn't the time to get caught in the spiderweb of escalating thoughts that would only muck up his thinking and make it harder to find Lauren.

Her building came into view, and he forced himself to slow down. He kept a sharp eye on every face, every vehicle, every damn crack in the sidewalk. Anything that could clue him in to where Lauren had gone.

The soft sound of an animal caught his attention. He whipped around, searching for the noise that competed with the sounds of the city.

A dirty ball of fur slinked out of an alley, keeping its body pressed against the smooth stone of the building beside Lauren's.

His pulse raced. *Sissy!*

Crouching low, he extended his fingers and made a clicking sound with his tongue. "Come here, kitty. I won't hurt you."

She stared at him with large blue eyes and he swore she was pleading with him to help.

He tunneled his hand through his hair. He was losing his damn mind. Taking another small step forward, he kept his gaze locked on the cat. "Do you remember me? I'm a friend. I promise. Come see me."

She pranced his way, and he scooped her into his arms. Bursts of color shone through the puffy fur around her neck, and he brushed the long strands aside. Lauren's bracelet looped around the cat like a collar.

His heart dropped to the sidewalk. Thoughts clicked into place and formed a picture that made complete sense. Lauren had tried to rescue her pet and left whatever she could behind so he'd know what had happened.

Lauren had been taken.

Grabbing his phone, he called Shelly. "I'm outside. Buzz me in. Fast."

When the door sounded, he sprinted inside and jogged to Lauren's apartment. "I'm at the door," he said, Shelly still on the line.

The door opened a crack, then was flung wide. "Oh, thank God," Shelly said, throwing her arms around him.

He gave her a quick squeeze, Sissy howling in protest, then hurried her inside. He didn't have time to offer her reassurances or comfort. He set Sissy on the ground, and she stared up at him and meowed. Nolan stood for a second, pressing his palms to his temples, and centered his frantic thoughts. "Shelly, did Lauren say anything to clue you in to where she went?"

"No, she just said she had to run outside and to lock the door." She wrung her hands together.

"I think she went outside because she saw her cat," he said, nodding to the noisy animal on the floor. "I think she was used as bait to lure Lauren outside."

Shelly's hand flew to her mouth. "We should have never come here. What was I thinking? We should have stayed at the hospital, reading through those blasted names and searching those pictures until someone could escort us back."

"Wait," he said, dropping his hands. "You all went through the spreadsheet of names?"

She nodded. "We split them up. Didn't get through a ton, but we have the list at least cut in half."

"Can you get it to me?"

She winced. "Rebecca and I can. Lauren was working on her phone. She left it here, along with her bag, but I'm sure it's locked with a password."

"Get ahold of Rebecca and ask her to send me what she worked on. I need to make a call."

He heard Shelly fumbling for her phone and speaking to Rebecca as he crossed to Lauren's room and contacted Jack.

"Hey," Jack said. "Something else come up?"

"Lauren's missing," he said, emotion cracking his voice. "She went back to her apartment with her roommate's mom to grab some things. I think this asshole used her cat to lure her outside then grabbed her. I have to find her."

"Any new names to investigate? Any clear idea who's behind all this?" Jack's brisk questions spoke of authority and competence, which snapped Nolan back into focus.

"Jim Pearl. Driver who was friends with both Malcom and Kevin. Also friends with Thomas. I hadn't gotten a chance to look him up yet."

A few beats of silence pulsed through the phone. "Don't think he's your man. Skin is too dark with black hair and a beard. If your theory is right, which my gut says it is, he isn't the one we're after. No way he could pass himself off as the other two victims whose vehicles were stolen. Not even if the passenger paid very little attention."

"I want to talk to him anyway. He might know something."

"I'll do that," Jack said. "Shouldn't take long to get some answers from him. Hopefully they help."

A beep interrupted the line, signaling a text message had arrived. "Keep in touch. I gotta go." Nolan disconnected then opened the message from Rebecca. He scanned the list of names she'd sent then swore under his breath before calling her.

"Hello?"

"Rebecca, it's Nolan. I just opened the document you sent. Are you sure you only kept the names that matched the physical description Lauren gave you?"

"Yes. Light skin. Blue eyes. I made some allowances for beards and such."

"But I see a name on here that I know personally. He has brown hair. Not blond."

"The man had a hat on when he attacked Lauren," Rebecca said, voice shaking. "If the other features are a match, the hair color doesn't have to be spot-on. I know it makes the list longer, but I didn't want to leave anyone out."

Dammit, she was right.

"How do you know this guy?" she asked, cutting into his thoughts.

"He's friends with two of the drivers that were killed. I've talked to him twice where he works days at an autobody shop."

Rebecca sucked in a breath. "Oh my God. Oil. Gasoline. The smell."

"Rebecca, slow down. What are you talking about?"

"The hand that covered my mouth smelled like gas and oil. Like I'd walked into a body shop. I didn't remember that until now. Like your words triggered a memory I'd repressed. I'm…I'm so sorry. How did I not remember that?" Soft sobs poured through the speaker.

An image of the first time he met Thomas flashed in his mind. The red handkerchief used to wipe the oil from his hands. The oil refusing to be removed. Shit, how had he not seen the role Thomas had played before?

"Our brains forget a lot when we experience a traumatic event," he said, moving back into the living room to find Shelly. His heart beat triple time. "But you remember now and that's what's important. I'm walking your mom back to the hospital then you two can get out of town. But I have to get off the phone. I need to find Thomas Beetle."

Shelly stared at him with wide eyes, cradling the cat like a baby. "Any news?"

"I think I know who has her. I need to get you back to the hospital. Take whatever you packed for Rebecca."

She nodded then dropped her gaze to Sissy. "What about the cat?"

"I'll make sure she has food and water then we leave her here. She'll be fine."

Following through on his promise, he quickly filled the food and water dish on the kitchen floor, gave Sissy a loving pet, then rushed Shelly out the door. He redialed Jack, filling him in on what Rebecca had told him, then called the autobody shop. If Thomas was still at work, his theory was dead in the water.

"Big Al's Autobody Shop. How can I help you?"

"Al, this is Detective Clayman. Is Thomas around?"

An annoyed rumble practically vibrated the speaker. "I told you not to upset him. He was so worked up after you left, he had to head home. Now we're slammed and I'm short-staffed."

Validation quickened his pace. No way Thomas leaving work right before Lauren went missing was a coincidence. Not with all his other connections to the case. "I need to know his address."

Al snorted. "Why would I just hand that information over?"

"Because your employee is a suspected murderer who I'm pretty sure just kidnapped a woman. I can find his address as soon as I hang up, which will take me a few extra minutes and piss me off, or you can save me the trouble."

"You've got to be kidding, right?" A sliver of doubt sliced through the question still full of irritation. "Thomas wouldn't kill anyone. He's a good kid. Always has been."

Nolan wasn't surprised that someone close to Thomas wouldn't see the signs he'd kept so expertly hidden. Hell, he was a trained homicide detective, and he might have connected the dots too late. "Either tell me now or I'm hanging up. I don't have time to waste."

"Fine," Al said, as if through clenched teeth, and rattled off the address.

"Thanks," he said, ending the call and pulling up Jack's information again as the hospital came into view. As soon as Jack answered he jumped right into the newest developments. "Forget about Jim Pearl. Thomas Beetle is our man. The driver who works days at the autobody shop. Got his address from his boss. Apartment in Brooklyn, close to the shop. We need officers there as soon as possible."

"I already talked to Jim. He was broken up about the deaths of his buddies and mentioned how he'd requested time off. When I pushed him harder, he confided Thomas hasn't driven for the past two weeks due to family issues."

The automatic doors for the emergency room whooshed open, and Nolan waited for Shelly to enter before stepping behind her. He lifted a finger, asking her to wait a second. "What family issues?"

"The guy didn't know," Jack said.

"Well, finding that out takes second place to getting to Thomas's house and seeing if he's there with Lauren."

"We need to plan this out. I know you want to go in there fast and get her out, but this guy has proven he's smart. We can't make a mistake. Where can I meet you?"

"At his house. I'm grabbing my car and making my way there now. I want to call the local precinct, get them in on this, but we better be quick. Thomas is dangerous. Lauren can't be in his clutches one second longer than necessary or we might be too late. I'll shoot you the address." He disconnected and focused on Shelly.

"You know who has her? You know where she is?" She clutched the purse strap dangling over her shoulder, her body wincing with every person who passed by.

"I think so. I need you to go be with your daughter. I'll let the guard know he is to walk you to your car. Take Rebecca home."

She tightened her jaw and nodded. "I will, and you… you go get Lauren. Bring her home safe."

"I will."

The promise played on repeat in his head as he hurried to the parking garage and climbed into his SUV. He'd do whatever it took to find Lauren and keep her safe, but his stomach churned at the thought of failing her again.

And this time, the price of failure would be her life.

Chapter 25

Awareness trickled into the darkness of Lauren's mind, waking her little by little. Her eyelids fluttered but remained closed. A wall of oppressive heat smashed down on her and stole her breath. Beads of sweat rolled along the side of her face, and her tank top was practically glued to her moist skin.

She reached up to wipe her hair off her forehead, but her hands were bound. She attempted to move her legs, but the same binding sensation kept her ankles pinned together. Panic tightened her throat, and the tinny taste of fear coated her tongue. Her eyes flew open, and terror grew exponentially as she took stock of her surroundings.

She lay curled on her side on an unmade bed, duct tape wrapped around her wrists and ankles, and the

comforter under her dirty and ripped. The walls were
painted a dusty pink with chunks missing, as if things
had been thrown across the room and chipped away the
drywall. A dresser was shoved against the wall, littered
with papers and beer cans and Lord knew what else.
Mustiness mixed with the scent of decay, threatening
to activate her gag reflex.

Holding her breath, she listened for any sounds—
any clue that someone else was in the room with her.
Fear kept her from turning around and facing whatever nightmare waited. Nothing but the hum of electricity met her ears. Slowly, she shifted onto her back
and pain throbbed against her head and slithered up
her stiff neck, reminding her of what had brought her
to this hellhole.

A man. A gun. A car.

Oh God. How long had she been unconscious? Fear
slammed against her. Spasms constricted her chest,
hitching her heart rate higher and higher until she
thought her heart would burst from her mouth. She
squeezed her eyes shut, trying to draw on everything
she knew about how to stop a panic attack. Spiraling
out of control wouldn't do a damn thing to help her.
She needed to figure out where she was, who had taken
her and how to get the hell out of here. With any luck,
someone had found the bracelet she'd left with Sissy and
alerted Nolan. He wouldn't stop until he found her. But
she needed to do everything within her power to save
herself, or at least keep herself alive until then.

Taking deep breaths in through her nose then pushing them out her mouth, she focused on the first problem
she needed to solve. No way she could defend herself

with her hands and feet taped together. She summoned all the courage she could and sat up. Nausea swam in her gut and her head spun. She gritted her teeth. She couldn't focus on the pain or fear right now. She needed something sharp or jagged enough to cut through the tape holding her hostage. There had to be something in the room she could use.

The floor was a mess of garbage and clothes. Stains covered the bits of carpet visible beneath the clutter. She swung her feet over the side of the bed and stood, hopping toward the wall. Her balance was out of whack, and she struggled to stay on her feet. But she kept moving, kept shifting the barrage of someone's tragic existence to the side as best she could in hopes of finding something useful underneath.

A flash of movement caught her eye in the corner and a puff of brown fur streaked by. She bit into her cheeks to quiet the scream dying to break through her lips. The critter poked its head through a sweater, and she stumbled backward, landing hard on her bottom.

Tears stung her eyes, and she pushed away from the large rodent. Something scraped the back of her calf, and she twisted to push aside an empty liquor bottle and a months-old newspaper. A silver edge emerged, and she used her forefingers to shove everything aside, revealing a metal picture frame.

A photo of a tall, stoic groom with a military-style buzz cut stood beside a long-haired bride wearing a floor-length white dress with puffy sleeves. The woman in the image beamed up at her husband, who stared grim-faced at the camera. She studied their features, trying to recognize anything about them but came up short. But that didn't matter. What mattered was she'd just found something that could help her escape.

Pushing her back against the wall, she sat with her feet flat on the floor and knees close to her chest. She wedged the frame between her knees, corner facing up, and sawed the duct tape over the sharp metal. Her heartbeat pounded against her temples. Her fingers shook and her head throbbed. The stagnant air burned her lungs. But she kept the steady motion of her arms, back and forth, yanking her hands in opposite directions.

The tiny sound of ripping tape lifted her spirits and urged her on. She pulled hard against her sticky restraints, the tape tearing. She moved her arms faster until shards of duct tape came loose like strings and the tape burst apart, freeing her hands.

A silent sob caught in her throat, but she couldn't stop now. Couldn't savor her small victory. She circled her wrists quickly and shook them out then used the edge of the frame on the binding around her ankles. After a few minutes, the tape broke apart and she slumped against the wall, a dim ray of hope breaking through the bleak clouds over her head. She'd overcome a huge obstacle—now it was time to conquer the next.

She studied the frame again. The metal had been perfect for the tape but was big and awkward as a weapon. But the glass inside could work. Flipping over the frame, she pulled the backing off and tossed it, along with the sad picture, to the side. She turned the rectangular glass over in her hands. Good, but it could be better. She jumped to her feet and slammed the glass down on the dresser, cringing as the sound echoed off the dirty walls.

The glass splintered, one half crumbling into a hundred little pieces, one half creating a jagged sliver perfect for concealing from her kidnapper before she needed to use it. Hurrying to the door, she pressed her ear to the thin wood. No sound. She turned the knob, but the door refused to budge.

No!

She was locked in from the outside. She turned in a circle, considering her options. There was no window in the small room and banging against the door might just alert her attacker that she was awake. He may not have killed her yet, but she was under no illusion about what he had planned for her once he returned.

The sound of heavy footsteps pounding against groaning steps slipped beneath the crack under the door. Alarm shot her heart up her throat. She had no options, no routes for escape. Determination surged through her. If she couldn't make a run for it, she'd have to be smart. Trick him the same way he'd tricked her by luring her out of her apartment.

Decision made, she buried the discarded tape under the mess on the floor and scurried back onto the bed. She curled onto her side, facing away from the door, and gripped the sliver of glass as hard as she could without it puncturing her skin. She evened her breaths, making it appear as though she were still passed out.

The footfalls stopped. The door creaked open. She squeezed her eyes shut and waited.

The energy in the room crackled, and a slight stirring of air leaked in from the open door. Heavy breathing made her wince. The carpet and clothes and whatever else lay on the floor padded the footsteps, but she could feel him moving closer. Feel his presence near her.

The mattress dipped beside her. Fingertips brushed against her bicep. She fought the urge to whimper, to coil away from his touch. The smell of…gasoline?… mixed with the putrid scents of the disgusting room. He moved closer against her back, fingers slithering up her shoulder to the side of her throat.

She shot forward as fast as she could and turned toward him before plunging the glass into the side of his neck. The glass pierced her palm, but she didn't register the pain through the adrenaline pumping in her veins.

"You bitch!" He howled, clawing at the makeshift weapon.

Flinging herself off the bed, she ran for the door. Her pulse raced and dizziness swam in her head. Beads of sweat pooled between her shoulder blades. She reached a short hallway, a set of stairs three feet away. She ran.

A feral growl sounded behind her.

She wanted to glance over her shoulder to see how close he was but couldn't take the risk. She had to move fast. If she could just get out of the house, she stood a chance.

Lauren leaped down the first step. The front door came within view. Excitement squeezed her chest. She could do this. She *had* to do this.

A hard yank on her hair reared her head back.

"Let me go!" Her words came out in a hysteric screech.

"Never. You need to learn your lesson, dammit!"

She slapped behind her, using her nails to dig into the thick skin around his wrist.

His grip tightened.

She leaned forward, ignoring the pain erupting in her skull. She jumped to the next step, and her foot slid as he pulled her backward. She bounced off the hard wood, breaking loose from her captor, and tumbled down the stairs head over heels.

She landed in a heap on a small landing, the front door ten feet away. She braced her palm on the floor and tried to lift herself up.

An evil laugh reached her seconds before the man stood over her, smile wide, blood trickling down his neck. The shard of glass gone from the open wound. The same piercing blue eyes—the eyes she remembered from the driver's face—that lived in her nightmares stared down at her, but his hair was brown. He pulled back his hand and slapped her across the mouth.

Stars exploded in her vision and her entire head throbbed in agony.

"Oh, you're going to be a whole lot of fun." Scooping her into his arms, he climbed back up the stairs. Away from the front door. Away from escape. Away from freedom.

Nolan yanked the steering wheel hard to the right and skidded to a stop in front of an old brownstone that had been turned into apartments. He'd called the local precinct, and squad cars filled the driveway. An ambulance was parked in the street, and a handful of officers blocked off the road from both directions.

He shut off the engine and jumped out of the car. He spotted Jack talking to a member of the SWAT team and hurried over. "What's everyone just standing around for? Get inside!"

Both men frowned at him. Annoyance on the SWAT member's face, pity on Jack's. But he didn't give two shits if his outburst was unprofessional. Standing around outside Thomas's house wouldn't help Lauren. Wouldn't stop whatever types of torture were being inflicted on her while everyone twiddled their damn thumbs.

"You must be Detective Clayman. I'm Officer Nick Steele, head of the SWAT team," the man said, his hands firmly latched around a large gun. "I understand your sense of urgency with this situation, but we have a process. We can't just charge in without a plan. Without a set course of action."

"How long does it take to figure out that plan? Seems pretty simple to me. Knock, then when no one answers, break down the damn door and get your asses inside."

"Nolan, calm down, man." Jack rested a heavy hand on his shoulder.

He shrugged it off. "Seriously? If that was Olivia inside, would you be telling people to calm down and just stand around?"

Jack winced.

A twentysomething man decked out in SWAT gear jogged down the street, slowing as he approached. "Single door in the back. Locked. No alleys or clear paths from the front of the structure to the back. All houses are attached up and down the street. We need men positioned in the front and the back, enter at the same time."

Nick nodded. "Thomas Beetle rents out the second-floor unit. No one answered the door or acknowledged our calls from the first-floor unit. Doesn't mean people aren't inside, so proceed with caution. Our goal is to get upstairs but know the suspect could be anywhere on the premises. Take Officer Holeman with you around back. I'll give the signal to go in. Have your radio nearby to hear the call."

He nodded, signaled for another SWAT member to join him, then jogged back the way he'd come.

"I want to go in," Nolan said, the energy around him buzzing with anticipation.

Nick shook his head. "No. We train as a team and work as a team. I'll clear you to come inside as soon as we can."

Anger and fear swirled around his gut, but Nolan wouldn't argue. There wasn't any point. He'd stand at the ready and charge to Lauren's side as soon as he could.

Nick led the rest of his team to the front door. He took control, announcing himself in a booming voice then pounded on the door. He waited a few moments, spoke into a radio attached to his shoulder, then used his heavy equipment to ram open the door. The small group swarmed inside like a pack of angry bees.

The sound of heavy footsteps and warning shouts poured outside the house and shot Nolan's anxiety through the roof. He stayed rooted to his spot in the driveway beside Jack, his pulse racing and terror growing with each passing second. He tapped his foot against the gray concrete, silently urging someone to come and tell him to get inside. That they'd apprehended Thomas and Lauren was safe.

The team filed out the front, one by one, shoulders hunched forward and defeat on their faces. Nick hurried over to him, his jaw set, and eyes narrowed. "No one is here."

Panic tightened Nolan's throat, stealing his ability to respond. His heart crumbled, and his head spun as he tried to figure out where the hell Lauren could be.

"Is there anywhere else Thomas would have taken her?" Jack asked, voice soft and low as if understanding the thin leash securing Nolan's sanity.

He shoved his hands through his hair, and beads of sweat glided over his fingers. "I don't know, man. He's not at work, he's not at home. The other victims were killed in a car he stole. Would he do the same to Lauren? Strangle her in a car and dump her body in an alley?" His stomach turned at the thought that Lauren could already be dead. That he was already too late to save her. There was so much he hadn't told her. So much he'd bottled up inside, afraid to scare or rush her in any way. He'd thought they'd had plenty of time to figure things out. Plenty of time to plan a future together.

A wave of grief slammed against him, but he refused to let it swallow him. "The murders started after Thomas took time off from At Your Service. That can't be a coincidence."

Al's words rushed back to him. "Thomas's boss said Thomas had been through a lot as a kid. He warned me not to upset him. Said he was a good guy despite his childhood or something like that."

"That jives with what Jim Pearl said about him taking time off due to a family issue," Jack said, his phone already in his hand.

A rumble of hope beat back the growing despair in

Nolan's core. "We need to find out what happened to his family. It could be the key to not only finding out why Thomas snapped, but where he took Lauren."

Chapter 26

Lauren thrashed and screamed as her kidnapper threw her back onto the dirty bed. She bounced once then scrambled off the side. No way she'd make this easy on him. She'd fight for her life with her very last breath.

He smiled, showing off crooked teeth. His brown hair was cut short and blue eyes shone with excitement. Blood slid down his neck from the gash where she'd slammed the glass through his skin. "You can run all you want. I won't stop chasing you." His smile disappeared, replaced by a sinister sneer. "You need to be taught a lesson. You all do."

Anger flared to life inside her. "What the hell are you talking about? I don't even know who you are. Just leave me alone. Let me go."

He shook his head and hiked a knee on the bed, keeping one foot planted on the floor.

She took a step backward and her back bumped against the wall. She couldn't be sure if he planned to launch himself across the bed or go around the end. Either way, she'd be prepared to flee in the opposite direction.

"I thought you were different than the others," he said, tilting his head to the side as if studying some exotic creature. "You shouldn't be hopping from one bar to the next. Making bad decisions. But you disappointed me. You're just like the rest of them. You're just like her."

She didn't have the faintest idea what he meant, but if she could get him to keep talking, maybe it'd buy her some time to come up with a plan. "Just like who?"

The question caught him off guard and the tense lines of his face faded away. He rubbed a hand over his chin, and the dark stains on his knuckles triggered the flash of a memory from the first time Nolan had interviewed the employee at the auto shop. The young man had wiped his oil-stained hands with a handkerchief before disappearing into the office. "Thomas?"

His eyes widened for a split second then narrowed to slits and he pressed his lips into a thin line.

The man before her transformed and pieces of information clicked into place in her mind. "The picture that was in the frame. Is that your father?"

He clenched his jaw and balled his hands into fists at his sides. "Don't talk about my father."

The vein that pulsed above his eye should have warned her to stop prying, but curiosity and sheer desperation spurred her on. "Why not? Are you close to your father?"

His cheeks puffed out as his breathing grew heavier. "My father is the best man I know."

The force of his words had her head rearing back. Her heart pounded in her ears. She grappled to come up with a response that would calm Thomas's growing temper. "I'm sure he is. Do you see him a lot?"

"No," he said, punctuating the word with a pound of his fist against the wall. "And it's her fault. It's all her fault."

"Whose?"

"My mother," he said through clenched teeth.

The smiling bride flashed in her mind. "The beautiful woman in the picture? She looked so happy. What was her fault?"

"Everything," he yelled, letting his arms fly wide. "Look at this mess. Look how she lived her life. What do you think that was like for me?" He jammed his thumb against his chest.

She surveyed the room with a fresh perspective. The empty beer cans, the liquor bottles, the busted walls and dirty clothes. Was this how his mother chose to live her life or was it the effect of living with an overbearing man and the son he'd groomed? Asking would clearly not win her any points with Thomas.

"That must have been hard," she said, choosing instead to zero in on how tough of a childhood Thomas had. She needed to find the right string to pull to get him to open up instead of lighting the fire of his fury. "Is this her room?"

He rolled his eyes. "What do you think? All she cared about was her booze. Sat in her room looking for the bottom of a bottle every damn day of her life. Not caring about anyone or anything. Didn't care if she had mouths to feed. No matter how much my dad tried to teach her, hoped punishing would get rid of all her bad habits, nothing changed. Nothing helped. So she'd sit in this shithole, drinking until she couldn't drink anymore."

The use of the past tense set her nerves on edge. Not to mention the fact that if he swore his mother did nothing but sit in her room and drown her sorrows in alcohol, where was she now?

Red crept up his neck and flamed his face. "She's not a problem anymore. That's all that matters. But just like always, her selfish ways took down my dad. Do you know how much he hated doing the things she made him do? But he didn't have a choice. *She* didn't give him a choice."

Lauren winced at each sharp, angry pronunciation of his words, and her heart broke for the woman who was forced to sit in this ruined room with no one to love her. With no one to care for her.

"He should have punished her sooner," Thomas said, cutting into her thoughts. "Then none of this would have happened. I have to do better than he did. I can't let women like you wander the streets, ruining good men like him."

He lunged across the bed, his arms outstretched and aimed at her neck.

She screamed and brought her knee up as fast as she could, jamming the hard cartilage against his groin.

Groaning, he fell to his side on the mattress.

She shot around the end of the bed. The door was left open and beckoned her ahead.

Thomas moved in a flash, scrambling toward her. His long arm stretched. He snagged the end of her shirt.

She flailed her arms and dove toward the door.

His arm latched around her waist and her feet lifted off the floor.

She fell and used her forearms to brace herself before slamming headfirst into the carpet. She clawed at the ground, coming up with dirty laundry and crumpled newspaper clippings. She threw them backward and fought for every inch she could until her hand came down on the neck of another liquor bottle. Gripping it, she swung her body around and smashed the bottle on the side of his head once, twice, three times until his hold on her loosened and she struggled to put distance between them.

Staggering to her feet, she threw herself at the doorway. She had to make it out this time. Failure wasn't an option. She refused to be another lonely woman who lost her life in this depressing room. She had people who cared for her. People who loved her.

She had Nolan.

Her heart skipped two beats as his handsome face flashed in her mind. She'd left so much unsaid, so much undetermined. She'd been so afraid of losing him that she'd guarded herself. And now she was the one in danger, and Nolan had no idea how much he meant to her. When she made it out of here, she'd confess all and never hold herself back.

A subtle clicking reached her ears, and she glanced over her shoulder. Crushing defeat froze her in place.

Thomas stood over her, blood gushing from his temple and a gun in his hands—aimed at her chest. "I told you I'd never stop chasing you. You'll never get away from me."

Not trusting himself to drive, Nolan hopped in the car with Jack and grabbed his phone to call Officer Jeffery.

"Where am I going?" Jack asked, starting the car and waiting for instructions.

Nolan didn't have a location but went with the safest bet. "Lower East Side."

Jack nodded and pulled onto the road.

He was convinced the line was about to go to voice mail when Officer Jeffery answered, her breathing hard and wispy as if she'd run to answer the phone. "Detective Clayman. I have information you might need regarding Thomas Beetle's family. Before I dive into the specifics, let me text you the address of his childhood home."

The line beeped, and he pushed the speaker button so he could look at the address. Validation pulsed through his veins as he typed the address into the GPS on his phone.

Jack flipped a switch by the steering wheel and the siren on top of his vehicle roared to life. "You called it. Lower East Side."

"The connection is there," Jeffery cut in. "Thomas has ties to both places. Makes sense he'd dump the bodies of his victims near where he grew up."

"Tell me what you uncovered," Nolan said, bracing for the worst.

"Thomas Beetle's father was arrested close to two weeks ago for the murder of his mother." Jeffery's voice turned hard as stone. "The father, Peter Beetle, had no prior arrests or dings on his record, but the autopsy report on the mother shows years of injuries. Poorly healed ribs, evidence of broken fingers, both old and fresh bruises all over the body. Most likely endured at the hands of her husband but never reported. Cause of death, strangulation."

He tightened his jaw as Jack maneuvered past road construction that never seemed to end. He and Lauren had discussed what could motivate someone to strangle innocent women and being a witness to constant domestic abuse had been high on his list. But being right wouldn't mean shit if he didn't get to Lauren on time. "With the father in jail and mother dead, the house would be empty. Is it a single-family home or apartments?"

"Single-family," she said. "One of a handful still left in a run-down neighborhood. Has been in the family for years."

"Good work, Jeffery. I'll pass this on and pray I get there on time." He clicked off then called dispatch to report what he'd been told. He had Jack with him, but more backup was needed. The SWAT team would be beneficial, but he wouldn't wait for them. Not this time. Not when hours had passed since Lauren had gone missing and he had a better idea of what he was working with.

"Ten minutes out," Jack said, pressing harder on the gas as they sped through red lights.

The sun sat low in the sky, and the city flew by in

a blur. Lights turned on, popping up like stars in the industrial wasteland they entered. Run-down buildings and graffitied sidewalks took over. The wailing siren didn't even attract curious glances from people sitting on their stoops or carrying groceries toward their homes.

Nolan made his calls then slid his phone back in his pocket. The estimated time on the GPS told him they were close. The streets grew narrower. Long shadows fell across boarded-up houses. Chain-link fences surrounded condemned properties. He unhooked his seat belt and sat on the edge of his seat. He double-checked his weapons—Glock tucked into the holster at his side and another strapped to his ankle.

Emotions threatened to drag him into a pit of fear and uncertainty, but he pushed them away. Forced them all to the deepest corner of his soul. He needed a clear head and steady hand to get Lauren out alive. And she had to be alive—because picturing a world without her in it broke him into a million pieces.

Jack made a final turn before sliding into a spot in front of a dilapidated house. "We're here. Light's on upstairs. Don't see anyone around. We should wait for backup."

"Like hell I will." Nolan charged out of the car and ran toward the front of the house.

"Knock it off," Jack hissed from behind him. "Think this through at least."

Nolan blew out a long breath. "Sorry, man. You're right. Running in and getting myself killed won't help anyone. There's a narrow street to the side of the house. One of us should go to the back, cover that exit. Once we're both in position, we head inside. Clear the bottom floor then head upstairs together."

Jack nodded. "I'll go to the back. I'll let you know when I'm ready."

Nolan watched him jog around the side of the house then secured his gun in his hands before walking to the front door. His heart pounded against his breastbone and sweat coated his palms. He waited, listening for the signal from Jack.

His familiar whistle rang into the night.

Nolan tried the doorknob, but it refused to turn. He didn't want to clue Thomas in to their arrival but couldn't just break down the door without a warrant or cause for concern. As much as his gut told him they were in the right place, a judge wouldn't care.

A piercing scream penetrated the thin walls.

Aiming the gun at the lock, he shot once and ran inside the house. "Lauren!" he yelled, sweeping to the side and finding a dingy living room deserted.

"Nolan!"

The panic in her voice squeezed his lungs. He pounded up the steps, taking them two at a time until he reached the hallway. A door on the left stood wide open, a dull light illuminating the figures standing just over the threshold. Thomas faced him, one arm hooked around Lauren's neck while his other hand pressed the barrel of a gun to her temple.

Nolan kept his gun trained straight ahead as he tiptoed forward. His weight shifted the floorboards, and they groaned with each movement. "Drop your weapon, Thomas. There's no way out of this for you. Let Lauren go."

"Not one more step," Thomas shouted.

Lauren winced. Tears tracked down her cheeks. She had both hands curled round Thomas's forearm as if trying to pull it away from her throat.

Nolan moved a little bit closer. He had to get Lauren away from Thomas but needed to make sure Thomas didn't squeeze the trigger before he could get to her. The best way was to make Thomas focus on him. "You don't want to do this, man. This won't fix anything. She's not your mother, and you're not your father."

"I said don't move," Thomas screamed, and the gun bounced a little in his hand.

Nolan stopped and took note of the blood caked on his face. "I can call a medic. Get you help. Clean you up. There's no need for anyone else to get hurt here, especially you. You've been through enough."

Thomas sniffed and used the crook of his elbow to wipe the crimson ooze from the side of his face. "She did this to me," he said, shoving her forward. "She needs to be punished. She's just like my mother. Always looking out for herself. Always causing trouble. I can't let her get away with it."

Lauren squeezed her eyes shut as if accepting her fate. The tight lines of her face smoothed and she let her hands fall to her sides.

Confusion moved him an inch forward. What was going on in her mind? What was she doing? He wanted to comfort her, to tell her everything would be okay. But he couldn't make those promises. Not when a deranged criminal held her at gunpoint, and Nolan was helpless to stop him from putting a bullet in her brain.

Thomas stilled and flickered his attention to Lauren.

The subtle movement relaxed his hand, the gun dipping slightly toward the ground.

Nolan aimed his weapon and fired.

Lauren's scream combined with the explosive gunfire. She fell to the floor, hands over her ears, and curled into a ball.

Thomas jerked back, blood blooming from his shoulder. His terrified gaze landed on Nolan, and he fired his weapon before falling to the ground.

The force of a bullet slammed into Nolan's hip. Hot, searing pain stole his breath. He crumpled on the dirty carpet, a few feet separating him from the threshold where Lauren still lay on the floor in the room, his weapon clattering to the ground in front of him.

"No! Nolan!" she screamed and scrambled to her feet.

Thomas climbed to his knees, gun dangling from his hand. He wobbled from side to side but kept his gaze locked on Lauren. He lifted his weapon.

Nolan gritted his teeth and summoned all his strength to sit up, grab his gun and lift it one more time. He didn't come all this way to watch the woman he loved get shot.

Footsteps pounded up the stairs, but there wasn't time to wait. He struggled to hear past the beating of his heart, even out his ragged breaths that wheezed from his open mouth and fire his gun.

Thomas fell to the floor.

Jack appeared from the stairwell and sprinted into the room. He crouched beside Thomas, checking his pulse before restraining him.

Lauren sobbed and wrapped her arms around Nolan as he collapsed.

He coughed as agony encased his body. Blood pumped from his wound, saturating the fabric of his pants. Chills danced up his arms, and he shivered despite the sweat pouring down his face.

"You're okay. You're going to be fine. Just keep your eyes open and talk to me, okay?" Lauren's face hovered above his, fear clear in her wide eyes despite her calm reassurances. She gently roamed her hands down his body until she landed on his hip.

He hissed as she pressed her palm down on the wound but stared at her beautiful face instead of focusing on the stinging pain. Numbness crept along his limbs. He licked his dry lips, having so much to say to her but no energy left to push out the words.

Jack appeared with a phone pressed in his ears. "Yes, suspect is unconscious and apprehended. Officer down. Need ambulance immediately."

Black spots danced in Nolan's vision, and he found Lauren's hand with his and squeezed it hard. His head spun, and his eyelids fell closed for a second before he yanked them back open.

Lauren pressed her lips to his cheek, his jaw, his mouth. "No sleeping. Stay with me, babe. You can't leave me. Not when I finally found you again. I can't lose you. I can't do this life without you."

He managed a small smile then cradled his palm against her cheek. She was so strong, so fierce. "Getting a chance to love you is the best damn thing that's ever happened to me."

Another coughing fit shook his body, and he doubled

over as the pain took control, blocking out everything else. His eyelids fluttered closed and his body went limp, the sound of Lauren's cries growing distant as he retreated into the blessed oblivion of darkness.

Chapter 27

Terror kept Lauren's hand firmly gripped in her mother's as she sat in the waiting area of the emergency room, hoping to hear a crumb of information about Nolan. Jack sat on her other side, writing down every word she said as she rattled off her statement. But she could have recited the alphabet for all she remembered. Her thoughts were firmly on Nolan.

Jack flipped his notepad closed and stood. "I appreciate you going over this with me right now. You've been through a lot, and I know you're worried about Nolan. But he's a tough guy. He'll be fine."

"Is there any way you can get an update?" she asked. "I'm not family so no one will tell me anything. But since you're a detective, you might have better luck. I mean, it's been over an hour. Surgery should be done by now, right?"

"I'll see what I can find out." He dipped his chin toward her then her mom, and strolled to the nurse's station.

"How are you holding up?" Brenda asked, giving her hand a little squeeze.

Sighing, Lauren rested her head on her mom's shoulder. Gratitude pushed back the tears misting in her eyes. "I'm a wreck. Nolan is lying in a hospital bed, fighting for his life again, because of me. This is my fault. How can I ever be okay if I'm the reason the man I love—" Her heart tripled its speed, and she snapped her mouth closed.

"The man you love?" Brenda asked, astonishment clear in her tone.

Lauren shook her head. "I don't know what I'm feeling except scared I'm about to lose this amazing man who's stepped back into my life. Who I thought was my enemy until a week ago."

Shifting, Brenda tucked her index finger under Lauren's chin and gently lifted her head from her shoulder. "Baby girl, look at me."

Lauren did as she was told, but kept her rambling thoughts locked up tight.

"You have always known your heart—your mind. Ever since you were a little girl. So if you say you love Nolan, don't doubt yourself."

The tears she'd held back for so long fell forward and spilled on her lap. "It's too soon."

"Honey," Brenda said. "I fell head over heels for your father the minute I set eyes on him. That love has grown into something deeper and stronger all these years, but nothing and no one could convince me my heart didn't belong to him. Loving your father has been the greatest adventure of my life and I wouldn't trade one second of it. And I sure am glad for those early days. Every single one of them. So don't you tell me it's too soon for those feelings."

Lauren covered her face with her hands and let her head fall forward. All the emotions she'd tried so hard to keep at arm's length flooded over her, shaking her shoulders and jumbling her insides. These feelings might bring happiness and joy into her life in a different situation, but not now. Not when guilt ate her up from the inside out as she waited for news on Nolan.

The sound of someone clearing their throat lifted her head. Madi stood in front of her, with an older man and woman huddled together just behind her speaking with a doctor in green scrubs. Jack hovered nearby, as if sensing Lauren's apprehension and at the ready to jump in if Madi launched into another lecture about staying away from her brother.

Madi folded her arms over her chest. Her messy hair fell in her eyes, but she let it linger, as if wanting to hide the obvious puffiness from crying. "Nolan's out of surgery. He's in his room and waking up. My parents and I just left him."

Relief sagged Lauren's shoulders and she filled her lungs with air for the first time since Nolan had been driven away in a screaming ambulance. She rubbed the palm of her hand over her chest and let the news sink in before standing. "Thank you for telling me."

The woman behind Madi broke away from the doctor and hurried over, hooking an arm around Madi's shoulders. She had the same brown eyes as Nolan, now filled with both fatigue and kindness. "You must be Lauren.

I'm Nolan's mother, Patty. How are you, dear? Feeling okay?"

Lauren nodded, words escaping her.

"I hope you're a hugger." She threw her arms around Lauren. "Nolan's awake and waiting to see you. We thought we'd give you two some privacy. Is this your mother?" she asked, nodding toward Brenda.

Brenda rose and extended a hand. "Yes, I'm Brenda Mueller. It's nice to meet you."

Patty folded her hands over Brenda's. "You as well. Do you mind if we sit with you awhile? I'm not ready to leave yet."

"Of course."

"Madi will take you to Nolan's room."

She swallowed a refusal to the assistance and offered a warm smile instead. "Thank you. Mom, I'll be right back."

"Take your time," Brenda said, settling back into her chair. "And remember, don't doubt your feelings."

She pressed her lips together and gave a brief nod before following Madi down the wide hall. This might not be the same hospital where Rebecca had spent the night, but the scenes she passed by were all familiar. Overworked nurses hurried from room to room, patients with ugly hospital gowns were wheeled around or clutched a rolling IV stand as they shuffled about, and worried visitors carried balloons or flowers into loved ones' rooms.

Madi led her up a flight of stairs. She kept her arms wrapped around her middle and gaze fixed straight ahead. Awkward silence pulsed between them with each step. She stopped in front of a room with the door cracked open and faced Lauren. "I'm sorry for what I said to you before. I just… I love my brother and hate seeing him hurt."

"Trust me. I understand." She'd have done anything for Charlie—and she had in an effort to clear his name. Lauren just wished Nolan's sister hadn't made such valid points. Points that couldn't be ignored. "I don't want to hurt your brother."

"I know. He cares about you, which means you must be all right." She cracked the slightest grin, then turned and walked back down the hall.

Lauren watched her go, giving herself a minute to calm her racing heart and face Nolan. She pushed open the door and peeked inside. The lights were dimmed, and the bed laid flat so Nolan could rest. A noisy machine beside him announced his vitals. She tiptoed inside, not wanting to disturb him if he'd fallen asleep.

"Lauren?"

"It's me," she said, inching farther into the room. She wanted nothing more than to throw herself into his arms and wrap him up tight, never letting go. But she couldn't. Not now when doing so would hurt his battered body. And maybe not later, when he was healed but she was too afraid to ever put him back in this place. "Are you up for some company?"

He pressed a button that lifted him into a seated position and beamed at her. "For you? Always. Come here." Extending a hand, he wiggled his fingers.

Her heart pounded with each step. She grabbed his hand and he yanked her to his side. She allowed herself one minute to study his features. Tired eyes and an ashy pallor were the only indicators he'd had another brush with death. "How can you be smiling?"

He tilted his head to the side as if her question didn't make any sense. "How can I not? Thomas is no longer a threat, you're safe, and we can start building our future together."

Her bottom lip trembled, and she pressed her knuckles to her mouth to stop a sob. "You're here, in this hospital bed, injured, because of me. I can't be in your life if I'm constantly getting you hurt. I couldn't live with myself if something else happened to you. I love you too damn much." There. She'd said it. She trusted herself and her feelings enough to know the truth, but that didn't mean she was meant to be with Nolan.

His smile grew. "You didn't put me in this bed. Thomas Beetle did because he's a bad man who made bad decisions. I was doing my job—protect and serve and all that. You just happened to be caught up in this whole mess. Something I hope never happens again."

"Caught up? No, I was the target. I was the beginning. I sucked you into my drama again."

Grimacing, he shifted on the bed to allow a sliver of space. "Sit with me for a second."

She shook her head. "I don't want to hurt you."

He gave an exaggerated eye roll. "We've established that already, but humor me."

Sighing, she gingerly sat on the edge of the bed, and he lowered her beside him. She curled against him, his arm tucked around her, and stared into his deep brown eyes. She longed to run the pad of her thumb along his stubbled jaw—to kiss his full lips.

"My job is dangerous. No matter who the target is. I'm trained and I'm capable. Being a detective is part of who I am just like your music is a part of you. I help people and fight for what's right in a world that's often a pretty scary place. Your brother showed me that this city needs officers like me."

The mention of her brother lifted her lips. "He'd love knowing that."

Nolan's smile finally fell. "You are not to blame for the tragic turn of events that put me here. You are the reason I fought so damn hard to wake up. You are the reason I'll battle through rehab for my hip until I can get back on the streets. I love you, too, Lauren. You don't hurt me. You make me whole. Please believe that."

She sniffed back tears and kept her gaze locked on his. "I don't want to ever lose you."

"Then don't. Don't be so afraid of the what-ifs that it stops you from enjoying what's right in front of you. Let me love you. Let me love you every damn day."

Happiness overflowed inside of her, bursting free in a bubble of laughter. She rested her palm on his cheek and pressed her lips to his. Savoring the feel of his mouth, the taste of his lips. She pulled away, her grin matching his. "Every damn day, huh?"

"Too much too soon?"

She shook her head. "Not nearly enough."

A blast of wind blew a handful of colorful leaves down the sidewalk and past the door of On the Rocks. Nolan watched the signs of autumn swirl around before being stomped on by the busy foot traffic of the Friday evening crowd. He leaned against the glass counter and waited for Lauren and Amy to run through their end-of-the-night checklist.

"Are you sure you want to go out?" Lauren asked,

flipping off the lights and shrugging into a denim jacket. "I'm exhausted. I'd be fine with heading home and ordering Chinese."

The word *home* made a slow, lazy grin grow on his face. After he'd left the hospital a few months before, he'd needed more assistance than he'd realized while he'd recovered from surgery. The shot to his hip had caused a lot of blood loss but minimal damage, but that didn't mean the physical therapy he needed to heal properly wasn't a complete bitch. With Rebecca staying at her parents' home, Lauren agreed to bring Sissy to his place and stay until he could get around a little better on his own. The temporary move had turned permanent, and he'd never been happier.

He looped an arm over her shoulder and pressed a kiss to her head. "I'm sorry you're tired. We won't stay out long. Promise."

She puffed out a breath that pushed a strand of brown hair off her forehead. "If I'm with you, I don't care what we're doing."

"You two are just the cutest," Amy said and grabbed her things before preceding them outside.

Lauren laughed. "See you later."

His pulse raced as he waved goodbye to Amy then led Lauren out of the store and waited for her to lock up before leading her a few blocks away. They walked hand in hand, companionable silence cocooning them from the bustling traffic and city sounds. He ran the evening he had planned through his mind again, just like he had a hundred times in the past two days. Everything was mapped out to the last detail, and pressure mounted on his shoulders to make this perfect.

Not like Lauren would know any different if things altered off course a little. Hopefully, she'd be ecstatic at the end of the night even if everything he'd set into motion blew up in his face.

Everything except those four little words that sat on the tip of his tongue.

Turning the last corner, he pressed his hand to the small of her back and ushered her toward The Songbird.

She eyed him with intrigue pinching her face. "The one night I don't play here, and this is where you want to go?"

Keeping his thoughts to himself, he shrugged and opened the door before recapturing her hand and leading her inside. He walked straight to the table right in front of the stage—the one where he'd sat and watched her play and knew he'd fallen hard. He pulled out a chair for her then slid the other one around the table so he sat right in front of her.

"What's going on?" she asked, casting curious glances around the darkened room. "Are those my parents in the corner?"

Ignoring her questions, he lifted a finger toward the young man up on stage. Music danced from the piano. A server appeared and set an ice bucket with a bottle of champagne and two glasses on the table. He refocused all his attention on Lauren.

She widened her eyes, amusement clear on her pursed lips. "You must have pulled some strings to get such great service here."

"I have some connections. Do you remember this song?"

She tilted her head then smiled. "Of course. I played

this the first time you saw me perform. When you were sitting right here, and I almost had a panic attack. That was the night I knew I could count on you for anything."

"That was the night I knew I loved you." He drew in a shuddering breath, needing to get out all of his jumbled thoughts before he burst. Not wasting another second, he pulled a velvet ring box from his pants pocket and dropped to one knee. "Our love took us both by surprise. Each day since the night I sat in this chair and you completely captivated me, I've fallen deeper and deeper. I know it's soon, but, baby, nothing about us has been conventional. I want you to be my wife. To have and to hold forever and ever."

She gasped and reached for his hand. "Do you really mean it? Are you sure you're ready?"

"I've waited for you all my life. Please. Say you'll marry me."

"I'll marry you." She threw her arms around his neck and squealed.

Joy exploded inside him along with the whoops and cheers around them. He hugged her tight, pressing kisses to her face as the people they loved most surrounded them with congratulations. His parents and Madi, her mom and dad, Rebecca and Jack.

Everything fell into place, just the way he'd planned, and now a future he never thought possible could begin. A future with the woman he loved and the music they'd make together.

* * * * *

HARLEQUIN
PLUS

Try the best multimedia subscription service for romance readers like you!

Read, Watch and Play.

Experience the easiest way to get the romance content you crave.

Start your **FREE TRIAL** at
<u>www.harlequinplus.com/freetrial</u>.